C000176898

HARBINGER

WAR MAGE CHRONICLES

CHARLES R CASE

Edited by
JEN MCDONNELL

Illustrated by
BOGNA GAWRONSKA

CASE BY CASE PUBLISHING

Copyright © 2018 by Charles R. Case

Case by Case Publishing

All rights reserved.

No part of this book may be reproduced in any form or by any electronic
or mechanical means, including information storage and retrieval systems,
without written permission from the author, except for the use of brief
quotations in a book review.

CONTENTS

CHAPTER 1

"IT'S EMPTY," Mezner said, tucking a lock of blonde hair behind her ear.

"What do you mean 'it's empty'? I can see cities from here," Sara said, zooming in the projection of the planet's surface to show a continent dotted with modern cities.

They had warped into the system an hour and a half ago, and this was the second planet they had visited. The first, while able to support life, only had single-celled organisms teeming in its vast, yellow oceans.

"I'm seeing the cities, ma'am. But there's no one in them. It looks like they've been abandoned for quite some time, if these readings are right," Mezner said, her fingers dancing over the controls of her station.

"How are the cities still standing, then? If they were abandoned, wouldn't they be grown over?" Sara asked.

"Not necessarily, ma'am," Connors spoke up. He was looking at the reading along with everyone else. "I'm getting some odd power signatures, but nothing on the scale of a civilization. However, some of the signatures appear to be moving. It could be that the cities are being maintained by a robotic workforce."

"I'm seeing the movement as well, ma'am," Mezner confirmed.

"Okay, if there's no more people, what happened? I need ideas here," Sara said, pacing back and forth.

"It could be that they had to run again," Grimms said from across the projection table.

"Maybe they died off from a disease?" Connors suggested.

"Unlikely," Mezner dismissed. "If it were a disease, there would be some survivors. Even the black plague was only seventy percent successful. I'm seeing no signs of life whatso-ever beyond plants and small animals. Not to mention there are no radio signals or Aether bursts coming from the surface. Even if there were only a few humans, we would see something—especially with a society as advanced as this one would have to be to build these cities."

"Mezner's right," Grimms said. "I don't think it's a disease. Are you seeing any signs of ships on the ground or in orbit?"

Mezner focused on her console for a few seconds before answering, "No, sir. I'm not reading any reactors of any kind. I am seeing a few small things that could be ships in orbit, but more than likely, they're just small asteroids or moons. Asteroid farming would be in-line for a society this advanced."

"Then Grimms is right, they must have run. But from what? Did the Teifen find them here?" Sara asked, petting Alister with an absent-minded hand when he jumped up on the projection table.

He pushed into her hand with his eyes closed and began to purr.

"I don't think so. If it were the Teifen, they would have

left people on the surface. This planet is far too valuable in terms of resources and placement to leave it empty," Grimms said, looking over the data.

"It's a little far from their empire," Sara mused.

"True, but it would give them a wonderful base to attack the Elif from behind," Mezner said.

Grimms nodded, "She's right, the Teifen are not known for giving up an advantage, and this planet would definitely give them that. Are we seeing any signs of battle anywhere?"

Mezner scanned the surface a few times in different spectrums before finding what she was looking for. Her eyes lit up as she answered, "Yes, sir. I missed it at first because I was only scanning for life forms, but there is indication of some irradiated fallout. However, it's quite old, and well within habitable ranges. It could indicate nuclear weapons, detonated hundreds of thousands of years ago."

"That's what I thought. Captain, we should send somebody down there to take a closer look," Grimms said.

Sara bit her lip, thinking about their directive, and wondering if she should take any risks that were not plainly spelled out. Alister sat on the table and cocked his head at her, confused by her sudden need to follow the rules.

Sara grimaced, "Don't look at me like that, you know how much trouble we got in."

Grimms smiled over at his captain. "I'm sorry, I wasn't thinking. We should follow orders on this one."

Sara waved a hand at him. "It's all right. We really do need to know what happened here, especially if we're going to try to seek out the ancient humans for help."

Cora spoke up at that. "Sara, we don't even know that they're going to help us. For all we know, they ended up killing themselves in some sort of war, or war was brought upon them. Either way, we can't spend too long out here. The attack on Effrit to take back the Elif home world is being planned as we speak; we can't embroil ourselves in too long of a search."

Sara considered that, then looked to Mezner. "I want a scan of the entire system; I don't care how long it takes. I need detailed information on every celestial body in the solar system. Let me know when you're done. I'll be in my room. Grimms, you have the bridge."

"We may want to consider retrieving one of those robots. They could hold some information, and the UHFC will want one for study," Grimms said, as she turned to go.

"You're right. Have a Marine detachment go down and get one, but make sure they come right back. We need to get out of here as soon as the UHFC calls. I don't want to piss them off any more by being late."

Grimms gave a sharp salute, then turned back to the holo-projection and began zooming in on various cities.

Sara stepped off the bridge, and Alister jumped on her shoulder as she began heading toward her rooms. After a moment's consideration, she opened a comm channel to Boon; after further consideration, she closed it, and opened a new channel for Baxter.

"Are you busy, big boy?" she said with a smile.

It took a second for her bonded guard to respond, but when he did, she could hear the smile in his voice. "Not particularly. Did you have something in mind?"

Sara blew out a frustrated breath, not able to keep up the charade. "I just really need to talk. I feel a little lost, and a few words of guidance would help."

"I'll be there in three minutes," Baxter said, all amusement gone from his voice.

"I'll have a drink waiting for you," Sara said, opening the door to her room.

"You know I'm still on duty, right?"

"Fuck."

CHAPTER 2

Silva spun in a circle before finally settling down on the bed in a tight ball, to Boon's great annoyance.

"Will you calm down? You've been agitated all day. What's going on with you?" Boon asked, looking up from her tablet. She had settled in for the night and was wearing a pair of pajamas that Gonders had said, jokingly, made her look like a child, but Boon didn't give a crap; they were comfortable.

Silva chattered at her, and sent a spike of irritation through their bond. Boon put her hand up defensively. "Okay, okay. Sorry I asked."

She turned back to the tablet, and began reading again. Gonders had given her several texts on the art of war and fighting, saying that she would be tested later. This warning was accompanied by a suggestive wink, which confused Boon a little.

Her performance on the dreadnought, while powerful and able to turn the tide, had been lackluster, and she needed to work on her tactical thinking.

She would be a lot further along if the text wasn't so damn boring.

How can reading about the most creative ways to kill someone want to put me to sleep? I think I would rather hit my head on the wall over and over, just to see if it knocks something loose, than read another word of this.

Silva fidgeted again, which made Boon want to scream, which made the ferret even more agitated. That's when it hit her. Silva wasn't agitated; *she* was, and her agitation was being projected onto her familiar.

She reached over and gave the pixie a soft pat. "Sorry, I just realized what was happening. I'll try and calm down. It's just the stupid texts are boring me out of my mind. Who knew it took so much knowledge to blast people out of their boots?"

Silva opened an eye, and somehow got across, *'I thought everyone knew that'* with just a glance.

Boon raised an eyebrow. "Okay, I guess everyone but me."

The door to her small room slid open, and Sara stuck her head in. "You busy in here? I was wondering if you could join me and Baxter in my room."

Boon powered off the tablet and tossed it on the bed in one quick move, making Silva jump out of the way. "Hell yes. I'm free," she said, jumping to her feet.

Silva chattered at her, then leapt onto her shoulder and chattered again in her ear.

Boon leaned her face away from the animated ferret, and held up a hand. "I can get back to it when the captain's done with me. It's not like we're on a super crazy time crunch here."

"I'm sorry, did I interrupt something?" Sara asked, confusion in her eyes.

"No, no. I was just studying, but I can get back to it

whenever. What's going on?" she asked, heading for the door.

"You want to put some clothes on?" Sara asked, raising an eyebrow at Boon, who was still in her pajamas.

Alicia looked down at her matching sleep shirt and pants, and the various kittens posed on its sky blue background. "Is this a 'change into my uniform' kind of talk?"

"I guess not. But Baxter will be there."

Boon waved a dismissive hand. "If it's just the three of us, I would rather not. I'm not on shift again for another six hours, and I'm probably gonna hit the sack after we talk."

Sara gave a shrug and turned down the hall as Boon exited the room, and they headed for the captain's quarters.

"How is the studying coming?" Sara asked, as they stepped through the door into her room. She headed for the small kitchenette that only the captain's quarters had, and pulled three glasses out of the cupboard.

Boon rolled her eyes, and flopped down on the couch. "About as well as can be expected. I just don't get why so many things are considered when planning a battle, if most of it just gets thrown out as soon as the bullets start flying."

Silva and Alister hopped up on the far side of the couch, and curled up against one another in a pile of cuteness that made Boon warm and fuzzy.

"Well, you have to have a plan to adapt from. Going in guns blazing gets a lot of people killed. Do you want some whiskey?" Sara asked, turning and waggling a bottle of the brown liquid suggestively.

Boon thought about the first time she'd had the stuff, sitting at the very table Sara was standing behind, and shook her head in the negative. "No thanks. I'll just take some juice or something."

Sara smiled. "Wuss."

But she poured some orange juice from the wall

dispenser into Boon's glass. The other two glasses received two fingers of single malt and a few ice cubes. She brought all three to the coffee table.

Just as Boon was reaching for her glass, the door opened, and Baxter walked in. He was all smiles until he saw the small, blonde woman in her PJs, sitting on the couch. His smile faltered, but returned once he reread the situation.

"Hello, Boon. I didn't realize you would be joining us," he said, nodding to her.

Sara handed him one of the glasses of whiskey, and smiled up at him. "I told you I just needed to talk some things out. What did you think was going to happen here?"

Boon gave a chuckle as Baxter looked down at the red-haired captain, his grin plastered on like his life depended on it. "Nothing. Just a talk, I guess," he said with forced joviality.

"Mm hmm," Sara said, her eyes suspicious slits. Then she smiled and gave a laugh herself. "Relax. Me and you can chat after."

"I'm still on duty."

She looked down at the glass she was holding. "Well, shit. I don't know where my mind has been lately," she shook her head, and downed one of the glasses in one go. After choking a little on the burning liquid, she croaked, "You want some coffee?"

"Uh, I'm good. Why don't you tell me what's up?" Baxter invited, a look of concern on his face.

Sara held up a finger to indicate she would get to the question in a minute. "Cora, are you there?" she asked the room.

"I am. I figured you would want me here, after the way you left the bridge," her twin sister said through the room's speakers.

"Good." Sara flopped down into one of the chairs at the

table. She put the empty glass down and took a sip from the still full one. "I have a confession to make, and you three are the people I trust the most, besides Grimms. But to be honest, I'm afraid to tell him."

The room waited for her to gather her thoughts. Baxter sat across from her, and Boon tucked her bare feet under herself, leaning forward in anticipation. Even Alister and Silva perked up and focused on her.

Sara leaned her head to one side, then the other, cracking her neck with loud pops. She rolled her shoulders and took a deep breath.

"So, you know how I tend to play things close to the vest?"

There was a round of nods, and a "Boy, do I" from Cora.

"Well, I may have fucked up with the brass," she admitted, taking another sip of whiskey to strengthen her resolve. "I haven't told them about the dreadnought buried in the Atlantic Ocean."

"What?" all three of them said at once.

"Or that Boon is a War Mage."

Boon slapped her forehead with the palm of her hand. "You have got to be kidding!"

"It's not like I wouldn't have eventually, but I wanted to find out what secrets the dreadnought held before it was off-limits to us. I figured we would deal with the Teifen invasion, then I would be able to continue exploring the ship with Boon. But then the whole incident at the embassy happened, and the battle, and then we had to run off and destroy the Teifen governor and his ship. And then when we got back, they had a lot to say to me at UHFC, as you know, and I guess it never really came up," she finished lamely.

"It never really *came up*?" Cora said incredulously. "How could two of the most important things to happen to this crew in recent history fail to come up?"

Sara made a pained expression. "I may have practiced a little 'malicious compliance'. I answered everything they asked of me, but they didn't think to ask if I had found an ancient city ship in the ocean. And Boon never came up at all."

"You're telling us that not one person on this ship has said a word to anyone at Command? There are eight hundred people onboard, and they all happened to not say anything?" Boon asked, now wishing she had taken the whiskey.

Sara bobbed her head reluctantly. "Grimms is the only other person who reports directly to Command, and he keeps his reports on-topic, almost to a fault. Now that I think about it, he may be covering for me a little."

"He would do that for his commanding officer," Cora agreed thoughtfully.

"Once the hearing was over, they wanted to get us as far from the Elif prince and empress as possible, so they latched onto the idea that there may be more humans out here, and sent us to look. They just wanted us out of their hair," Sara explained. "It's not like they can stop using us; we're far too valuable a resource."

Baxter had kept calm through the whole ordeal, and finally spoke up. "Why are you keeping this from the UHFC, and why are you telling us now?"

Sara smiled. *Leave it up to Baxter to see the fire through the smoke.* She took another breath. "There is a small part of me that doesn't trust, I don't know... humanity?"

The room was silent while everyone tried to process that.

Baxter got there first, to no great surprise of Sara's.

"You think it's too much power to hand over. That the UHFC will just use it for personal gain?" he guessed.

"Not so much personal gain as revenge. We were betrayed by the one race that says they are our friends. And the more I look into the Teifen and their society, the more I am convinced that a small, power-hungry contingent is pulling the strings. Most of them don't want anything to do with the war; they just want to live and raise their families," she said, becoming agitated. "The Teifen remind me of the old human governments, before the Elif came—politicians and corporations vying for power at the expense of the public."

Baxter nodded. "I have been getting the same feeling. Dr. Hess and I had quite a few talks before he left with the prince and empress."

Sara gave a nod. "If you look at the Elif network's info on the Rim, planets are constantly leaving their respective empires to become independent. Hell, half of them have populations of Teifen and Elif living and working together. It's just such a small percentage of the empires as a whole that it gets swept under the rug."

Boon held up a hand. "What does this have to do with not telling the UHFC that we have a dreadnought, and that I'm a War Mage?"

Sara blew out a breath. "Honestly, I don't know exactly. I think it's something the governor said to me before I crushed him."

"Wait. The Teifen governor? Why would you listen to anything that maniac had to say?" Cora interjected.

"Because he didn't have anything to lose when he said it. I don't know, maybe it was the way he said it that made me think," Sara said, taking another absent-minded sip.

"Well, what did he say?" Boon was nearly bursting with impatience.

Sara gave her a sad smile. "He said that we were the monsters."

CHAPTER 3

Mezner found nothing more of interest with her deep scans of the ravaged planet. There was no sign of the huge dreadnought that should have been there, and the Marines confirmed it was a ghost town when they subdued one of the small worker bots.

The bot didn't fight them as they had feared, but instead complied with their prodding it onto the dropship, and stood still as they strapped it in. When the dropship reached orbit, the squad reported that the bot powered down, and that they had not been able to get it started again. It was now resting in a crate, awaiting delivery to the white coats back at the UHFC.

The *Raven* had received the call to return to Earth promptly, to prepare for the retaking of Effrit. Sara inferred that what had happened was the prince and empress had been picked up by the Elif and were no longer in the system.

"So, tell me again how this is supposed to be relaxing?" Boon huffed, balancing on one leg in Warrior Three.

As the ship made its way back to Sol, Sara insisted that Alicia join her for some yoga.

"It trains your body and mind to work together," she imparted. "It's saved my butt on two occasions, when my powers were starting to get out of control." Sara was barely glistening with sweat.

Boon pulled the bottom of her shirt up and mopped her forehead, noting that it was already drenched. "I can barely do the moves, let alone center my mind. I don't know that this is for me," she complained, but still went into Standing Triangle.

"It takes years of practice, but trust me, it's worth it. I mean, come on, how do you think I have such a rockin' bod?" she said with a smile.

"Genetics. Probably. Remember that I've seen Cora, and you two look pretty much the same."

Sara laughed as she returned to Plank and then pushed into Chaturanga. "Well, that's part of it. But I'm a lot stronger than Cora."

"Only physically," Cora qualified snidely from the speakers.

"When you get out of that tank, I'm going to wrestle you to the ground, then beat you at chess," Sara taunted, looking up at the ceiling.

"One of those things is true," Cora allowed lightheartedly. "Speaking of—Teichek says that, when we get back, I need to come out of the tank for maintenance."

Sara raised her eyebrows. "Really? Awesome. I haven't been able to kick your butt since you went in."

"It will be nice to actually touch someone again," Cora said longingly.

Boon flopped to her butt and brought her feet together to stretch out her groin. "I can't take anymore. I'm done. We've been at this for forty-five minutes. I need a break."

Sara laughed, but rolled to her butt and began stretching

as well. "Okay. That was pretty good for your first time; next time, I'll start us off a little easier."

Boon groaned. "Ugh, 'next time'? Kill me now."

"She used to try and get me to do it with her. I never understood her obsession with yoga," Cora said sympathetically.

"That's because you never gave it a real try. You would do three poses, then tell me it was too hard."

Boon grimaced. "She isn't wrong. It is pretty hard."

"Too bad you don't have a choice," Sara said to the still-sweaty Boon. "This is about control. Control of your mind. There is far too much at stake to let ourselves run amok with our powers, so every little edge that we can get, we need to take."

Boon held up a hand to stop her. "I know. It just kinda sucks is all. I'm not quitting."

"Good. I like it when you push yourself. Being a War Mage is about more than power; it's about control and dedication," Sara said, taking a sip of water from the sports bottle beside her.

Boon got a distant look in her eye. "What's it going to be like when there are other War Mages? They're not all going to do hours of yoga to stay centered."

Sara had been thinking about this herself, and she was no closer to an answer. "I think it's something that we will just have to wait and see about. Now that we know that being a War Mage is genetic, maybe every candidate will have markers that make them better able to handle the power?" She looked over at Alister and Silva. "Or, maybe their familiars will temper them better. I know that mine and Alister's connection makes me look at the universe in a new light."

Boon glanced at the two pixies, piled on top of one another. "That's true. Silva and I have been talking in the

Aether quite a bit, and she has really opened my eyes to a few things."

Sara was thoughtful for a second. "I think we should all meet tonight. We need to discuss the future, and I want Alister's and Silva's opinions."

Both familiars raised their heads and gave nods of approval, to Boon's amusement. "I think they agree. Okay, I'll see you tonight." She rolled to her feet and began rolling up her yoga mat.

"I really wish I could join you. What's it like?" Cora asked, her words dreamy.

Sara cocked her head, "That's actually something we need to talk about. You need to become a War Mage."

Cora laughed. "And how am I supposed to do that from this tank?"

"Well, you have a maintenance cycle coming up..." Sara reminded her with a shrug. "Think about it."

CHAPTER 4

SARA CLIMBED into bed and snuggled up to Baxter's side, laying her head on his chest, sighing contentedly.

"You all right?" he asked, reaching an arm around her and lazily combing his fingers through her hair.

"Mmhm," she hummed, shifting under the covers and enjoying the feel of his soft skin on hers. "I just know its going to be a busy few weeks to come, so I'm trying to enjoy myself."

"I know what you mean," he said, moving his fingers from her hair to lightly rubbing her back. "I have the Mages working double practices to adapt to mine and Gonders' improved Aether control. It's already made a huge difference."

"I'll bet. Your tactics will be completely different, with the two of you being able to take twice the fire on your shields," Sara said, her mind immediately thinking of how she would utilize such abilities, if she were in Baxter's shoes.

He gave a laugh. "I don't know about twice the fire, but a solid fifty percent more isn't unreasonable."

Alister hopped onto the end of the bed and high-stepped across the covers until he was directly behind Sara, then curled into a ball against her butt. To her slight irritation, he liked to sleep against her, and more often than not, she was on her side cuddling with Baxter, so her butt was the most accessible part of her. She reached behind her and gave him a scratch on the head.

"I keep getting a feeling of unease from you," Baxter said quietly before leaning down and kissing the top of her head. "What's that all about?"

Sara hesitated. "I've just been tired lately. Searching the galaxy for a group of 'other humans' is stressful," she said with a shrug.

"If you don't want to tell me, that's fine, but you don't need to make excuses," he said smiling. "Remember, I can feel what you feel, if I focus a little."

She sighed. "Oh, right. I forget sometimes." She looked up at him with a half-smile. "I'm worried that my decisions are putting the crew in danger."

His eyebrows rose, "More than usual?"

She slapped him playfully on the stomach. "Yes, smartass, more than usual."

He grunted at the sudden impact and laughed. "Is this something more than the bombshells you dropped on us about keeping the UHFC in the dark?"

"Honestly, it's just some ideas I've been kicking around about humanity's place in the universe."

"Do you want to talk about it?" he asked, stroking her hair lightly.

She hummed in the negative and snuggled down tight against him. "Not right now. Right now, I just want to be here with you and not worry about it."

He pulled her in tight. "That works for me."

SARA OPENED her eyes to the all-encompassing white of the Aether. She took a deep breath and relaxed, letting the calming feel of the space fill her.

"Still haven't mastered the whole *clothes* thing yet, have you," an amused baritone voice teased.

"Shut up, Alister. Let me enjoy this for a bit," she said, taking another breath.

After a few seconds, she willed herself into her familiar blue sundress and sat up. Alister wore his black pants and shoes, with a royal blue vest over a crisp, white shirt. He sat in a leather, high-backed chair, and sipped from a brandy snifter.

"Hello," he said with a wave.

Sara smiled. "You are the oddest person I've ever met, you know that?"

He nodded. "By far."

"Where are Silva and Boon? Shouldn't they be here by now? I didn't get to bed 'til late," Sara admitted, looking around the empty, white expanse.

"They must not have fallen asleep yet. Silva said she would be here as soon as Boon was out," Alister told her, taking a sip of brandy.

Sara willed a beer into her hand and joined him in imbibing. "You know, we never talk."

Alister shrugged. "Well, we tend to go from one crisis to another. There's not a lot of time, I guess."

"Boon mentioned that she talks with Silva all the time. We should really make an effort," she pressed, raising an eyebrow.

He nodded. "Not as much as Silva and I talk, but they do communicate quite a bit."

Sara put up a hand. "Wait, you and Silva meet here? Without us? I didn't know that was possible."

He gave her a look that said a lot. "Of course we can. It's how most pixies communicate over distance. Why do you think we're always napping together?"

Sara shrugged. "I don't know, I figured it's just what cats and ferrets do."

"You know we're still pixies, even if we are in animal form, right?"

"Duh, but you like rough pets, and you purr, and do cat things all the time," she pointed out, getting a little defensive.

He gave a short nod. "Well, it is true that we tend to be very animal-like in our forms, but that doesn't mean we are those animals. We're more like half and half. There are some instincts that take over, but on the whole, we're still us." He gave her a hard look. "Besides, who says I don't like a good spanking as a pixie?"

Sara blushed, then realized he was joking when he burst out laughing.

"Oh, god, your face!"

She rolled her eyes. "Okay, asshole, you got me. Seriously though, I don't know all that much about you."

He wiped a tear from his eye. "What would you like to know?"

She shrugged. "Everything? What did you do before I summoned you?"

He cleared his throat, and took another sip of brandy, his face still red from laughing. "I was a tailor."

"You made clothes?" she asked incredulously.

"Yeah. I had a little shop outside the academy where I sold them to the local community. I was talking to a customer, and BAM, I was summoned. It took me a while to figure out what the hell was happening; by the time I got the customer out, I was already transforming into my cat shape."

Sara stared at him, trying to process everything. "You owned a shop? In a community of pixies?"

He nodded. "Yeah. The shop was actually my father's, but he decided to move back to the larger city, so I took over. The communities outside the pixie cities are pretty sparse, but they tend to cover a lot of ground. We pixies are everywhere. We are just usually in our animal forms, so no one is the wiser."

"I didn't know that," Boon said, sitting up from where she had just appeared—fully-clothed in pajamas, to Sara's chagrin. "Silva, you never said there were communities of pixies all over the place."

"You never asked," came Silva's voice, and Sara swiveled her head to see the beautiful pixie stepping around Alister's chair.

Silva smiled down at the dapper pixie, and put a hand on his shoulder that Sara couldn't help but notice.

"Are you two..." Sara asked, waggling her eyebrows.

They looked at one another and shrugged. Alister spoke up. "Pixies are pretty familiar with one another."

Silva smiled, and sat on the arm of his chair. "Well, it's just the two of us here, so we don't really have many other friends to talk to."

Sara frowned. "I suppose you're right. Sorry, I never considered you would be lonely."

Alister shrugged. "I'm not lonely. I'm with you all the time, and now that Silva is here, I have a friend that understands. Besides, we're War Mages, and that's pretty badass."

"About that, we should probably get down to business. Isabella gets up pretty early, and I don't want to scare her if I don't respond," Boon said, only turning slightly red.

"Right. Okay. The dreadnought. What do we do about

it? And we need Cora to become a War Mage, so how do we make that happen?" Sara said, focusing on the task at hand.

It was Silva who took the lead. "I'm not sure what we should do about the dreadnought, but as far as Cora is concerned, we need to get her a volunteer as soon as possible. The histories say that a War Mage being in the position of controller on a starship is incredibly powerful. She would have capabilities we can only dream of."

"Capabilities like what?" Sara asked.

Silva hesitated. "Uh, I'm not really sure. I just heard stories growing up."

"Yeah, the stories are kind of a thing in pixie society, but they're a little abstract, like Greek mythology. I do agree that she needs to get this done, though, and soon," Alister concluded.

"Okay, how do we do that if she's always on a ship in space? She said she was coming out of the tank for a maintenance cycle, but I'm sure she will be going right back in as soon as possible."

"We could go find a volunteer," Boon suggested. "We should talk to the pixie council anyway to make sure the dreadnought stays a secret, if you're still wanting that to be the case."

Silva perked up. "That's a great idea. We could go down when we get back. The Keepers of the Record will want to have a chance to get someone who's been trained as a familiar in the position."

"They train for it?" Sara asked, raising an eyebrow.

"Yes, it's tradition. There is always a class who is prepared for a pairing, even though it's been thousands of years," Silva said.

"Huh, I bet Cora would like that her familiar is already trained up. Might make the transition easier for her. Okay, Boon. You and Silva head down to Atlantis and talk with the council. I do want to keep the dreadnought under wraps for now; at this point, I'm already going to be in trouble for not mentioning it, so what's another few weeks? Me and Alister will convince Cora she needs to do this, and then you will have to get back here quickly so she has time to adapt. I'm not sure how long we will have; if I know anything about the speed of government, it's going to be longer than the 'immediate return' order is hinting at."

CHAPTER 5

WITH A FAMILIAR FLASH, the *Raven*'s view screen resolved into the familiar sights of the Sol System. Earth hung to their left, her blue and white surface looking very inviting after the two weeks the *Raven* and her crew had been out scouring the galaxy for humanity's distant cousins.

"Captain, I have a communication from the UHFC," Mezner reported.

"Hopefully a detailed timeline and attack plan," Grimms said from beside Sara, as he flipped through his tablet.

"Put it onscreen."

The screen changed to a recording of Admiral Franklin, his white hair shining in the afternoon light from his office window. "Captain Sonders, it is good that you are back, and I look forward to hearing what you have found. As you may have noticed, the Elif battlecruiser the *Regent* is still in orbit. The prince and the empress are aboard, and are preparing for the retaking of Effrit. The plans are coming together nicely, and we will be prepared to leave when the scattered Elif forces are gathered at the rendezvous point in six days' time.

In the meantime, you and the *Raven* are to dock at Xanadu and resupply.

"I apologize for the early callback, but the Admiralty was getting anxious with the new War Mage recruits, and wanted you close in case they had any questions that the Alant program couldn't handle." He gave a smile. "To be honest, I think they may have realized just how much power a War Mage has, and want to keep you all under watch. You officially have the next five days off for leave, so be sure to rest up. This is going to be quite the battle."

The admiral reached to shut off the recording, but stopped. "One more thing. Two of the War Mage candidates have received their familiars. We are outfitting one of the battleships, the *Catagain*, for a tank system. They will be leading the assault on Effrit with the prince. The *Raven* will be handling the battle for Suttri, the second habitable Elif planet in the system. We don't want to cause an incident between us and the prince by forcing you two into close proximity. I understand, and even agree with your actions, but this is a political matter. I hope you understand."

The screen changed back to the view of Earth, and Sara could make out the huge Elif battlecruiser, the *Regent*, coming over the horizon.

"Well, I guess Boon and I are not the only War Mages anymore," Sara said, feeling a little at a loss for words at the notion.

"We knew it was coming. It had to, or we would never survive this fight," Grimms reassured her.

She nodded. "I know. I'm just not sure what we're fighting for anymore. Not really. We have positioned ourselves as the Elif's hammer, on a conquest to take down their enemies, but is that what's best for humanity?"

Grimms frowned. "Best or not, it's what we've been ordered to do."

"I know. I'll follow orders, you don't have to worry about that. I just feel like there is a lot more going on behind the scenes than we're being told," Sara mused. "There is a change coming; something festering just out of sight."

"I agree," Grimms said, leaning on his elbow as he stared at the Elif battlecruiser from his seat.

THE *RAVEN* BUMPED GENTLY against the airlock of Xanadu Station, Ensign Connors making the move so smoothly that the only indication they had made contact were the green lights informing them of a good seal.

Grimms sent out the leave rotation from his ever-present tablet, as Sara requested over the comm that Boon, Gonders, and Baxter meet them in her ready room.

She and Grimms entered the small room off the bridge, and Sara immediately began preparing five coffees. She had gotten to know each of her crew so well that she knew how they liked theirs without asking.

Grimms and Baxter, if asked, would say black, but that was just posturing. In reality, they liked it with a touch of cream and sugar. Gonders, on the other hand, actually did like it black, and strong. And of course Boon, sweet Boon, liked her cream and sugar with just a splash of coffee.

Sara had yet to decide how she liked her own coffee. She had been drinking it for twenty years, and would change it up regularly depending on her situation.

Right now, she liked it black; not because she actually liked it black, but because she felt like she was wasting time if she tried anything else. It was probably a byproduct of her not knowing what she would have to do next, or how long she had to do it.

She passed out the steaming cups as each member of her

crew entered. The room was small, but there was a bench along one wall, and two chairs in front of the small desk, along with her own chair behind it. Everyone found a seat and sipped quietly on their coffee while Sara organized her thoughts. Alister and Silva had both climbed into Baxter's lap as soon as he sat down, seeing as he had the largest lap of the bunch.

Finally, after what felt like forever, Sara spoke. "We have five days, and a lot to get done in that time. Cora, I am sending Boon and Gonders down to get you a familiar. You need to get on our level if we are going to come out of this war alive."

"Find me something cute. I don't want my familiar to be a badger or something," Cora said lightheartedly.

The statement made Sara cock her head in confusion before she remembered that non-War Mages didn't know that familiars were actually pixies in animal form.

"Don't worry, I'm sure whoever it is will be adorable," Sara said, rolling her eyes. "Grimms, we are going to need to transfer that robot we picked up to the science division. Make arrangements, and be sure that they know to report their findings back to us, in addition to the UHFC. We are still tasked with finding the other humans out there, so it shouldn't be a problem to get the info to us."

Grimms gave a nod. "I've already drafted my report to the science team. I'll be sure to reiterate the need to get us the info."

"Baxter," Sara said, moving on. "I have something a little different for you. I need to know more about what life is like in the Teifen and Elif empires far from the centers of power. What do the common people think of the war, and where do they fall, allegiance-wise, when the shit hits the fan? I have a feeling that things are not as black and white as they may seem. Use whatever resources you need, but if it were me, I would start with the Elif researchers we picked up on Colony Seven-Eighty-Eight. A lot of them are still on Xanadu, working with the UHF to get the tank systems up and running."

He nodded, taking a sip of coffee. "I'll see what I can find out. Is there a particular angle you're looking for?"

"No, just the truth. Try and cut through the nationalism and get the meat of it," Sara said.

She took a gulp of the black brew and set her mug down, looking at each of them in turn. " 'Something is rotten in the state of Denmark', as the bard once said. I want to know what it is. If this whole war is nothing more than the political maneuvering of two empires who have nothing better to do than fight amongst themselves, I want to know."

Grimms cleared his throat. "Ma'am, while I appreciate the idea of us not being in the dark, I don't know that we are in a position to do much about it. The UHFC would need to reconsider their position before we can change direction."

Sara pursed her lips. "The UHFC will be in the loop, but they are slow to react, like any government organization. I cannot stand by and watch human lives get thrown into the fires of war because one empire says so. I have a duty to protect my people, whatever the cost."

"You're not a law unto yourself," Cora said, concern in her voice.

"No, I am not," Sara lied.

CHAPTER 6

BOON LOUNGED in the shuttle's co-pilot seat, one leg
thrown over the armrest, as she watched Gonders pilot the
craft toward the Azores. She smiled at the look of determined
concentration on her bonded guard, and full-time lover's,
face.

"Why are you staring at me, weirdo?" Isabella said with a
false irritation that made Boon grin even more.

"Because I want to make sure you're not just a figment of
my imagination," she replied, tucking a strand of blonde hair
behind her ear.

Isabella looked over at her, and smiled a bright white
smile of her own. "Fair enough. I tend to do the same thing,
but I have the common courtesy to do it while you're
asleep."

Boon laughed. "Who's the weirdo, again?"

The island of São Miguel came over the horizon, green
and vibrant against the deep blue of the surrounding Atlantic
Ocean. As they circled the island, Silva climbed onto the
dashboard and watched through the windshield, chattering

excitedly when the small forest that held the pixie city of Atlantis came into view.

"That's odd," Gonders commented, looking at the shuttle's scanner.

"What?" Boon asked, craning her neck, looking for anything out of the ordinary.

"There's a shuttle in the meadow beside the forest. It's UHF, but it doesn't have a ship designation. Probably one of the unmarked ones from Command."

A spike of fear ran up Boon's neck. "Why would someone from Command be here? They shouldn't even be able to get past the pixie wards around the area."

"I don't know, but I'm guessing we're about to find out. I'm going to put us down right beside it,"

BAXTER STEPPED into the bar from the main promenade on Xanadu Station. He had been stopping in at every establishment along the way, looking for a very particular set of people. Looking over the heads of the patrons seated at tables and bellied up to the long, wooden bar, he was about to step back out and continue on to the next establishment when he saw what he was looking for.

At the back of the small place was a table dimly lit, with a group of Elif packed around it, sitting on high stools. Stepping closer, he thought he even recognized one of them as the medical doctor from Colony 788.

Dr. Lister, if I remember correctly.

Baxter moved through the crowd, trying not to get too pushy, but having to move a few people to squeeze through. A few gave him hard looks, which surprised him, until he remembered he was out of uniform, and his jeans and black tee shirt were not exactly screaming 'Sergeant Major'. He gave them nods and pushed on past, relying on his superior size and friendly face to keep him out of trouble.

The sea of people finally parted, and he found himself standing next to the group of Elif that were huddled close around their table. They seemed comfortable enough, just in quiet conversation. At least, as quiet as the music blaring over the sound system allowed.

Baxter reached out and put a hand on the doctor's shoulder, making her turn to face him. "Hello, doctor. I saw you from across the bar, and thought I would stop over. How have you been?" he asked, his voice raising to compensate for the background noise.

It took a few beats, but then recognition flooded the doctor's face. "Sergeant Major Baxter, I never expected to see you here. Please, join us," she invited, her pretty face splitting into a grin as the rest of the Elif shuffled around to make room for him at their table.

"Thank you," he said, puling an empty stool over and crowding into the tight group.

When everyone leaned in, the sounds of the bar fell away somewhat, making conversation less of a shouting match. The number of beautiful faces present was a little intimidating to those not used to the Elif's natural looks, but luckily, Baxter was well-versed.

"I'm surprised you're still on the station. I would have thought you would have shipped off when we got back from Colony Seven-Eighty-Eight," he admitted.

The doctor tugged on her long, pointed ear—a habit a lot of Elif had—before saying, "We would have, but the UHFC offered us an opportunity to study the tank systems, and how they interact with the cores we've found. They wanted a medical team to supervise the candidates, and they thought my team and I would be perfect," she said, indicating the half-dozen Elif with them.

"Where did you get a core to test with?" Baxter asked, surprised they had access to one, considering there were only three in the known universe. Well, four counting the one on the dreadnought, but the UHFC didn't even know about the ship.

"Oh," her voice tinkled with laughter, "we don't have a core. Most of our data is coming from the readouts from Captain Sonders' tank. We are still going over the data from the tests that were performed right before the battle with the Teifen governor."

Baxter wondered if Sara and Cora knew that their information was being scrutinized this closely. He shook his head and pushed forward, despite wanting to know more.

"Where are you from, Dr. Lister? Originally," he asked, raising a hand to a waitress and gesturing that he would like a round for the table.

"Oh, thank you, Sergeant," Dr. Lister said, acknowledging Baxter's generosity, then she pointed to a pair of male Elif on the other side of the table. "Chezzi, Gran, and myself all come from the same planet: Kister. It's a little out of the way, closer to the Rim. It was actually by chance that we met at university on Suttri while getting our medical and spell training."

Baxter raised an eyebrow. "The Rim? What was that like?" he asked, as the waitress passed out the new round of drinks.

Dr. Lister smiled in a far off way. "Very different than life in the core. Much slower paced," she said, nodding to the waitress as she set down her glass. "A lot less political," she continued.

Baxter laughed. "Sounds great. I feel like we can all use a little less politics from time to time. Why did you leave?"

Dr. Lister shrugged. "Suttri has the best medical school in the galaxy." She gave an ironic smile. "It also has compulsory civil service attached to it."

Baxter and the group of Elif talked late into the evening, both sharing stories of growing up in their respective communities. By the time the bartender shouted last call, Baxter had the distinct impression that the Elif Royal Family was not held in quite the esteem the Royals thought they were.

"They're a bit antiquated," Dr. Lister said, her cheeks red with drink.

Gran laughed, "Antiquated? More like 'in the way', if you ask me. It's nearly impossible to get funding for any kind of new research. They want to keep everything just the way it is."

"That and the military acts like a little lost puppy without them," Chezzi said, rolling her eyes before downing the last slug of whiskey in her glass. "It's a little hard to get funding when every credit is spent on new ships for the fleet."

The round of grumbles that followed Chezzi's last statement was all Baxter needed to realize the Elif were not all of the same mind. He gave a smile behind the rim of his glass, *Sara was right. It seems the Royals forgot the most important rule. Keep your people happy, and they stay loyal.*

BOON STEPPED down from the shuttle's ramp as soon as it hit the grass, Gonders right on her heels. They had decided to wear hiking-appropriate clothes for the trip to Atlantis. Boon had warned Isabella that it would take a while to make it through the forest to the city proper, so Gonders printed them up some athletic tights and zip-up performance shirts, along with hiking boots.

They either looked like a pair of experienced hikers, or a pair of young, rich girls who had never hiked a day in their lives.

Boon checked out Gonders' ass as she passed by to check on the other shuttle. "Hey! Did you make my pants tighter than yours?" she said, twisting at the waist to try and check out her own ass.

Gonders turned her face Boon's way and flashed her a bright white smile. "I would never do such a thing." Her denial was dripping with sarcasm.

"You bitch!" Boon said, her mouth open in disbelief at the thought of Gonders trying to show off her girlfriend's ass.

Gonders slapped her own muscled butt cheek, and winked. "Sorry babe. I just thought you would want to look your best."

"Oh, my god, you are the worst! We're on an important mission here, and you're thinking about how my ass looks?" Boon said, ignoring the irony of that statement.

Gonders turned back to the shuttle as she approached the open ramp, but the smile was obvious in her voice. "Oh, babe, I'm always thinking about how your ass looks."

Boon flushed, and couldn't help but smile. "Well, as long as you're consistent, I guess."

When Gonders spoke, her voice told Boon that the flirting was over for now. "It's empty. Looks like they got here maybe half an hour ago, if the matted down grass is any indication. I'd say we have some company."

Silva began to chatter, and circled Boon's neck so that she was looking behind them, toward the forest. Boon turned and saw several small figures in Aetheric armor stepping from the woods, their small coil rifles over their shoulders.

"Izz, we have company," Boon announced, getting Gonders' attention.

The soldiers spread out, letting a female figure in robes step past them. She pulled her hood down, and Boon recognized her from her previous visit as Nyx, the Keeper of the Records.

The two women approached one another, and when they were a few meters away, Nyx gave them a polite bow from the waist. "War Mage, it is good to see you once again. Are you here to see your brothers?"

"Holy shit," Gonders mumbled beside Boon, making her turn in surprise at the uncharacteristic behavior.

Gonders' mouth was open, and her eyes were wide enough that Boon could see white all around her irises.

"Oh, that's right. You've never seen a pixie before." She glanced at Silva sitting on her shoulder. "Well, not in their true form, anyway." Boon gave a bow to the pixies, "Nyx, it is good to see you, as well. This is my bonded guard, Isabella Gonders. Izz, this is Nyx Morenna, Keeper of the Records."

Gonders gave a wide-eyed wave. "Hello."

Boon smiled at her girlfriend's brain overload, and turned back to Nyx. "You said something about meeting our brothers? Is that who came in the other shuttle?"

Nyx gave a nod. "Yes. I assumed you had come to meet with them. Is this not the case?"

Boon shook her head, sending her blonde ponytail dancing. "I had no idea they would be here. Actually, we've never met them. This should be interesting."

Nyx motioned to the path she had just come down. "Then we should make our way to the city."

Boon laced her fingers through Gonders', and a smile, pulled her along behind the retreating pixies. "Pretty cool, huh?"

"Amazing," Gonders replied, looking at the small, white ferret on Boon's shoulders as if for the first time.

Silva gave Isabelle a wink before turning to watch the path ahead.

"Holy shit," she reiterated.

CHAPTER 7

WITH A HISS, the top of Cora's tank split, and each side hinged open until the still surface of the light blue liquid was revealed, still as glass. Sara sat cross-legged on the small plat-form around the top of the tank, wearing a battlesuit and wringing her hands nervously.

"Calm down, Sara. This is a normal procedure, and it's going to be much easier now that the core is installed. The mechanical systems of the tank will take care of my extrac-tion; no coughing up blue liquid this time," Cora assured her through the speakers.

Dr. Green and Dr. Teichek were monitoring the various systems around the tank, and Green said, "We're all ready on our end, Cora. You're up."

"Thanks, Caroline. See you in a second. I'm going offline now," Cora said. Her voice was calm, a sharp contrast to the knots forming in Sara's belly.

"Be careful," Sara said, trying and failing to keep her voice from cracking.

There was no response. Instead, Sara could see a small circle open in the floor of the tank, and a segmented, metal, tentacle-like appendage snaked out, probing the tank until it touched Cora's foot. As soon as it made contact, it followed the contours of her body, up to her face.

Sara was doing everything she could not to use her magic to rip the tentacle to shreds, knowing it was just her fear of the unknown messing with her. Still, her heart would not stop racing.

I haven't seen Cora in the flesh in a couple of months. God, it seems way longer than that since we were living in the dorm together.

The end of the appendage suddenly folded open, like the gaping mouth of some sea monster, and latched itself onto Cora's face, covering her nose and mouth.

Sara jumped, calling up a force spell from Alister, who was sitting beside her. He provided the requested spell, but also sent her a feeling of calm that took the edge off her panic. She didn't power the spell.

There was a pregnant moment of silence as everyone stared at Cora's still form. Finally, a series of bubbles came from under the tentacle mask, and her body shuddered. Then a spasm sent her drifting toward the edge of the tank, but the gravity supporters pulled her back to center. Another spasm sent her up toward the surface, and Sara reached out for her sister, but Cora sank back to center. Another series of bubbles flowed from the mask, then another. Soon, the bubbles were coming at what Sara judged to be normal breathing intervals, and she relaxed a little.

Cora's eyes popped open, as she jerked to consciousness. She looked around in confusion for a few seconds, before making eye contact with Sara through the blue haze of the Aetherically-sensitive liquid. Sara saw Cora's cheeks rise, turning her green eyes to slits as she smiled under the mask, and Cora raised up a hand for Sara to grab.

Sara didn't hesitate, and reached into the liquid, holding

onto the railing to keep her balance, and grabbed her twin's wrist while Cora did the same. With a grunt, Sara pulled Cora up until she came out of the gravity field and floated up to the surface. As soon as her head broke the surface, the tentacle mask detached and retreated into its hole, closing the opening behind it.

Sara and Cora stared at one another for a few seconds.

Eventually, Sara quietly asked, "Are you okay?"

Cora smiled again. "Oh yeah. You better have gotten me a cheeseburger, though, or I'm going to thump you good."

Alister gave a "Meerow!" at the mention of cheeseburgers.

Cora looked over at him and gave a chuckle. "Hello, Alister. It's good to see you. Don't worry, I'll be sure you get your own burger."

Alister began to purr unabashedly, to the sisters' great delight.

SARA WAS SITTING at the table in her room, across from her twin sister, who was stuffing as much cheeseburger into her mouth as she could. Alister was sitting on the table eating a meat patty with nearly the same gusto.

"Careful. Just because you haven't been breathing air for the last two months doesn't mean you don't need it now," Sara said with a smile, as Cora swallowed down her current bite with minimal chewing.

Cora wore only a bathrobe, not having taken the time to put on clothes after her shower and medical exam. Her bare feet were crossed and swinging like a child's under her seat.

"Hey—" She coughed on a bit that she hadn't quite gotten down, and swallowed again. "I haven't eaten in a while. Don't tell me to mind my manners," she retorted, taking another heroic bite.

Sara laughed and slid her untouched burger toward her ravenous sister, who snaked out a hand, and snatched the plate to her side. "Fanks," she said, blowing a bit of burger onto the table.

Sara laughed, her blue eyes twinkling with mirth. "God, I've missed you."

Cora forced the bite down and gave a toothy grin. "Missed you too, sis. So, how have you and the big guy been getting on? Things good?" she asked, taking a sip of beer before chomping the last of her burger in one go and chewing noisily.

"You've been here. Haven't you seen?" Sara asked, cocking her head to the side.

Cora scrunched up her face in disgust. "Ew, gross. I'm not going to watch you two in here. I have no idea what you get up to."

"We're doing pretty great. The whole bonded thing took some getting used to, but when you can't hide your feelings, communication becomes pretty easy. I can't say 'I'm fine' if he can feel that I'm not. So, it's the most honest relationship I've ever been in," Sara said, leaning back and taking a sip of her own beer. She squinted her eyes in contemplation. "He's pretty amazing. The only person I've ever trusted this much is you. I didn't know it could be like this," she said dreamily.

"*Gaack*," Cora said, as she mockingly shoved a finger down her own throat. "Oh, man. You are way further gone than I thought."

Sara laughed and threw her napkin at Cora. "Shut up. You asked."

"Yeah, but if I knew it was going to be so syrupy sweet, I wouldn't have requested dessert," she said, waggling her eyebrows at the tray of brownies on the kitchenette's counter.

Sara swung out of her chair and walked over to the counter. Picking up the knife beside the tray, she began to cut oversized brownies.

"Boon and Gonders are getting you a familiar," she told her sister, redirecting the conversation.

Cora was quiet as she took another bite.

Sara turned her way, and saw that Cora had a bit of a deer-in-the-headlights look as she chewed.

"You knew this was coming. What's wrong?" she asked, plating the two brownies and placing one next to Cora's second plate before taking her seat again.

Cora swallowed and took a drink before answering. "I just worry that I won't be able to adapt quickly enough. We're set to lead a planetary invasion in five days. What if I have the same troubles you did with Alister?" she asked, looking over at the black cat.

Alister was laying on his side on the table, the burger patty half gone. He didn't even raise his head at the mention of his name. His distended belly rose and fell with the shallow breaths of one who had eaten so much, there was no more room for air in their lungs.

"It'll be different for you. We were the first in a long time, and had no one to guide us. But look at Boon; she got the hang of it in just a few days. Hell, she led the assault on the Teifen dreadnought," Sara said, taking a bite of the gooey chocolate cake.

"Yeah, but she didn't have the fate of an entire ship to worry about. If she didn't get the hang of it right off, it wouldn't mean that the ship couldn't warp, or defend itself if we were attacked. I just don't know that it's worth the risk."

"There's no question that it has to happen. There is already a new set of War Mage twins at the UHFC, and they are going to be taking command of the battleship *Catagain* in the next few days. The fleet is down to a couple dozen ships after the battle with the Teifen. We need every advantage we can get. In the next year, the fleet might be able to get back to where they were before the attack, but that's a pretty big maybe," Sara said, leaning back in her chair and giving her twin a hard look. "We need this, Cora. If it means we don't participate in the battle for Effrit, then so be it; in the long run, we will be better off as a species if you take this familiar. I can't fight this battle alone. I need you to come with me."

Cora gave Sara a half-smile and held up her brownie. "When did you become so forward thinking?"

Sara took a swig of beer. "Probably around the time I was ripping a Teifen carrier in half over the skies of Colony Seven-Eighty-Eight."

CHAPTER 8

CORA SAT in Sara's room, her feet tucked under her on the small couch as she contemplated the next few days and what she should do. She was still in her bathrobe; she wasn't planning on leaving the room until Sara got done with her shift.

She was biting a nail and twirling a strand of her fire-engine-red hair around a finger as she stared off into space, when the door chime sounded, jarring her back to the present.

"Come in," she said, before remembering she was only wearing a robe that came to mid-thigh.

The door slid open, and Grimms stepped in, a smile on his handsome face. He froze when he saw she was not fully dressed. "Oh, should I come back later?" he asked, gesturing to her bare legs.

Cora turned a little red and stood, trying to pull the robe down further, but ended up exposing more of her chest, to her horror. Grimms, to his credit, just turned around to face away from her as the door slid shut in his face.

"Uh, sorry. I kind of forgot I wasn't dressed. Give me a

second, I'll put something on," she said, quickly stepping over to the closet and opening it up.

The closet held a large collection of battlesuits and uniforms, but she rummaged in the bottom for a pair of yoga pants and a tank top.

Cora checked on Grimms over her shoulder, saw that he was still looking at the door, and dropped the robe, quickly slipping on the pants and tank top. That's when she noticed her nipples were poking the thin material in a rather obvious way. She rummaged some more, found a red pullover hoodie, and slipped into that. Judging that she was now properly covered, she turned back to the commander.

"Okay, I'm decent. Sorry about that, Charles. You can turn around."

He did so, but cautiously, as if worried she was mistaken. "Ah, good to see you walking around, Cora," he said, his smile flashing behind his meticulously trimmed, white beard.

She gave a laugh and flopped back down on the couch. "It's good to be out, but there is a little part of me that misses it," she said, her eyes going out of focus for a second before she waved a hand to dispel the thought. "I guess I just have to give it a few days; then I'll be wishing I was out again," she laughed.

Grimms laughed with her. "I know the feeling. Every time I went on vacation, the only thing I could think about was all the work I had back on base. Then when I was behind the desk, all I could think about was being on vacation again."

Cora patted the couch beside her. "Have a seat. Was there something you wanted to talk about, or were you just stopping by to say hello?"

He came around the coffee table and sat at the opposite end of the couch. "I was speaking with your sister, and she mentioned that you were having some trepidation about completing the Familiar spell. I thought maybe talking out your fears with me would help... get an outside perspective, if you will."

Cora pulled her knees up to her chest and sat sideways on the couch to face him. The couch was small, so her bare feet were only a few centimeters from his thigh, but he didn't make a move to put any distance between them.

Cora gave a smile at that, and wiggled her toes before speaking. "I guess I do value your opinion more than most. What would you do in my position? Take the chance and become a War Mage, but potentially lose your magical abilities right before we are supposed to go into battle, or not take the familiar, and let us operate at a disadvantage?"

Grimms glanced down at her wiggling toes—just for a second, but Cora didn't miss it.

He cleared his throat. "You're forgetting about option number three: you take the familiar, become a War Mage, and kick serious ass. You can't think in the negative, Cora. Take it from this old man; you need to take chances sometimes, or you end up regretting not doing so later."

"You're not an old man, Charles. You're fifty. Maybe thirty years ago fifty was old, but with the arrival of the Elif and the advanced medicine and magic they brought? You're early middle-age at best," she said with as warm a smile as she could make.

Charles Grimms rolled his eyes, and Cora nearly fell off the couch in surprise. She had not been expecting that from him; he was always so reserved.

"I'm old enough to be your father... that makes me too old," he said, looking away from her.

She lifted her left foot, and lightly jabbed him in his tight stomach. He jumped at her prodding.

"You have a six-pack, Chuck," she teased. "I don't know any old men who have six-packs." She put her foot down on the cushion, making sure her toes were touching his thigh, and waited for him to make eye contact. "Old is a state of mind. And I don't want to regret the decisions I didn't make."

Grimms looked at her for a long time before saying, "We're not talking about you becoming a War Mage anymore, are we?"

Cora shook her head. "I had already decided to go through with it before you got here."

"Then what are we talking about?" he asked, raising an eyebrow.

Cora's green eyes sparkled, "I don't care what we talk about, as long as you don't leave."

He stared at her for a long second, at war with himself. "It's not right, Captain."

She smiled. "Actually, I checked. There's nothing in the rules of conduct that explicitly forbids... this."

Grimms kept his expression neutral. "There isn't? That seems like an oversight on someone's part."

Cora leaned forward, dropping her knees to the side. "From where I'm sitting, it seems like they knew exactly what they were doing."

He put a hand on her shoulder. "I don't think we should. We need to keep a professional relationship, for the crew's sake."

"Charles, I live in a tank of blue liquid ninety-nine percent of the time. Don't make me beg." She held his gaze and bit her lip.

He smiled. "You're the devil."

She smiled back. "Only when I need to be."

Then she leaned in and kissed him on the lips.

CHAPTER 9

BOON AND GONDERS followed Nyx through the large double doors into the pixie council's chamber in the center of the city. Gonders had yet to close her mouth from the shock of seeing an entire city filled with the fifteen-centimeter-tall pixies, going about their daily routines.

Standing in the center of the chambers and facing the ornate, wooden platforms where the pixie council sat were two human men. Even from the back, Boon could tell they were identical twins, and the small gray cat and black mongoose at their feet identified them as the War Mages that Nyx had mentioned.

The mage on Boon's left was speaking as they entered. "Our familiars recommended that we come seek counsel for our future brothers and sisters. The UHFC has twelve sets of twins trying to finish the Familiar spell as we speak, and Niff," he indicated the gray cat at his feet, "said they would have a much easier time in their transition if we were to come and collect volunteers."

"Finally, a sensible thought from a Chosen One," the

crotchety councilmember that Boon remembered well from her last visit said. "We will have members of the Keepers find suitable pixies. About time they started pulling their weight." He leaned to the side, noticing Nyx approaching with the newcomers. "Ah, speaking of the Keepers. Nyx, we need to find some volunteers for these two."

The twins turned, and Boon saw that the men were older than she would have first guessed—maybe in their mid-thirties. Both had black hair and blue eyes that seemed to glow with an inner light. Each was wearing their military uniform, with the name 'Rodgers' over the left breast. They wore matching shocked expressions at the sight of the approaching pair of women.

"Who are you?" the second twin asked, his mongoose turning to regard Silva, draped over Boon's neck.

At that moment, Boon was happy that she had insisted they not come in military clothing, and hoped she could keep her identity secret, or at least ambiguous. After her conversation with Sara about the UHFC not knowing she was a War Mage, she didn't want word to get back without Sara knowing.

Shit, I'm going to have to get creative with these two.

"Hello," she said, approaching them and offering her hand. "My name is Alicia, and this is my friend Isabella."

The first twin took her hand and gave it a hard shake, and the second did the same, but with much less force.

"I am Gordon, and this is Reese. We are the new captains of the *Catagain,*" the first twin said, eyeing the two women suspiciously. "I thought the only other War Mage was Sara Sonders, captain of the *Raven.*"

Boon put on her most innocent face, and hoped she was better at misdirection than outright lying. "Oh, I wouldn't know how many other War Mages there are. What's a *Catagain*?"

Boon could feel Gonders' eyes on her back, but their connection told her that she was going to play along, even if she didn't like it.

Gordon cocked his head. "The *Catagain* is the newest battleship in the fleet. Are you not in the UHF?"

Boon gave a light laugh and indicated hers and Gonders' hiking clothes. "Do we look like we're soldiers?"

"If you're not in the military, how did you become a War Mage?" Reese asked.

"Not all mages start in the military," Boon said, cringing at the weak excuse.

Nyx stepped forward and addressed the twins before they could ask Boon for clarification. "You are seeking volunteers? I can take you to the Hall of Records. Please follow me." She turned and walked out the doors they had just entered, not waiting for the twins in the least.

Gordon looked at her retreating back, then back at Boon's smiling face. "We need to talk to you some more. Stay here and wait for us. The UHFC will want to know about you," he said firmly, before jogging around them to catch up with Nyx.

Boon gave him a really shitty impression of a salute.

When they were gone, she let out a breath she didn't realize she had been holding.

"Why don't you want them to know you are part of their organization?" the silver-haired female pixie on the council asked. Boon couldn't remember her name.

They stepped closer, and Boon gave a short bow at the waist. Gonders followed suit. "Sara wants to keep me a secret for now. I must admit that I'm not entirely sure why, but she is my captain, and I follow orders."

The silver-haired female nodded. "If that is what the First Mage wishes, we shall keep it quiet as well," she said, adjusting her robes. "What brings you here, War Mage? Do you require assistance?"

Boon smiled. "Actually, we need a volunteer, as well, for Cora Sonders—Sara's sister. And we need to speak to you about the dreadnought," she added on a whim. Then, after a moment's consideration, "And your safety."

CHAPTER 10

"You want us to keep knowledge of the dreadnought from the rest of the War Mages?" the silver-haired pixie clarified. Her severe eyebrow rose ever so slightly.

"If you can, that would be for the best. Sara wishes to study its contents before she is restricted access by our government," Boon said, realizing she was saying that Sara wanted, in some respects, to betray her leaders.

"We can do this, of course. We will have an Aether meet, and let the populace know the First Mage's wishes," another female pixie said, her black hair cut short in a bob.

"An Aether meet?" Boon asked, her face a mask of confusion.

The grumpy councilmember cleared his throat loudly. "Yes. We will have a Moot in the Aether. All pixies will be there, and we can make the announcement. Is there anything else the First Mage would like us to keep from her people?" he asked, somewhat flippantly.

Boon looked at Gonders, who shrugged. Silva climbed to Boon's shoulder and put one of her small paws on her Mage's cheek.

A feeling of needing safety filled Boon's mind, and she knew what the ferret was trying to say.

"Right, thanks, Silva," she said with a smile before turning back to the pixie council. "Sara is concerned about the safety of this city, and the pixies in general. If every new War Mage comes here, it will become apparent to the UHFC that there is something here they might want, and they'll investigate. Even if we can't talk about the pixies with anyone but a bonded guard, or another War Mage, our actions could be interpreted by our commanders."

"We have had the same concerns. I propose that during the Aether meet, we begin to funnel War Mages to other cities to speak with the leaders around the globe. We do not want to draw too much attention to this place. We appreciate the First Mage's concern for our safety," the silver-haired one said with a slight bow of her head.

"You keep calling Sara the 'First Mage'. What does that mean?" Boon asked.

"We are referring to her rank," the grumpy one said with a huff.

"Rank? Because she is a ship's captain?"

"Her rank among human organizations is irrelevant. She was the first War Mage on Earth, therefore she is ranked first among them," said one of the other councilmembers.

"Uh, so what rank am I?" Boon asked cautiously, fearing the answer.

"You are the Second Mage."

"What does the ranking mean?" Gonders asked, stepping up beside Boon.

The grumpy pixie gave her a disapproving look, but answered her. "It means that Alicia's word is law above all but Sara's. If Alicia gives an order, it will be followed as law until Sara countermands that order."

"Oh, shit," Boon said, her eyes wide. *This could turn into a clusterfuck really easily*. She looked up and asked, "So the two Mages that just left... they are Third and Fourth?"

"Correct," he said, as if it were the most obvious thing in the world.

"Shit. We need a volunteer for Cora right away," Boon said to the council.

The answer came from behind them, and Boon and Gonders swiveled their heads to see who was speaking.

"I have already volunteered for that position. We were just waiting for you to return," Nyx said, walking back into the chamber.

The twins were not with her, to Boon's relief.

As if reading her mind, Nyx continued, "It seemed that you did not want to speak with the new War Mages, so I am keeping them busy, selecting from the pool of Keepers. If you wish to avoid them further, as I think you do, we should leave soon."

"Oh, that is wonderful, thank you," Boon said with a smile. She really did like the pixie, and believed she and Cora would get along famously. "I think we have covered everything Sara wanted us to talk about. When can you leave?"

"I am ready now," Nyx said with a small bow.

CHAPTER 11

SARA AND CORA stood next to each other, leaning into the projection table and observing the plans that had been sent a few minutes before by the UHFC. Grimms and Baxter were on the opposite side, and Alister was lazily sprawled on Sara's captain's chair. The bridge was empty except for the five of them, the rest of the bridge crew being on leave.

The holo projection showed the Elif home system. The worlds of Effrit and Suttri were highlighted, with the most recent Teifen troop movements playing out around the system.

Grimms explained the situation while the simulation played. "The Elif admiral in charge of the operation," Grimms glanced at his tablet, "Admiral Zett, has a double attack strategy in mind. He wants each attack to be led by a War-Mage-controlled ship, but he wants us to play a minimal role, if possible. He has expressed his concerns that most of the fleet does not know that humans are back in the game, and our presence could cause problems."

"How can they not know about us? Every Elif we have met didn't seem all that surprised to see humans," Sara said.

"The Elif we have come into contact with were warned in advance. It seems that the move to bring humans back into the war was not a universally approved idea. The late emperor was funneling resources into uplifting humanity as a sort of last resort. Only the higher-ups knew about us," Grimms concluded.

"From what I gathered, talking with the Elif I found on the station, humans are seen as a kind of boogeyman throughout the galaxy; a monster they tell their children about to keep them in line," Baxter added.

"Okay, but if we show up and lead the assault on Effrit and Suttri, won't they see us? I mean, we can't very well lead them in battle if they don't know we're there," Cora said.

"Admiral Zett is telling them that we are a secret military branch they have been working on. Essentially, we will be like their Delta team, or their Green Berets. In and out without any actual contact with the main forces," Grimms summated, scratching his beard and pointedly not looking at Cora.

"So they are telling the Elif fleet that we are Elif?" Baxter inferred.

Grimms gave a gruff laugh. "That's what I got from our conversation. The admiral made it sound like their people would be too afraid of us monsters of legend to properly concentrate on the battle."

Everyone gave a laugh except Sara. She stroked her bottom lip in contemplation before saying, "This is what I've been talking about. I think we may have been misled by our benefactors from the start. What if we really are the monsters? Is there something about humanity that turns us into a terror when we get too much power? Some kind of predisposition at work?"

That sobered the rest of the team up, and they exchanged glances before Cora said, "We do have a tendency to play a heavy hand when the opportunity is presented. World wars should never have been a thing, but we were in two in less than a generation. I could see how that kind of thinking would scare the shit out of a bunch of Elif. The Teifen, though, seem just as aggressive as we are, if not more. To be honest, I think the only reason the Elif have lasted this long against them is that the Teifen have been fighting a two-front war, with the Galvox on the back side."

"What I got from talking with Dr. Lister and her companions is that the attacking Teifen we are seeing are from the core of the system. The outer worlds are not nearly as aggressive; they just want to get along with their neighbors and build a life for themselves," Baxter said.

"You're saying that these are the zealots? There are millions of them, though. I don't know if the case can be made that these are just bad apples," Sara said, cocking an eyebrow.

"Don't forget we are talking about an empire that covers hundreds of systems, and has a population in the hundreds of trillions; everything we have seen from the Teifen so far wouldn't even constitute a rounding error," Baxter replied.

"Regardless of why they are fighting us, we need to be prepared for the worst. Though, the Elif have quite the empire backing them, as well, even after the system was taken. The numbers are just incredible; we are outmatched in all possible aspects of this conflict," Grimms admitted, stroking his beard.

They stood in silence for a few minutes of contemplation before Grimms brought them back on track. "We should go over the attack plan," he said decidedly, and started the simulation once again. "The Elif forces will be split into two units. The one attacking Effrit will be led by the *Catagain*, and the attack on Suttri will be led by the *Raven*. We will have twenty-seven hundred ships in our attack force, which will be coordinated by the battlecruiser *Hast* and her commander, Admiral Vorst," Grimms said, bringing up a hologram of the ship in question.

It was a very aggressive ship design for the Elif. There were obvious nods to the human ship designs, having more sharp edges than rounded corners that had been the standard.

"The admiral has made it clear that they only want us to engage if needed; otherwise, he wants his own forces to take this victory," Grimms continued. "I do believe Admiral Vorst is a bit of a speciesist, if not a complete narcissist."

Sara switched the holo back to the system view and took in all the Teifen ships surrounding the two Elif planets. She grinned. "I suppose I don't mind what he is, as long as it means we don't have to take the brunt of the attack."

CHAPTER 12

Sara kicked her feet up on the small desk in her ready room, and let out a breath of exasperation as she punched in a few more words on her tablet. Alister lifted his head off his paws and regarded her with a raised eyebrow from the couch.

"Don't give me that look. You're not the one who has to do all the reports around here," she grumbled.

"Merp?" he replied.

She frowned. "Yeah, I suppose Grimms does the brunt of the work. But it's still a bitch. Honestly, I don't know how he makes the time; this is beyond tedious."

Alister gave her a smile and laid his head back down.

"God I wish I was a cat. You have it so easy," she said longingly.

Alister just flipped an ear in reply, but he still had a smile on his little, black, furry face.

The door chime sounded, and Sara practically threw her tablet down in excitement as she said, "Enter."

The door slid open, and Boon and Gonders walked through. Silva was hopping along behind them. Then, to

Sara's amazement, a pixie in a long, brown robe with a deep hood came walking in behind Silva.

"Uh, what the fuck?" Sara asked, her mouth not quite able to close.

The small figure dropped the hood to her shoulders, and the captain immediately recognized her.

"Nyx? Is that you? How the fuck are you just walking around the ship? Aren't you scared someone will see you?" Sara asked, jumping up and quickly sticking her head out the door.

The bridge was empty except for Mezner, who was sitting at her console, working on a report of her own.

She saw Sara stick her head out, and gave a short wave. "Is there something I can do for you, Captain?"

Sara looked down at her feet and met gazes with Nyx, who was looking up at her with a small smile on her face.

Sara turned back to Mezner and narrowed her eyes. "Did you see anything... suspicious come through here?"

Mezner wore a look of confusion as she replied, "No, just Ensign Boon and Specialist Gonders going in there. Was there something else?"

Sara looked down at Nyx, then back to Mezner and shook her head. "No. Uh, thanks."

"No problem, ma'am." She looked back to her tablet and resumed typing.

Sara stepped back into the ready room and closed the door, then knelt down in front of the newcomer. "Hello, Nyx. It's good to see you, even if no one else can." She smiled and held out her hand.

Nyx took one of Sara's fingers in her hand and gave it a shake. "It is good to be here, First Mage."

Sara looked to Gonders and Boon, both of whom were still dressed in their hiking gear. "Can you two see her? Or am I going crazy?"

Boon laughed. "Of course we can see her. We brought her here."

"Then how did Mezner not notice you?" Sara asked the blonde pixie.

"Remember when I told you about the spellform Alant and Altis gave us?" she asked, and continued once Sara nodded, "Well, it extends beyond the city. It puts a kind of shroud around us so that normal humans and mages don't perceive us. It wears off eventually, but for a few weeks after we leave a city, we are very difficult to spot."

"You're invisible to humans?" Sara asked.

Alister jumped off the couch and greeted Silva, engaging in their usual romp, before coming over to Nyx. He sat in front of her, and offered his paw to shake.

Nyx took the offered paw. "Hello, Alister. It is good to see you again." She turned to Sara and continued. "I am not invisible, I'm just not something they notice. I suppose it is possible to come across a human that is so perceptive, they might think something is there, but it is incredibly rare."

Sara stood and put her hands on her hips. "Huh, that's crazy. I had no idea it would be this easy to get a pixie on a ship."

"Yeah, we were pretty worried about it ourselves," Boon said.

Gonders rolled her eyes. "*You* were worried. I figured Nyx knew what she was doing."

Boon's jaw dropped at the statement. "That is such a load of horse poo. You were sweating like a drug smuggler when they checked our bags at the station gate."

Gonders shrugged. "It was hot."

"It's a space station. It's always the same temperature," Boon said.

Gonders just smiled at her.

Sara rounded her desk and sat down. She avoided

looking at the tablet, and instead leaned forward with her elbows on the desktop and gazed down at Nyx.

"So, why have you come? I though Boon was going to bring back a volunteer for Cora."

Nyx nodded and spread her arms. "And here I am, First Mage."

"You? I thought you had important work to do back in Alantis?" Sara asked, surprised.

"There is no greater or more important work than being a War Mage, First Mage."

Sara narrowed her eyes. "Why do you keep calling me that?"

Nyx opened her mouth, but it was Boon who answered.

"I asked the same thing. Evidently, there is a hierarchy to War Mages. You were the first on Earth, so you are First Mage. I was second, so I'm Second Mage. The *Catagain* War Mages are third and fourth, meaning Cora will be Fifth Mage, as long as we can get her to cast the Familiar spell quickly enough."

"Knowing Cora, she will put you and me to shame with how fast she gets it," Sara said. She switched on her comm when it beeped in her ear. "Speak of the devil. Hello, Cora, we were just talking about you."

"Oh? I thought my ears were burning a bit. Grimms just informed me that Boon and Gonders are back; did they bring a familiar for me?" Cora asked, her voice bright and cheery.

"They did," Sara said, smiling at Nyx.

The pixie had no idea what was being said, and kept her face neutral.

"What is it? Is it something cute, like a puppy?" she asked, laughing.

"Uh, I'm not sure."

Cora sobered slightly. "Haven't you seen it?"

"Uh, it doesn't really work that way. Tell you what, why don't you come to my ready room, and we can explain?" Sara suggested with a shrug to herself.

"Okay. Give me three minutes to put some clothes on, and I'll be right there." She cut off the connection.

"She's on her way. Should we, I don't know, hide you, or something?" Sara asked Nyx.

"I'll be fine. I will just sit over here with Alister and Silva," she said, indicating the couch.

True to her word, three minutes later the door opened, and Cora came in. She had gotten dressed, but Sara noted that she was wearing the bare minimum: a tank top and a pair of Sara's yoga pants. She didn't even have any socks or shoes on.

"Okay, Where is the little bugger?" Cora asked, excitement plain on her face.

Sara heard a tinkling laugh come from Nyx, but Cora didn't seem to register the sound.

"Well, that's the thing," Sara began. "You don't get to see her 'til you complete the summoning. It's kinda part of the deal. Trust me, you'll understand after."

Cora gave Sara a withering look, then noticed Boon and Gonders standing next to the couch. She gave a wave.

"Oh, hey. Didn't see you there. How are you two getting on?" she asked in what Sara recognized as their mother's 'unexpected company' voice.

Boon smiled at Gonders. "We're super good."

Gonders smiled back, but spoke to Cora. "Are you enjoying your time out of the tank?"

Cora got a faraway look on her face. "Oh, you have no idea how much."

Sara cocked her head at that, but Cora continued before

she could make a comment. "Boon, your pants look a little tight, do you want to borrow a pair?"

Gonders gave Boon's butt a quick pat, and said, "Nope, she's fine. They're just right."

Boon's face turned as red as Sara's and Cora's hair, which made the twins laugh out loud.

Then Cora clapped her hands and dropped to the floor in a cross-legged position. "Okay, let's do this thing."

Sara was taken aback. "Just like that? I figured we would have to convince you more."

"Nope. Grimms made a really good argument, and I have to agree with him. The sooner I do this, the faster I can adapt to the new casting. I want to be ready in a few days when we ship out for Suttri."

"Uh, okay. Wow. I didn't think you would be so gung-ho about this. Do you remember the spellforms?" Sara asked, coming to sit beside her sister.

Cora gave her a look like she was an idiot, and Sara found herself missing that look. "Of course I remember," she said tartly. "I made them."

"Okay," Sara replied with a laugh. "I was just checking."

Cora shook out her hands, closed her eyes, and took a deep breath. "Okay, I'm going to do it."

"It's okay if it takes you a while. Boon and I both took..." Sara trailed off when Nyx began to glow with a bluish Aetheric light.

"Holy shit, is she getting it on the *first try*?" Boon asked incredulously.

"Showoff," Sara grumped, but there was no real heat behind the words, and everyone watched the glow around Nyx grow in intensity.

Cora slowly began to float off the ground, like Boon had on the beach; unlike Boon, Cora didn't seem to be fighting the spell at all. In fact, she wore the most serene expression Sara had ever seen on her sister's face.

The power built up, creating a static charge around them, and Sara was shocked several times from the carpet. A humming started up in a frequency that was felt more than heard.

Sara looked to the pixie on the couch. She was glowing so brightly that it was hard to look directly at her, but Sara wanted to see what was going to happen to her, so she continued to watch even after her eyes began to water.

Nyx stood and walked to the edge of the couch, her arms held up like she was praying, but she seemed to be growing shorter with every step. It took Sara a moment to realize the pixie wasn't getting shorter; she was morphing into another shape altogether. By the time she had taken three steps, she fell forward, landing on all fours, and her hands grew into thick but tiny paws. Pointed ears began to sprout from her head, while her nose and mouth pushed forward into a snout.

The glow became too much for Sara to stare into. She had to look away, or she would be seeing spots for days. Just when she turned her head, there was a flash of blue, like a flash bulb, then the room was back to its normal luminosity.

Sara turned when she heard Cora squeal with delight and clap her hands a few times.

There, on the couch, was no longer the regal, blonde pixie, but a tiny, blonde fox with giant ears.

"Oh my god, a fennec fox!" Cora said, holding her hand out to the familiar.

Nyx jumped off the couch and came forward, stopping in front of Cora—who had somehow not passed out or fallen over, to both Sara's and Boon's slight irritation.

"Oh my god. Pixies? Are you shitting me?" Cora said,

staring at Nyx. Then, after a beat, she held out a hand and shook one of Nyx's paws. "It's a pleasure to meet you, Nyx Morenna. I'm so honored that you chose to pair with me."

Cora looked over at Sara, a smile threatening to split her face in half. "This explains so much."

CHAPTER 13

THE SMALL SHUTTLE jumped and bucked slightly as it dove through the ever-thickening atmosphere of Earth's northern hemisphere. Sara and Cora had decided that they needed to find some open ground where Cora could practice her new abilities without the restrictions of an Aether dampener, like they had used in their final exams.

After a few calls to the UHFC, Sara got the clearance to go ape-shit out in the northern territories of old Canada. They were heading to a spot just north of the Arctic Circle, where there was the least likelihood of causing serious damage.

Sara hadn't told Cora that she was keeping both Boon's and Cora's new abilities secret from the UHFC for now, but she couldn't shake the feeling that the secrecy was going to save her ass at some point.

I really should trust my government more. Oh well.

Boon and Gonders were strapped into seats in the back, while Sara piloted and Cora sat next to her, petting and talking with Nyx. Alister was somewhere in the back; probably curled up on a seat with Silva, if Sara had to guess.

"Do you have any ideas about how you want to test your powers?" Sara asked, when Cora finally stopped fawning over the appreciative Nyx.

"Well, I wanted to start with some of the balancing you were talking about. The last thing we need is for me to go berserk while I'm in the tank," she said, craning her neck to see the green treetops that spread out in all directions when they punched through the clouds.

"Yeah, we're not all that good at it yet, either," Boon shouted from the back, and Sara had to nod in agreement.

"She's right. On the dreadnought, I was nearly gone before I remembered to center myself. The power can get away from you rather quickly if you're not careful," Sara warned.

Cora looked down at Nyx, who in turn looked back at her for a second. Then Cora said, "I think we have a few ideas. I'll try them out, and we can see how effective they are."

" 'We'?" Sara asked, looking over at her sister with a raised eyebrow.

Cora gave her a smile. "Yeah, me and Nyx. I think we can figure out a few combinations that could work."

The treetops quickly began to thin the further north they traveled, eventually giving way completely. The ground was covered in fluffy, white blankets of snow and ice. Sara could only tell that they had started crossing the Arctic Ocean because the sensors on the shuttle told her so.

"There it is," Cora said, pointing out the window.

Sara craned her neck, but couldn't see a difference between the white area Cora was pointing out and the rest of white surrounding it.

"Uh, how can you tell? It all looks the same to me," she said, checking the navigation computer. To her ever-so-slight irritation, Cora was right. They were above Bathurst Island.

"I don't know," Cora said, cocking her head to the side in thought. "Maybe it has to do with the time I spend in the tank, using my powers to transport us places." She looked over at her sister, watching her maneuver the ship around for a landing. "It's like when you mark a place on your viewing bubble; I don't know where that place is, but I can suddenly feel its location. You were a controller when we were training at the academy... wasn't it that way for you?"

Sara thought about all the hours they had spent in the simulators, back when they thought she was going to be the controller twin, but she had never felt what Cora was describing.

"Actually, it was nothing like that. I'm sure it's a property of the tank system and our connection. When we were using the standard setup, the locations were a calculated number that I just sort of inputted into the spellform for a warp. But on the *Raven,* we don't use the navigation computer except to confirm our location. When I pick a jump point, I'm using my intuition, and then I think the Aether provides the details according to my wishes," Sara said, deploying the landing skids and bringing the shuttle down the last fifty meters onto what the sensors said was a level landing zone.

It was such a glaring white outside that Sara was starting to see purple spots, and she regretted leaving her aviators on the *Raven*. For all she could see, they could have been landing on a cliff face, and she wouldn't know.

"That would make sense as to why I don't get the 'calculated position' feeling. When you input a location, I just know where it is," Cora said, pulling on her bottom lip in contemplation. "You would think it would make our warps and jumps less accurate, but the *Raven* is far more exacting than a standard ship."

The shuttle rocked slightly as it settled fully on the struts, and a billowing cloud of snow and ice blew up from the disturbance made by the gravitic engines.

Sara shut them down, but left life support on to keep the ship from getting too cold inside while they were out. She turned to Cora and continued their conversation. "I think it makes perfect sense. Our computers can only calculate inside the parameters we input. Space is so vast that leaving the hundredth decimal place off a calculation could lead to thousands of kilometers' difference in the final calculation. With the Aether, I'm not choosing a location so much as a place."

"Isn't a location and a place the same thing?" Boon asked, following the conversation from the back.

Cora shook her head. "No, I think I know what Sara is saying. A location is a calculated spot; like this island, for example. It has a longitude and latitude that corresponds to a point on a map. But a place is just that, regardless of its location. The universe is always moving and expanding, so locations change. But places stay the same. Earth is a place, but its location in the galaxy is constantly changing as it hurtles through the void."

"Right. So when I mark a place on the viewing bubble, I'm actually marking a place I want to be, and the Aether I use to send that marker to Cora translates it exactly. I say I want to put us three kilometers away from a ship, instead of requesting the specific coordinates, because the coordinates are constantly changing for us and the moving ship I want us to end up beside," Sara said, looking back at the blonde woman, who had a thoughtful look on her face.

"I get it," Gonders said, jumping into the conversation. "Though it's a little spooky, when you think about it. It's like the Aether can think for itself."

"Who says it doesn't?" Cora and Sara said at the same time.

They both gave an identical laugh, then laughed again at their mimicking of one another.

"Twins are creepy sometimes," Gonders said quietly to Boon, as the sisters continued to laugh.

Boon turned to her with a sickly sweet smile. "I'm a twin, babe. Am I creepy?"

Gonders leaned back from the too-large smile, "You are right now."

Boon laughed at her girlfriend's expression before unbuckling her restraints. "Come on, we need to get into our armor so we don't freeze to death out there."

"What about these guys?" Gonders asked, waving a hand toward Silva and Alister as they began to stretch awake.

Cora came out of the cockpit and said, "Oh, I made something special for them."

CHAPTER 14

"Oh, my god. You three look *adorable*!" Boon nearly screamed with excitement as she squatted down in front of the three familiars and clapped her armored hands together with clanking booms.

The three pixies-turned-animals were all wearing custom-made Aetheric armor of their own. Each set was designed with their animal form's natural movement in mind, and was powered with a wireless link to their owner's suit. The armor was matte black, like the human armor, but where the human armor glowed blue at the seams with the power of the Aetheric, the seams on their armor were a deep red. In addition, each suit featured a small plate above the left breast, bearing the pixie's name.

"Why is their power red, and not blue?" Sara asked Cora, as she admired her sister's handiwork.

"I don't know," she admitted, tugging on her lip. "I didn't do anything different with the power design, except make it wireless. There are plenty of examples of wireless Aether power transmission, and it's never changed the properties of the Aether itself. I honestly don't understand why the color is different."

"Could it be dangerous?" Sara asked, looking Alister over with concern.

The light coming from the familiars' suits began to change from red to orange, then to a kind of green, and finally fell into the blue spectrum. After maybe thirty seconds, they were the same blue as the rest of the armor.

Nyx cocked her head at Cora, and they stared at one another for a few seconds, before Cora slapped her armored forehead.

She was not used to wearing the armor, so the slap was far harder than she intended, and her head snapped back with the clanging impact.

"Ow, shit. How do you ever get used to this?" Cora complained, trying in vain to rub her sore head through the helmet.

Sara burst out laughing, as did Gonders. "You just need to practice. Honestly, I still forget sometimes," Sara told her.

Cora growled with frustration, then said, "Anyway, I think I know why the color changed. The suits work off of our power, but they need to be in range to charge; I'm not sure what that exact range is, so I installed a small Aether battery in the suits. Anyway, when the power is being used up, the color will probably change to indicate how much they have left."

"You don't know for sure?" Boon asked, helping Silva onto her shoulder. There was a clicking sound as the ferret's tiny gauntlets magnetized to her shoulder plate.

"I didn't actually design them. Well, not completely. They were stored in the core," Cora said, stepping up to the ramp controls, and pressing the button to open the back of the shuttle.

The back ramp began to lower, and a strong gust of wind

caught in the opening, rocking the small shuttle with a shudder. Snow and ice swirled into the compartment, announcing the Arctic winter they were about to step into.

"How did you even know to look for something like these?" Sara asked, holding out a hand to Alister, who climbed into it. She raised him to her shoulder, while Cora did the same with Nyx. Both familiars locked onto their mage's shoulder plates.

"It just made sense. War Mages were constantly going into battle, and I was sure they didn't carry their familiars in their pockets. I thought there had to be something already designed for them, and I was right," Cora said, her smugness barely audible.

"Why didn't I think of that?" Sara wondered, as they made their way down the ramp.

"Because you've been a little busy lately," Cora said, and Sara could hear the smile in her voice.

She smiled herself and blushed inside her armor, then took in their surroundings.

The landscape was beyond barren. Bathurst Island was really nothing more than a 16,000 square kilometer, flat-topped boulder, sticking out of the Arctic Ocean. There were slight variations in the terrain, but nothing more than a few rolling hills that became lost in the endless whiteness of it all.

"A blank canvas," Cora observed, putting her hands on her hips, taking a slow deep breath. "Let's fuck it up."

FIRE RAINED FROM THE SKY, sending up plumes of white snow and steam where the flaming orbs landed. Great swaths of ice were torn from the ground as force blades sliced them free, and shield walls batted them like person-sized baseballs across the frozen tundra. Walls of ice and stone were formed from the ground, only to be shattered by blasts of Aether, similar to what the cannons on the *Raven* launched.

That's a new one. I never thought to use the cannon blast spell, Sara thought as she watched her sister sling spell after spell into the frozen waste. *Kinda stupid that I didn't,* she admitted to herself.

Just when Sara was about to stop her sister before she threw herself too far out of balance, Cora knelt down and placed a hand to the ground. A familiar blue glow surrounded her, and the torn-up chunks of ice began to melt and recede back into the divots Cora had made.

Sara stood slack-jawed as she watched her sister mend the destruction she had wrought over the last twenty minutes.

When the area looked nearly the same as when they had stepped out of the shuttle, Cora stood and turned to the three mages. "That was freaking awesome!"

"Holy shit. You just mended all the damage! How do you feel?" Boon asked, excited to watch someone else use their power set.

"Well, I was starting to feel that tipping sensation you mentioned, so I figured the fastest way to get back to center was to fix what I had just done. Worked like a charm," she said, flexing her left arm comically.

"Combat is great, but you're going to be in the tank most of the time. We need to be able to test what you can do in there. Do you have any ideas about how to do that out here?" Sara asked.

"Actually, I do. And I'm pretty sure you two will be able to use it to your advantage," Cora said, looking over at Nyx, positioned on her shoulder. After a few seconds, she nodded and turned back to Sara and Boon. "So, we're pretty sure we can use the jump spell on ourselves. Nyx says the records talk about War Mages that could jump around the battlefield, so

I'm going to give it a try." She lowered her head in concentration.

"Did you just say that Nyx told you—"

Sara's words were cut off when Cora disappeared. The resulting shock wave that the air made as it violently filled the resulting vacuum slammed into the three mages, blowing them off their feet as the sound dampeners in their helmets kicked in and blocked most of the resulting blast of sound. Enough got in, though, that Sara had to blink away tears as her ears rang.

Then a secondary blast of sound pushed the cloud of snow and ice that the first implosion had flung into the air, moving it to the side like a gale-force wind.

Sara could hear the groans from both Boon and Gonders as they struggled to get to their feet. Alister and Silva stumbled over as Sara finally got to a sitting position, and the two familiars sat down, a little woozy from the blast, but Sara figured the sound dampeners on their suits were working just fine, because they were not writhing in pain.

"Oh, shit," Cora yelled, running over to them and sliding to a stop on her knees in front of Sara. "Are you okay? I didn't even think about the shock wave a vacuum that big would make."

Sara held up a hand, and worked her jaw a little to get the ringing in her ears to stop. "We're fine, but it looks like my armor took a thrashing." She looked down at the dented and warped plating of the super hard material. She noted that two of the polymer plates on the chest had even broken.

Cora reached out a hand and, with a push of Aether, began mending the suit. It only took a few seconds, and Sara took the time to work her jaw some more. She checked to make sure Alister's suit was okay, and determined that he must have been blasted free before any serious damage to his armor could occur. Sara had been the closest to Cora when she jumped, so she had taken the most damage.

"If I had been a few meters closer, that could have been really bad," she said when Cora had finished with the mending spell.

"Oh, man. I really should have thought about that. I'm so sorry," Cora apologized again.

"It's okay, we all make mistakes. At least this one had the added benefit of teaching us how to use a new weapon in our arsenal. You'll need to teach the spell to Alister and Silva; it could be extremely useful."

"I'll have Nyx teach them. She said she can give them spellforms in a way similar to how they give us spellforms," Cora said as she reached down and helped Sara to her feet.

"Yeah, about that," Sara said, checking to make sure that Boon and Gonders were all right. "Are you saying you can talk to Nyx?"

Cora cocked her head, her blank faceplate hiding her expression. "Of course. Can't you talk with Alister?"

"Uh, no. That would make things so much easier, though. How does she do it?" Sara asked, excited that she and Alister might soon be talking on a daily basis.

Cora looked over at Nyx, and Sara understood they were actually having a conversation, not just staring at one another.

She turned back to Sara, her shoulders slumped slightly. "Nyx says it's a skill that takes a long time to develop. She can do it because the Keepers are all taught the technique from a young age. She said she can try and teach Alister and Silva, but she doubts they will be able to do it anytime soon."

Sara felt a shocking amount of disappointment at the news, but her comm buzzed before she could say anything.

"Captain, you need to get back to the *Raven*," Baxter's voice told her. "They've moved up the attack. I'm recalling the crew, but you four are the only ones on Earth; everyone else is on Xanadu. They want us to ship out in three hours."

"Shit, why the sudden rush?" she asked, motioning for everyone to board the shuttle.

"The Elif intelligence network is reporting odd behavior from the Teifen. Evidently, they are moving ships out of the system, and the Elif want to take the opportunity to engage a smaller fleet."

"That sounds like a good strategy. We'll be up in ten minutes. Have Teichek and Green prepare Cora's tank when they get onboard," Sara ordered. She hit the button to close the ramp once everyone was on the shuttle, then headed for the cockpit, not bothering to take off her armor.

"They're already onboard, ma'am. They never left the ship."

"Good. See you in a few, Sergeant." She started up the engines and grabbed the flight stick.

"We're cutting our leave short?" Cora asked when it was clear that Sara was no longer on comm.

"Yeah. A golden opportunity has just presented itself in the Elif home system."

Cora cracked her knuckles. "Aw, yeah. Let's kick some ass."

"Damn, girl. A little taste of the familiar life, and you're practically an addict," Sara snorted.

"I just can't wait to see what the *Raven* will be capable of, now that we're both War Mages," Cora said defensively.

Sara just smiled to herself and jammed the throttle open.

CHAPTER 15

THE SMALL SHUTTLE cut through the atmosphere, rocking and shimmying as Sara pushed the acceleration hard. The ride was only bumpy for the first minute or so, just until the atmosphere began to thin, then the turbulence became less severe. As the ship rose, Sara put on more power, rocketing them out toward Xanadu Station.

The cabin quieted down until they were just listening to the hum of the gravitic drives as the shuttle fully entered open space. Then they picked up speed, once there was nothing holding them back.

"I think we may have a problem with the new War Mages." Boon broke the relative silence through her armor's comm.

"Why do you say that?" Cora asked, turning in her seat to look at the small woman.

She shrugged. "I don't know. They seemed..." She trailed off, trying to think of the proper words.

"Brainwashed," Gonders finished for her.

Boon nodded. "Yeah. They were a little too indoctrinated. Like they would do whatever they were told, as long as it was a direct order. I don't know, maybe I'm looking at it wrong. It was just a feeling."

"Regardless, I know what you're saying. But the real problem is not so much them in particular, but the idea that so *many* of them are coming directly from the UHFC," Gonders said, surprising everyone—she was supposed to be the play-it-by-the-book Marine. "I think what made the War Mages work in the past was that there were so few of them; if fifty suddenly show up, that could scare the shit out of our allies."

"I get the feeling the Elif don't really trust us all that much already. Especially after Sara stormed their embassy," Cora said thoughtfully.

"Hey, I did what I had to. I was right, after all. That little shit-stain had sold us out," Sara said in her own defense.

"I didn't say you were wrong, just that it happened. The problem is that it made the Elif nervous. Now imagine if they realize there is a whole army of people as powerful as you, traipsing around the galaxy," Cora said.

" 'Traipsing'? I don't traipse, thank you very much." Sara rolled her eyes.

Cora gave a chuckle. "You get the idea. From what I've gathered from the core, back when humanity ruled this galaxy, there were never more than twenty War Mages active at one time; not that they didn't want more, that was just how few there were. The UHFC has at least *ten* candidates working on the spellform right now. That's a lot of power to deal with. What if some admiral decides he doesn't like the way someone else is doing something, and he orders a War Mage to take out a space station?"

Sara cocked her head, immediately thinking about how she would take out a space station. She shivered when she realized how easy it would be for her. Compared to a warship, a space station may as well be made of paper bags.

"I see what you mean. Humanity is gaining power too fast to control it. All it takes is one War Mage saying that they're 'just doing their job', and we have a whole new war on our hands. The problem is that we can't hope to win the war we are in without a troop of War Mages leading the way," Sara said.

"Damned if you do, damned if you don't," Gonders summed it up.

"Maybe. Maybe not. We need to find the other humans," Cora said, seeming to change the subject.

"I agree, but what does that have to do with too many War Mages?" Sara asked, pressing a button to request a flight path to the *Raven*.

"Everything. There is a group of humans out there that remembers their powers and how to balance them. At least there were a few thousand years ago, if our readings on that planet were accurate. They took the dreadnought, so there had to be someone who still knew how to channel Aether," Cora reasoned.

"What if they scrapped the thing eons ago? That would explain why we couldn't find it," Sara argued.

"I don't think so. The War Mages in charge of it would have hidden it, like they did on Earth. I think there was a war, and a group of them escaped to find a new home. If they are out there, that means they used the ship to leave, and that means they are still using Aether. If that's the case, then it stands to reason they know how to balance the power," Cora said, reaching up to tap on her bottom lip before remembering she was still in armor, and the best she could do was tap on her faceplate.

Sara glanced over at the armored fox sitting in Cora's lap. "Doesn't Nyx know how they organized power back then? She is a Keeper of the Records, after all."

Cora and Nyx turned to one another for the briefest of moments before Cora said, "Yeah. We talked about it."

There was a long pause as Sara waited for Cora to finish, but it became apparent that she wasn't going to without prompting.

"Aaaaaand?" Sara pressed.

"And I don't like it. It wouldn't work with the way Earth is now," she said, looking out the window.

"How do you know? Maybe it would. How did they do it?" Sara wanted to know.

"Forget about it. I don't even want to talk about it," Cora said, still not looking at Sara when she spoke.

"Wait, does this have to do with the whole First Mage, Second Mage thing?" Boon asked, leaning forward in her restraints.

Gonders pulled her back, shaking her head, but it was too late. Sara saw Cora's head drop in defeat just a little, and knew Boon had hit on it.

"That's it, isn't it?" she asked. "So, what, does the ranking of War Mages mean that they get a vote or something? Or..." Sara trailed off, realization beginning to dawn.

Cora turned at her sister's loss of words. "That's right. It was all about rank. So in this case, you would be supreme ruler of the world, and Boon back there would be second-in-command. You wouldn't even be above the law; you would actually *be* the law. You still think the old ways would work?" Cora asked almost acidly.

"Uh, yeah. So maybe we should find another way," Sara said, swinging the shuttle around the station and catching sight of the *Raven*. She brought the small ship down to the level of the docking bay, and slowly maneuvered it through the plasma shielding, setting it down between two of the larger dropships.

Boon and Gonders unstrapped and headed to the back of

the shuttle to lower the ramp. Sara and Cora didn't move until the others were halfway to the storage lockers.

Sara turned to Cora. "But what if it's the only way?"

Cora laughed. "You think you're qualified to lead humanity? Are you shitting me?"

Sara raised a hand in surrender. "I'm just saying, governments are always going to have corruption. Even in this new world we've built, there is always someone trying to play the system. The only way to make sure they can't is to take the system away completely."

Cora stared at her for a good three seconds before she responded. "You aren't kidding, are you? You think the best option is for you to rule us all?"

"God no. I just think there is something to having one person with the final say, is all. It doesn't have to be me. Shit, I don't want it to be me."

"And how do you propose we pick this person? Random lottery? Vote? Have a computer do it? And what happens if their orders are ignored? Who deals out the justice then?" Cora asked, frustration plain in her voice.

Sara bit her lip. "Well, shit. When you say it like that, it kinda makes sense that a War Mage was in charge."

Cora threw her arms up. "You think I don't know that? If *we* can figure this out, what makes you think they don't have a room full of eggheads locked away in the sub-basement of the UHFC that hasn't figured it out already? You think they don't have a plan for this? I bet you anything they came up with a plan to control War Mages the second you touched down at the Elif embassy."

Sara reached up and pressed the button to retract her helmet. Her faceplate slid up, and the helmet split open, folding in on itself and lying flat against her back. Her face was a mask of concern as she looked over to Cora. "You think they consider me a threat?"

Cora opened her own helmet, and gave her sister a thin-lipped smile. "I don't think the UHFC considers you a threat; you've done too much for humanity. However, there are people in important places within the UHFC that will feel threatened, and they may try to do something about it."

Sara harrumphed. "If they can't control me then they'll kill me? Are there still people like that in government?"

"The old ones remember a much different world than the one we were raised in. Back then, governments were unsupervised behemoths that did whatever they wanted. When you showed up, slinging more magic than anyone ever thought possible, they saw something from the past come to life. You represent power and influence to those that think they can control you, but then you showed them that wasn't going to happen. You defied orders and took the law into your own hands when you confronted Prince DeSolin. I'm sure they didn't like that."

Sara nodded. "You're right, as always. I never even considered how that act would change the way I was perceived. I will always do what's right for humanity."

Cora put a hand on Sara's shoulder. "I know you will. That's why, even though you make me crazy sometimes, I'll always trust you. You would give your life for your people. I just don't want that to be anytime soon."

Sara nodded. "Follow the straight and narrow."

Cora smiled. "Straight and narrow," she agreed.

CHAPTER 16

Sara and Cora exited the shuttle and headed for the storage lockers to stow their armor. Boon and Gonders were already gone by the time the twins stepped off the shuttle's ramp, but the cargo bay was abuzz with activity.

There was a plethora of cargo containers full of delivered supplies strewn across the deck, most of which were open, their contents being stowed in cargo lockers. The resupply was quite thorough, but considering they were heading into a battle that could potentially last for quite some time, Sara was happy to have it.

She remembered that she still had to show Cora the proper way to step out of her armor so that it stayed put in the locker. When Sara turned to head out of the bay, she nearly ran into a short woman wearing an engineer's uniform.

"Oh, sorry, ma'am," the woman said, taking a step back as Sara stumbled to a stop.

"It's okay..." she looked at the woman's name tag, "Jeffries. What can I do for you?"

"Oh, uh, actually, I have something for Captain Cora,"

she said, handing a folded piece of cloth out to Cora when she turned from her locker.

"What's this?" Cora asked, taking the white square.

"Chief Sabine wanted me to deliver this to you as soon as you were onboard. He said he had it printed up for you from plans he found on the core."

Cora unfolded the small cloth, and revealed an entire bodysuit. It was so thin that it folded down to the size of a handkerchief.

"Are you kidding me? You can practically see right through this thing. What was wrong with my old suit?" Cora asked, holding the thin suit up to the light, and Sara could see that the garment was more translucent than not.

The woman suppressed a chuckle. "He said you would say that. He looked up plans on the core for the design. Your original suit was designed by the UHFC, but he noticed that your connection with the Aether-conducting fluid in the tank was not as strong as he thought it should be. So he decided to see if the core had anything, and this was it," she said, pointing at the super thin garment. "It has all the bio monitors the old suit had, but the thinner material allows for more of the fluid to flow freely against your skin. He says not to worry, that it isn't see-through."

Sara smirked at her sister's exasperation.

Then Jeffries mumbled, "He thinks," and Sara burst out laughing.

Cora rolled her eyes, but draped the garment over her arm. "Fine. I'll try it, but if people start lining up to stare at my naked body in the tank, you'd better charge money and deposit it in my account. Let's go. I need to get back in there," she said, pulling on Sara's arm.

"Uh, ma'am?" Jeffries said to Sara before Cora could drag her too far.

"Yes?" Sara asked, pulling her sleeve free and giving Cora a dirty look.

"Ma'am, I think something got mixed in logistics. We got a lot of supplies that are already topped off, but when I tried to return them to the station, they wouldn't take them. Most of it is just MREs and other ground supplies, but they delivered an entire crate of the new warheads, and I don't have anywhere to put them. The other supplies are just being kept in one of the empty crew quarters, but I don't want to store the weapons in there."

"Well, I guess having more weapons isn't necessarily a bad thing," Sara reasoned as she looked around the bay, trying to think of the best place to keep them. "We can't just strap them down to the deck in a corner over there?" she asked, pointing to an empty corner in the cargo bay.

"Uh, well, we could, but I would be afraid that they would break free during battle, and then we would have warheads rolling around the deck," Jeffries said, not wanting to piss off her captain, but also not wanting to shirk her duty.

"How about one of the dropships?" Cora suggested. "They have cargo storage that can withstand a drop through atmosphere; I would think that'll be safe enough."

"That's a great idea. Put them on Dropship Three; we hardly use that one," Sara said, pointing to the large craft closest to the doors.

Jeffries saluted. "Yes ma'am." She ran over to a large, black crate and activated the grav lifter, then pushed the now weightless box toward the back of the dropship.

"Too many supplies... Not a bad problem to have," Cora mused as she headed toward the doors. "You coming?"

"Yeah, I'm coming," Sara said, tearing her eyes away from the black crate, and jogging to catch up.

GRIMMS AND SARA stood behind the consoles surrounding Cora's tank, and watched as Teichek and Green prepared for Cora's return to the womb. Alister and Nyx sat at their feet, and Sara was surprised to see that the two were not nearly as familiar with each other as Alister and Silva had been from the very start.

I wonder if it has to do with Nyx's position in pixie society. Sara snorted a laugh. *Maybe it's just because they are a cat and a dog.*

Alister, Nyx, and Grimms all looked at her when she snorted, and she gave an unconvincing cough to cover it up.

"Have we received any more reports on the Teifen's movements?" Sara asked her XO, more to fill the void of silence than really needing to know. They were waiting for Cora to change into her skinsuit.

"Nothing yet, but that doesn't mean they haven't gotten any more news. Admiral Zett has been less than pleasant in our interactions; I think he is holding a grudge about what you did at the embassy," Grimms said with a frown.

"Eh, fuck him. I did what needed to be done. Maybe he should be more upset that his prince is a traitor," Sara argued, feeling a rising heat of righteous indignation in her chest.

Grimms looked over at her and raised an eyebrow—a sure sign he did not approve of her words. "I think it would be wise to keep talk of treachery to ourselves. You've already painted a target on our backs, no need to light it up as well," he reminded her quietly, so Teichek and Green didn't overhear.

"It's me they're pissed at, not the crew," she said, feeling a flash of guilt.

"A crew and her captain are the same thing. We're your people. We follow you. What you do impacts us," he said, his tone softening. "I know you are still relatively new to command, so I can give you all the slack you need. Just know that I've seen commanders and their men go down for less than what you've done. You ruffled some feathers, Captain; you can be sure that someone is upset. We just need to see if they're going to do anything about it or not."

"Now you sound like Cora; we had a very similar discussion not twenty minutes ago," Sara said, running a hand through her hair.

Grimms smiled. "She's smart. You should listen to her."

Sara squinted over at the older man. "She is smart. She makes good choices, too."

She was happy to see him turn slightly red before they were interrupted by Cora herself coming around the tank. She had ducked behind some of the machinery to change, seeing as there were no bathrooms in the engineering room.

Grimms' face went from slightly red to nearly crimson, and his eyes bugged at the sight of her. Sara even let out a little gasp at how thin the material was.

Cora was covered from the neck down in the white material, but you could see every nook and cranny she had.

"Well, at least it's not see-through?" Sara said with a shrug.

Cora spread her arms wide and looked down. The suit's material was thinner than the finest silk, and clung to her like pantyhose. "I don't really think it matters, do you?" she demanded with amused irritation. "It'd better be worth it, or I'm kicking Sabine's ass when I come out again."

Grimms' back was ramrod straight. Sara had to give him credit for not letting his eyes wander.

Not too much, anyway.

Cora smiled at his discomfort and waggled her eyebrows in a comically suggestive way in his direction.

Sara snorted again, and Grimms sighed in exasperation.

"Sorry, I'm just teasing you," Cora said, straightening

with an unapologetic smile on her face. "I do have a favor to ask you, though," she said to Grimms.

"You name it," he replied.

She smiled. "Can you look after Nyx? She prefers you, and it would be a big help to me. I left everything you'll need to take care of her in your room; just be sure she doesn't leave the ship, or our connection will become too distant for me to maintain spellforms."

He gave a nod and looked down to the fennec fox at his feet. "I will do my best, Nyx. Just let me know if you need anything special."

Nyx gave him a nod, and Sara could see that it caught him by surprise. He obviously had no idea how smart she was.

"Thanks," Cora said, leaning in and kissing him lightly on the cheek. "Okay, it's time to make the donuts."

She climbed the steep set of stairs that led to the top of the tank. The top was already open, and she stood looking down into the blue liquid for a few breaths. Then she looked up and met Sara's gaze. Sara smiled and blew her a kiss, which made Cora smile.

"I hate this part," she admitted, then stepped off the edge, plunging into the tank.

The liquid being thicker than water, the splash wasn't nearly as big as it seemed like it should have been, and the bubbles around Cora dissipated slowly. She gave a wink to Grimms, then opened her mouth to take a deep pull of the fluid. Immediately, she began to cough, sending a torrent of bubbles out as her lungs filled with the oxygen-rich substance.

After what felt like forever to Sara—but was less than a minute, in reality—Cora's body went limp and curled into a natural fetal position. The gravity field in the tank held her in place, and her hair spread out in a halo around her.

"Ugh, that's the worst," Cora's voice said over the ship's speakers.

"Everything is showing okay on our end, ma'am," Teichek announced.

"All right, let's see what this pony can do!" Cora said.

"Where do you come up with these sayings?" Sara asked, shaking her head.

"Old TV and movies, mostly. I have a lot of free time in here."

CHAPTER 17

THE *RAVEN* DROPPED out of warp only a few hours after disembarking from Xanadu. They had followed the rendezvous coordinates provided by the Elif, and Sara was surprised to see so many ships begin to appear on the holo display.

"I thought the bulk of the Elif forces were taken out during the attack on Effrit? There must be thousands of ships here," she said, gesturing to the tiny pinpricks of green light that were scattered throughout the area.

They were staging the attack a short jump from Effrit itself, only a few light years out in the blackness of space. The reports said that the Elif had been amassing their forces there since the initial attack nearly three weeks before; in that time, an impressive armada had formed.

"The Elif empire is quite vast, even if it is small in comparison to the Teifen's. They have many more ships still out, protecting other interests; these are just the ones they could spare," Cora said over the bridge speakers.

"Still, even with these numbers, I'm not sure the Elif will

be able to drive out the Teifen without significant losses," Grimms added.

"Do we have any updates on the Teifen ship movements in the system?" Sara asked.

Mezner answered without looking up from her console. "We have just received an updated attack plan along with the most up-to-date ship positions, ma'am. I'm sending it to the display now."

The holo projection table fuzzed and reformed, showing a close-up of Effrit and the surrounding traffic. Thousands of Teifen ships swarmed around the planet in all different planes of orbit, but a significant number of them were peeling away to warp out of system. They would gather in groups of ten or so, and then jump together.

"Are all the ships jumping on the same trajectory? It seems like they are *going* somewhere, not just leaving," Sara observed, squinting at the small shapes.

"They do seem to be following a similar path. Give me a minute, and I'll see if I can find a likely destination point," Mezner said, getting to work.

"How old is this data?" Grimms asked the ensign.

"About an hour," she replied after a quick check.

"It looks like they're abandoning the system. At this rate, I don't even think an attack will be necessary," Grimms said to Sara.

She reached up and gave Alister a scratch under his chin, and looked over her shoulder to find Nyx sitting in Grimms' chair, regarding them with her golden eyes. She gave the fox a smile, and turned back to her XO.

"You think the Elif are just going to wait this one out?"

He shook his head. "I doubt it. I think this is as much about payback as it is about liberating their home world," he said, then looked down at his tablet. "I think we're about to find out what they want to do; Admiral Zett just sent out a message."

He slid the file off his tablet, and it began to play on the main view screen. The Elif admiral was handsome in a very severe way, with the blonde hair that was common among Elif cut short in a military style that showed off his long, pointed ears.

Sara thought there was something slightly disturbing about him, and it took her a second to realize it was his eyes. They were so dark, she wasn't sure they were not just black.

"The battle will commence in a little less than thirty minutes. Every ship has been sent their orders for the initial attack, and I expect everyone to perform their duties to the letter. This is the day we strike back at our sworn enemies; they will pay for the transgressions they have enacted upon us with their lives.

"Each of the two battle groups will engage and destroy the air support above Effrit or Suttri, allowing our troops already engaged with the enemy to push forward. Without fresh troops and supplies, the Teifen armies will be engaged in a war of attrition that will quickly swallow them whole.

"We have enlisted the help of a special division that the emperor commissioned before his death; however, after review of the Teifen's movements over the last day and a half, the battle for Suttri looks like it will be particularly light, so the special forces unit, *Raven*, will be held in reserve.

"This is the hour of our victory. The Teifen have shown their cowardice, and are fleeing in droves. We will dominate the skies above our beloved core worlds by the end of the day.

"Fight with honor. Show our enemies the true cost of attacking our great empire."

Sara looked at Grimms when the communication went dark. "Well, that was pretty aggressive for an Elif."

"He does have the attitude of a zealot, from the transmissions I've seen. I think he is feeling the pressure of taking over the old admiral's command. He was pushed to the top, not because he deserved the post, but because everyone above him died in the first battle for Effrit," Grimms related, scratching at his chin.

"You think he's overcompensating?" Cora asked through their comms.

He smiled at her attendance. "I don't know that he is *over*compensating, but he is perhaps a little more *dedicated* than the average Elif. That's not a bad thing, necessarily; the Elif need a little more aggression in their campaign against the Teifen, if they want to come out on top."

"Ma'am, I have those calculations on the departing Teifen," Mezner reported, looking up from her station.

"Put it on the holo projector, please," Sara requested with a nod of appreciation.

The image of the Elif home system zoomed out until it was just another speck of light, and other stars began to appear at the edges of the projection, and quickly fall toward the center. Soon the view showed local space, and a blue line began to spear outward from Effrit, following a straight trajectory through the blackness of space to intersect with a system several light years away.

"How accurate is this model?" Grimms asked, leaning in and selecting the destination system with a finger. The point of light expanded, showing a binary star system with very little detail.

"The fleeing ships could be meeting at a point and changing course, but the number of ships leaving and taking the exact same course tells me that they are more than likely flying directly to their target. The computer puts the probability of that target being in this particular system at ninety percent, sir," Mezner said.

"What do we know about the system? The projection isn't giving me much detail," Sara said, scrolling through the limited data on the small display set into the side of the table.

"Not a lot, ma'am," Mezner admitted. "The Elif network marks this as a long-time Teifen system. They have not been able to send in probes and regularly retrieve the information. At the time of their last assessment, there was one habitable planet, and several moons with atmosphere thick enough to make ground bases possible without a complicated dome structure," she reported. "The Teifen had a strong military presence a few years ago, but this was mainly a colony world."

She looked back down at her console. "Ma'am, we have a call coming in from the *Catagain*."

Sara raised an eyebrow. "Put it onscreen, Mezner."

The image changed to a view of a bridge much like the *Raven*'s, though it was much larger in number of stations. The captain was older than Sara first imagined him to be—maybe in his mid-thirties—with black hair and intense blue eyes. His mouth was smiling, but the rest of his face was not playing along.

Sara immediately disliked him.

"Captain Sonders. It is so good to finally meet you. I am Captain Rodgers of the *Catagain*," he said, raising an eyebrow with a pompous air.

"I know who you are, Captain. I'm glad you could join us on the mission," she greeted, giving a dead smile of her own.

Why do I not like this guy? I've only just seen him, and I want to punch him in the face.

"Yes. It is unfortunate that you will be sitting this one out. Looks like they only want us to participate." He smiled a little larger. "I suppose that's what happens when you rough up a prince, am I right?"

Was that supposed to be a joke? Sara cocked her head to the side. "As I remember it, 'roughing up' the prince saved the human race; I feel like it was a fair trade."

"I suppose some good came of it," he allowed. "The UHFC was not very happy with you, though. Sometimes the politics are just as important as the actions." He smirked just a little. "Next time you find yourself in trouble, give us a call before you act; the Admiralty wants us to take the lead. Now that the Elif would like you to sit this one out as well, it would be best if you just let us take care of it. There are a few admirals back home that are hoping we don't have to clean up any more messes after today."

Motherfucker. That little shit thinks he's so hot... Sara took a calming breath before answering. "Sounds good, Captain. Happy hunting," she said, pressing the button on the holo table to end the call before he could piss her off anymore.

"Well, that was a little hostile," Cora noted.

"Yeah. I think we might better serve this mission by finding out where the Teifen are going, and staying out of everyone's hair. Mezner, get me Admiral Zett," she ordered, tapping her lip.

After a few moments of silence, the ensign spoke up. "Ma'am, they said he is unavailable and re-sent the orders for us to wait on the outskirts to provide backup."

I hate politics. What a waste of time and effort. They want us to play by the rules? Fine. We'll play by the rules.

"Very well. Everyone, prepare for battle. Or at least, prepare to *watch* a battle," Sara qualified before walking over to her command chair and flopping down into it.

Alister hopped up on her lap, and curled into a ball to wait. She gave him a few absent pets, then propped her elbow on the armrest and dropped her chin into her hand.

They want to push us to the sidelines? That's fine by me, she lied.

CHAPTER 18

Sara and the bridge crew watched as Elif ships started departing the staging area in droves. The slower Elif ship design meant that they had a fifteen to twenty-minute warp time to Effrit and Suttri, but the *Catagain* could make the trip in a little less than three minutes, so they sat and waited along with the *Raven* until the entire Elif fleet was on its way.

There was no more communications between the two War Mage ships, which suited Sara just fine.

At T-minus three minutes to contact, the *Catagain* sent a message that it was time to go, and warped away. Cora waited another two minutes before engaging warp for the *Raven*.

"Are we really that much faster than even another ship controlled by War Mages?" Sara asked no one in particular.

She was surprised when Connors answered her instead of Cora.

"Yes, ma'am. The *Catagain* has much more mass than we do, being a battleship, so it requires more power to get moving, even when using Aether to do so. Because the *Raven* is a corvette class, she can slip through the warp thread much easier—and Captain Cora has at least as much power as the other War Mage, so she can convert that power into more speed."

Sara smiled at the animated, red-haired man. "I didn't know you were so versed in warp physics, Connors. Your explanation makes a lot of sense. Thank you."

"No problem, ma'am. I took quite a few classes on warp mechanics at the academy; I had thought I might be an engineer. But it turned out I was pretty good at flying, so my advisors steered me that way," he said conversationally before adding, "We will be dropping out of warp in ten seconds."

Sara held her breath. The slightly compressed image onscreen grew until it finally flashed with blue, Aetheric light, and then the Effrit system sprawled out before them. Space was so expansive, though, that what they saw didn't really look much different from where they had just been, except now, the right bottom corner of the screen displayed a small, green and blue planet.

"We are in position, one light second from Suttri. I have confirmation that the battle has commenced," Mezner reported, reading her scans.

"Cora can you give me an Aetheric sensor sweep? I want to see what is happening closer to the planet." Sara placed Alister on the floor, and stood up from her command chair.

Instead of approaching the table where Grimms was, she stepped into her control ring, and shot a small amount of Aether into the spellform to activate it. A shimmering, golden bubble appeared around her top half, giving her a 360-degree view from the ship.

She zoomed in on the planet, and thousands of icons began to appear around it. A large number of them were red, signifying the Teifen forces, but it was obvious that the green-marked Elif ships outnumbered them at least three to one.

"Looks like this will be an easy battle," Grimms commented.

"It might be easier than they think," Cora said to the bridge in general. "The Teifen are continuing to evacuate. Some of the ships are fighting back, but it looks like they are just trying to give the rest of the ships time to escape."

As Sara watched the battle, she saw what Cora meant; more and more of the Teifen ships were warping out of the system. The defending Teifen had been quickly overwhelmed, and bright flashes of light indicated a few that had experienced catastrophic reactor ruptures in the onslaught.

"Why are they not fighting? I know they're outnumbered and it's a losing battle, but I've never heard of Teifen running from a fight. Just in the last two or three minutes, nearly half of what was remaining has jumped away," Sara pondered.

"Maybe they know the score and are planning on coming back at a later time. They could be regrouping out of system for a counterattack," Grimms reasoned.

"That doesn't make sense. Why would they counterattack when they could have just reinforced what they already had here? The governor is gone, but there has to be a replacement on the way," Cora said.

"Maybe there's a bigger threat somewhere else," Grimms theorized. "From what I've gathered, the Elif are not really a threat to the Teifen; they are not aggressive, and do not take out Teifen resources. They were really just a conquest for the governor of this region, a bid for him to become the new emperor."

He brought up a ship counter on the holo table that showed the number of active ships on each side. The Teifen counter was spinning down rather quickly, but the Elif counter dropped only a few ticks every couple of seconds.

"Hon, give me a scan of the surface. What are the ground troops doing?" Sara asked, trying to put it all together.

They watched the battle unfold for a few more seconds before Hon answered.

"Ma'am, it looks like the Teifen forces are evacuating. If I had to guess, I would say they have been doing so for quite some time. Most of their troops are off the field and waiting at staging areas, where troop transports are picking them up."

"Interesting. How long would you say it would take them to completely evacuate?" Sara asked the ensign.

At the rate they are going, I would estimate between half a day and a full day," Hon said, checking the numbers.

"Can you tell if they are taking prisoners?"

"It doesn't appear that they are, ma'am. But they could have taken them on earlier transports," he said.

"I don't think so. This is a total one-eighty in the Teifen's actions; they pushed so hard to take this system, and now they can't get out of it fast enough?" Sara mused, pulling on her lip. She looked through the translucent viewing bubble and saw Grimms regarding her with a raised eyebrow. "What do you think, Commander?" she asked him.

Grimms turned back to the holo table, and the battle taking place in miniature in front of him, while he considered. Eventually, he crossed his arms.

"I think we should find out what they are running to, not what they are running from. I believe our answers are at their warp destination."

"Get me Zett on the line," Sara requested again, making a decision.

"They are ignoring our hail, ma'am," Mezner said with a frown.

"Then send them a message that we are following the Teifen, and determining the new threat. Tell them we will return in..." she shrugged and looked to Grimms for an estimate, but he just shrugged back. She took a breath. "Tell them we will be back when we know something," she finished.

"Aye, ma'am."

"Cora, how quickly can we get to the system that Mezner mentioned as the most probable destination?" Sara asked.

"I could get us there in less than three hours. It's only a few hundred light years away."

"Let's do it. I'm marking the warp location now. Have we received a response from the Elif flagship?"

Mezner shook her head. "No, ma'am."

"Alright, it looks like the Elif have this well in hand. Let's go see what our horned friends are all in a tizzy about. Cora—"

Sara was cut off by Mezner. "Ma'am, we are being hailed by the *Catagain*."

"Fuck," Sara muttered, then louder, "Put it onscreen."

Captain Rodgers appeared, but the view of the bridge around him was gone, replaced with open space. Sara could see Elif and Teifen ships, moving together in battle behind him, and she realized she was seeing the inside of his viewing bubble.

"Captain, what is this I'm hearing about you abandoning your post? The admiral wanted me to contact you." His face was a mask of annoyance.

Sara needed to bite the inside of her cheek to keep from emitting a long string of curses.

"We are not 'abandoning' our post. We are scouting the enemy while they are otherwise engaged. We will find out their destination and return with the intel. That is what this ship was designed for, after all."

Rodgers' eyes shifted as he tracked an enemy, and it was obvious he was only half paying attention to the current conversation. "The UHFC ordered us to help with the battle here. You can't just ignore a direct command," he told her.

Sara closed her eyes in frustration before saying in an overly polite voice, "I am following my orders, which are to protect my Elif battle group. There is a reason the Teifen are abandoning this system, and I think it's pretty important to find out what it is."

Rodgers considered that for a moment. "Alright, be sure to come back right away, though. Would hate for something to happen to you while you're out chasing ghosts."

The last was said as he stared into the camera, sending a shudder down Sara's spine that she didn't like.

"We'll be safe. Sonders out," she said simply, then cut the channel. "Cora, get us out of here."

"Ma'am, we are receiving a second transmission from the *Catagain*. It looks like... Oh, wait. I'm sorry, it must have been an echo of the first," Mezner said, her face a little red.

"That's probably for the best; I really didn't want to speak with that... person right now, anyway. Cora?"

"Warp in three, two, one."

The view smashed down to a pinprick of light.

CHAPTER 19

SARA SAT IN HER ROOM, eating a light meal of salad with grilled chicken on top. She didn't really taste it, instead she mechanically took one bite after another while she thought about the possibilities of what they would find.

She was trying to imagine what would make a Teifen fleet abandon their prize and rush off to a system that, by all accounts, held no real military advantage. The system was inside Teifen controlled space.

When she brought it up on a star map, she could see that it was closer to the galactic rim than she had originally thought, but still well within their domain.

She took another bite of salad and chewed as she stared off into her mind's eye, until her door slid open and Baxter stepped in.

"Hello, you," he said with a bright white smile as he came over to the table and sat across from her.

"Hey," she said, her mouth still half-full of greens. "Why would you give up a valuable position even before you were being attacked?" she asked after swallowing.

He leaned back and ran a hand over his short-cropped, white hair. "Okay, we can talk about tactics." He laughed, but still crossed his arms and gave it some serious thought. "Well, it could be that the position is no longer valuable. It could be that the position is no longer worth the cost to keep it, or that there has been word that the enemy is about to sink considerable resources into taking it back."

"What about needing to send reinforcements somewhere else? Would you be ordered to give ground to keep other ground?" Sara asked, taking another bite.

"Again, that would depend on the value of the position, and the position that needed the reinforcements. War is all about balancing a spreadsheet. If you do the calculation, and your number is bigger than the enemy's at the end, you win," he said with a grim smile. "Why?"

"I'm trying to figure out the Teifen's motives. They have been pushing to take Effrit for years; why the sudden lack of interest in keeping it?"

Baxter scratched at his hair again, thinking. "That's a good question. What do you know about the system we're headed to?"

Sara shrugged. "Not much. The Elif haven't had a successful scan of the place in years. Last they saw, it was a one-world system mostly filled with civilians. There was a military presence, but no huge bases or anything."

"Could they be leaving to swear in a new governor?" Baxter asked doubtfully.

"There is no way they would sacrifice thousands—no, hundreds of thousands—of troops and ships just to make it to a ceremony," she said, shaking her head. "Though that does bring up a good point. Who is in command of the Teifen fleet? Maybe they have a different mindset from the old governor. If the Elif hadn't jumped the gun on the attack, the Teifen would have been out of the system completely by the time we showed up."

"That's true," Baxter said, pinching his chin in thought. "Let's say you're in command of the Teifen fleet. What would make you give up your old boss's prize? What would make you leave?"

She blew out a breath, making her cheeks puff out. "Shit, anything. The thing is, there is no real reason for the Teifen to want to conquer the Elif. It's not like they need resources the Elif are using… There's a whole galaxy of empty planets to exploit. The governor took over the Elif in a bid to win favor from the higher-ups and become emperor himself. If I were left in charge after he died, I would find any reason to get out of there. History has taught us time and again, it's never worth occupying hostile territory. Not in the long run."

"Okay, so what would give you the excuse to abandon the system and not lose face?" Baxter asked.

Sara thought about it and then her face lit up. "My people are being attacked. I need to get to them to save lives."

Baxter nodded. "It's not us, and I doubt the Elif have another armada stashed away for a sneak attack, so it has to be the Galvox."

Sara considered this. "That's pretty far from the Galvox territories for an attack. It would be a suicide mission, unless they are more powerful than we think."

"Or they have a weapon that we don't know about."

Sara let out an overly dramatic sigh, and rubbed her face in her hands. "I don't know. I'm so tired, I can't think straight. Grimms sent me to bed. He said I was falling asleep in my chair."

"You've been going pretty hard for a full day. Just this

morning, you were blowing shit up in the Arctic Circle," Baxter reminded her as he stood to help her to her feet.

He began to guide her toward the bed.

"Let's get you out of that battlesuit."

CHAPTER 20

Sara yawned into the back of her hand, then blinked and took a gulp of hot coffee, savoring the bitter brew. She leaned back in her captain's chair, watching the view screen begin its final expansion, heralding their arrival in the Teifen system.

"How many of the Teifen armada from Effrit should we expect in the system when we get there?" Sara asked Grimms, who was sitting beside her in his own command chair.

"We will be arriving a few hours ahead of the first ships. Our travel time is a magnitude faster than their fleet can obtain." He checked his tablet before continuing. "The Elif reported that the first large battle group left nearly two days ago, and it contained their capital ship and a good ten percent of the Teifen fleet. We should have time to settle in and enable Cora's cloaking ability to wait for their arrival."

Sara nodded, taking another gulp of the coffee. Alister sat on the ample chair beside her, watching the view screen along with everyone else. She reached down and gave him a pet before saying, "That's good. It will give us a chance to get a handle on what's happening. Cora, are you good on cloaking us right out of warp?"

"I am. It will be easier, now that I have Nyx to help. My precision has gone up twentyfold," Cora said through Sara's and Grimms' comms. "I also have a few tricks up my sleeve. I've been going through the core and looking at what the ship is actually capable of, now that I'm a War Mage myself. The list is pretty long, but I obviously have not had time to try anything. I was really hoping I would have more than a day and a half to get used to working with Nyx before we were thrown back into the fire."

"Yeah, sorry about that, but to tell the truth, you two seem to be working together really well," Sara said, looking over at the fennec sitting on the arm of Grimms' chair. The normally severe man and the slightly standoffish fox were getting along like the consummate professionals they both were.

Nyx glanced over at Sara and gave her a smile that somehow made the tiny fox look fierce. Sara smiled back and reached over to scratch her behind one of her too large ears. Nyx stiffened at first, then leaned into the scratch and closed her eyes in enjoyment.

"We really are," Cora agreed. "She is so interesting, with her vast knowledge. I'm really learning a lot from her. By the way, she really likes that," she said with a smile in her voice.

Nyx gave a sort of purring chirp that made Alister jump a little, and look over at the fox with wide eyes.

"Don't be a hater, bro," Sara laughed to him, and scratched him between his ears.

"Sixty seconds to end warp, ma'am," Connors reported, breaking up the Familiar lovefest.

"Thank you, Connors," Sara acknowledged, standing from her chair and stepping into the control ring. She powered it up, and her view showed the same expanding image on the screen.

Grimms stepped around the control ring and bellied up

to the holo table. He turned on the gravity anchor used to keep him in place during engagements, and turned his comm on to its ship-wide reach.

"Attention," he began. "We are heading into an unknown situation. Get to your battlestations."

The announcement rang through the ship, and the lighting turned an amber color around the ceiling, indicating the caution alert.

"Cora, are you ready?" Sara asked, setting her shoulders for the unknown.

"Ready. Preparing the gravitic drives for cloak," she said, and Sara saw the engines come online.

They spooled up, but at very low power, sending a slight tremor through the deck.

"You can run the engines while in warp? I thought that would disrupt the warp field," Sara voiced with concern.

"That's true of a normal controller, but I am far from your normal controller," her sister said mirthfully. "The core we have has picked up a few tricks over the millennia. Now that I'm with Nyx, I can actually do some of them. I have to say, I'm glad you and the commander convinced me to do this."

Sara recognized the pure joy emanating from her twin, and smiled in response.

"Ten seconds to end warp," Connors updated.

"Hon, as soon as we are out, charge up the gauss cannons. I want to be ready in case we need to use them. Everyone, we need to be on our toes, here. No mistakes," Sara said, gripping the command ring with white knuckles.

"Aye, ma'am," Connors, Mezner, and Hon chorused.

"Exit in three, two, one," Cora counted down.

The view screen and Sara's viewing bubble both flashed with blue Aetheric light.

"Cloak engaged," Cora reported, her voice all business

now that they had arrived. Even Nyx seemed to be more focused than usual.

"Mezner, give me a passive scan of the area. Let's keep our transmissions to a minimum. No need to let them know we've arrived. Cora, give me a low level Aetheric scan," Sara commanded.

"Passive data is coming in, ma'am, but we're pretty far out, so we won't get any planetary data for a few hours," Mezner said.

The holo table suddenly populated with Cora's Aetheric scan. Only gravitational elements and life signs were shown. The computer then extrapolated the data and gave a rough estimate of the size and shape of the objects in the system. It displayed what objects were there, but showed none of the capabilities of those objects.

The system was a wreck. Literally. There were broken ships and space stations littering every corner. It looked like a battle had raged here for a thousand years. Most ships were in pieces, spinning lazily in clusters, and the planet's surface was pocked with craters large enough to see from space.

"Ma'am, I'm not getting any life signs," Mezner said hollowly.

"You're not getting life signs from where?" Sara asked quietly, already knowing the answer.

"From anywhere. The entire system is dead, ma'am."

Sara was quiet for a moment as they stared at the massive destruction. "Can we move in and keep the ship cloaked, Cora?"

"Yes, though we can't make fast movements, or I won't be able to compensate. We can jump without problems, though," she said.

Sara sniffed and marked a location close to a relatively tight formation of wreckage. "Jump us here. I want to get some scans and see if we can't figure out who did this."

"Jump in three, two, one," Cora counted down.

The view in her bubble changed, and Sara was able to see that they had jumped half a million kilometers and now hung motionless in the midst of a spinning ballet of scrap.

As she watched, the view of the closest wreckage began to fill with technical details as the sensors picked up the information on the objects at the snail's pace of light waves.

"I'm picking up a lot of Teifen tech in the ships. I'm also getting Galvox signatures, ma'am," Mezner said her face close to her console.

"Well, that confirms it. Galvox are pushing in from the other side of Teifen space. It makes sense that the Teifen would abandon the Elif conquest if they need to fight off a force that can do this," Grimms said, leaning into the holo table.

"Where are the survivors? There should be someone left," Sara reasoned.

"Maybe they took off after the battle. Moved on to a new system," Connors guessed.

Sara shook her head. "That doesn't make sense. They would have left someone behind, even if only to warn the others that they were being followed. This looks like two forces met and fought each other to the death, but the probability of both sides killing everyone defies logic."

"True. If a force came to invade, they would have brought superior numbers, to assure victory. If they were losing, they would pull out, but that would mean there was some of the enemy left," Grimms mused, rubbing a thumb under his chin while he tried to work it out. "If they stayed and fought, that would mean that they were going to win, and there would be some Galvox left. The Galvox could have left and moved on, but an armada of the size it would take to do this kind of damage would need to be constantly outfitted with more weapons, and that would mean a supply line, which means there should be someone left. This makes no sense in any scenario."

Sara nodded. "Why would the Galvox come here, anyway? This system was not a military threat, and it's pretty deep in Teifen territory to just be a hit-and-run target."

The bridge crew was silent while they each tried to come up with a reason for the attack. The silence stretched on for what seemed like several minutes before Hon finally broke it.

"Ma'am, my targeting array is picking up an odd signature," he said, sending the data to her viewing bubble and the holo table.

"I saw it, too, but I thought it was another piece of wreckage," Mezner said. "But passive scan is identifying the mass as a ship locked onto a larger piece of debris."

Sara spun the image around to get a better look at it. The ship was boxy and compact, but had an impressive array of engines on it that she didn't recognize by design. It looked like it was bristling with weapons, but they were of such odd design she wasn't sure of their exact function.

"Are we getting any life signs?"

"No, ma'am, it's dark. I'm not getting any power signatures either, but that could be due to superior shielding," Mezner said.

"Cora, can you give me a deeper Aetheric scan? I want to see if the shielding is hiding life signs."

"Give me a second. I'm going to try something the core suggested," she responded.

"Okay, be careful," Sara said, biting her lip.

"Well, that's interesting," Cora said a moment later.

The holo display popped up with a 3D rendering of a small room.

"What are we looking at here, Cora?" Sara asked, zooming in on the room in question.

"It's an Aetheric scan of the inside of that ship. I think it's the engine room, but I can't tell."

"How did you get this?" Sara asked in amazement.

"I combined the jump ability with the scan ability, and opened a tiny hole inside the ship that I could take a peek through. It only lasted for a picosecond, but this is what I got," she said proudly.

The interior of the ship was not like any design Sara had ever seen. It didn't look like it would be easy to move around in, due to the close quarters and how much stuff was jammed into the small area. Nothing was familiar; there was not one component that seemed recognizable.

"How would the crew be able to do any maintenance? It doesn't look like they could even crawl through some of those openings," Grimms commented.

"Did you get any life signs on your scan?" Sara asked Cora.

"Nothing. It's as dead as the rest of these heaps."

Sara bit her lip again, then rechecked that there were no life signs in the entire system. She didn't want to reveal the *Raven*'s presence, but she needed more info about this strange ship. She took a breath and looked down to Alister standing at her feet.

He gave her a shrug and said, "Merp?"

"I suppose," she said to him, then made her decision. "Mezner, give me an active scan of that thing. Make sure the beam is tight, but I want to know its specs."

"Aye, ma'am," she said, her fingers dancing over her controls.

Sara felt an itch on the back of her neck, and turned to see Nyx still sitting on Grimms' chair. She was at attention, which Sara didn't think too much about, until she realized that the small fox was trembling.

Sara keyed her comm to link directly with Cora. "What's wrong with Nyx?"

"Scan complete, ma'am. I didn't get much, but..." Mezner's eyes went wide. "Ma'am, it's powering up!"

Sara snapped her attention to her viewing bubble, and observed the ship coming to life. Lights began to flicker on, and a blue jet of plasma shot from the strange engines.

"Oh, shit! Get us out of here now!" Cora nearly screamed over the bridge's speakers. "Emergency jump," she said, and the screen flashed to a new view.

Sara saw that Cora had jumped them nearly a million kilometers away from the foreign ship. The small, odd ship was accelerating at an alarming rate, but it was still a ways away.

"Cora, what's going on?"

"That ship. We need to get away from it. I'll explain later, but you need to get us far away, and now."

Sara trusted her sister. If Cora said they needed to leave, then they needed to leave. She zoomed out and selected a system close by at random.

"Take us here."

"Warp in three," Cora began, and Sara saw the small ship accelerate to an unbelievable speed in less than a second. "Two." The small ship began to blur on her viewing bubble, then it disappeared completely. "One."

The small ship reappeared right beside the *Raven*, and six beams speared out from the incredibly fast ship. Each beam was right on target to hit them, but the image froze and smashed down to a pinprick as the *Raven* entered the warp thread.

The slowly expanding view gave Sara the chills as she stared down the frozen image of the most aggressive ship she had ever seen.

"What the hell was that?"

CHAPTER 21

"As soon as we drop out of warp, we need to do it again. Pick a direction away from populated space, especially Earth," Cora said, her panic lessened now that the *Raven* was away.

"Okay, but you need to tell me what's going on," Sara said, looking at the frightened faces of her bridge crew.

"I will, I promise. But this jump was short, so in two minutes, I need you to jump again," Cora pressed.

Sara nodded, and they all waited as the image of the alien ship slowly expanded. With a flash, Sara's viewing bubble updated, and she immediately selected another system. The *Raven* went to warp, and they were on their way.

Sara had selected another relatively short jump, but one that took them to a binary system the Elif had surveyed many years ago. They knew that the radiation from the twin suns messed with sensors and gave false readings. Aetheric sensors would still work, but the constant need for shields kept anyone from spending too much time in the system.

Sara hoped the interference would help them hide, if the enemy happened to have a way to find them.

She waited patiently through the fifteen minutes it took to get to the system, only biting her lip half a dozen times as she tried to figure out who and what was following them.

She noted that Nyx was pacing back and forth in Grimms' chair as her fur stood on end, and there was a wild look in her eyes that spoke of disbelief. Sara raised an eyebrow at that and considered what the pixie might know that she didn't.

The screen flashed again, and Sara was nearly blinded by the intense light of the two suns. She had warped them directly between the astral bodies to take the best advantage of the radiation, but she hadn't known how close the large suns were to one another.

She immediately powered a shield spellform that Alister gave her, encasing the *Raven* in a golden blanket and keeping out the most harmful stuff that was being thrown at them. The amount of power she needed to focus into the shield was slightly alarming at first, but she soon had a comfortable stream of Aether flowing, and she felt confident she could keep it up for a long time before it became a problem.

"Boon, meet me in my ready room," Sara requested into her comm as she stepped out of the command ring. "Grimms, you have the bridge. You let me know the second that ship shows up, if it ever does. I'm keeping us shielded to give us a little breathing room if we are attacked."

He gave her a salute. "Aye, ma'am."

Nyx and Alister followed her into the ready room just as the bridge doors slid open, revealing Boon fastening up her battlesuit.

Sara stepped into the small room, and Alister and Nyx came in on her heels, jumping onto the small couch and looking at her attentively. She gave them a nod and poured herself a cup of coffee from the wall dispenser.

"You want one?" she asked Boon as she stepped into the small office.

"No thanks, what's this all about? I was watching on my room's monitor as that ship came at us. Who was that, the Galvox?" Boon asked, taking one of the chairs in front of the small desk.

"We're about to find out. Cora? What the fuck is going on?" Sara demanded, flopping down into the swivel chair behind her desk. She nearly spilled hot coffee down the front of her battlesuit, but was able to keep it in her mug, if only just.

"Nyx recognized the ship," Cora said, calming down now that they were not in immediate danger.

Sara looked over at the nervous little fox and raised her eyebrow. "I thought I saw recognition from you," she said, confirming what she had seen earlier.

The fox gave a curt nod, then closed her eyes.

"She wants me to relay what she says," Cora explained in a slightly monotone voice. "She says they are called the Vitas, and will destroy any life they come across without a second thought."

"Fuck me. How have we never heard of these assholes before? If they're that aggressive, shouldn't the Teifen or the Elif have had previous run-ins with them?" Sara asked, taking a gulp of coffee and mumbling a curse at the burning liquid as it went down her throat.

I should have gone for the whiskey.

"Nyx says they are an ancient enemy of the pixies, and have been hunting them throughout time." Cora stopped and addressed Nyx. "I thought humans and pixies were from the same planet. How can they be hunting you and not us?"

There was a moment of silence as Nyx presumably answered her War Mage.

"Well, that's news to me," she mumbled. "She says the

pixies are not actually from the same planet as humans, but came to us early in our development and made the pact with us to protect themselves from the Vitas."

"That was hundreds of thousands of years ago. How have they kept themselves hidden all this time?" Sara asked, powering on her tablet in its slot on her desk to keep an eye on the sensor readings. So far the coast was clear.

"They haven't. They just now got here," Cora said.

"The Vitas are obviously capable of warp, or they would not have been in a system toward the center of the galaxy. The Milky Way is only a hundred thousand light years across; it wouldn't take them a couple hundred thousand years to get anywhere in the galaxy," Boon countered, doing the math in her head.

"I agree." After a quiet moment during which Nyx was talking to her, Cora let out a low, "Oh. That's horrifying."

"What's horrifying?" Sara asked, narrowing her eyes at the cream-colored fox.

"They aren't from the Milky Way."

CHAPTER 22

"You're saying the pixies are from another galaxy?" Boon asked, turning her head to look at Silva draped across her shoulders. The white ferret gave a shrug. It was obviously news to her.

There was a moment of silence as Cora and Nyx spoke. Then Cora shook her head in frustration. "Wait. I'm just going to tell them as you say it, Nyx, okay?"

The small fox gave a nod, but kept her eyes closed.

"The pixies were an advanced race that came from a galaxy just over seven hundred million light years away," Cora related. She stopped. "*Seven hundred million*? Seriously? Okay, sorry. Please continue," Cora said, as the fox frowned.

"Their original galaxy was about the same size as the Milky Way, and as far as they could tell, they were the only sentient species in it. They explored every star system they could, and never found anything more intelligent than wild animals," Cora continued with the tale. "The pixies focused on exploration, and wanted nothing more than to find others to share the universe with. It became apparent that they would need to go a lot further from home if they wanted to accomplish that, so they started building ships that could travel between the galaxies."

"The dreadnoughts," Boon supplied, almost out of nowhere.

Nyx's eyes popped open, and she tilted her head to regard Boon. Then gave her a short nod of affirmation.

"Yes. How did you know that?" Cora asked.

Boon shrugged. "I don't know, it was a guess. But when we were on the dreadnought, it seemed to me that it had been one thing, and the human-sized stuff was added later. It was small things, like we passed an access hatch that was far too small for a human to get into. And the whole park in the middle; it didn't seem like something a human would put on a starship that was meant for battle."

"The Teifen had a park in their dreadnought," Sara pointed out, remembering her bloody march to the governor's chambers.

"That was pretty small when compared to the vast open space on our dreadnought. The Teifen used it as a sign of status, but our dreadnought had a park that took up huge amounts of space. It wasn't practical, unless people were raising families on the ship," Boon said with a shrug.

"So the pixies can fly the dreadnought? I thought they didn't have the Aether capacity to do things like that," Sara said, sitting up with interest.

"They used to be able to fly it. But when they made the arrangement with the humans, they reworked the ships to make them easier for humans to use. We're getting off-subject, though," Cora said irritably.

"Sorry, please continue," Sara said, shoving her idea to the back of her mind and refocusing.

"While some number of their species worked on the dreadnoughts, another faction was trying to build a way to achieve immortality."

"Why?" Boon asked, not getting the connection.

"Because, even with the dreadnoughts, it would take a long time to travel between galaxies. And if they needed to get to a new galaxy and still take the time to explore it, most of the pixies that left on the initial flight would not be alive when they finally found what they were looking for. So, they wanted to find a way to extend their lives. Eventually they found a solution: the cores," Cora relayed.

"Like the one connected to your tank?" Sara asked.

"I guess so. I had no idea," Cora said, taken aback. "I thought cores could only be made by War Mages."

"No, the Alant program told us that any four mages could make a core. It was the spellforms that made it possible, not the abilities of the War Mages themselves," Sara said, tapping her lip.

"So, you're saying that the Vitas are actually pixies?" Boon asked, skipping right to the end.

"Not exactly," Cora continued. "The Vitas are the result of several mishaps and abuses of power. The immortality project was actually pretty close to something humans are trying to figure out right now. The idea was that a core could be a computer that would hold and process all the information a sentient being needed to be considered alive. They were trying to upload their consciousness onto a hard drive."

"I don't get it," Boon said, shaking her head.

"It's a pretty simple concept. The idea is that a human brain works on electrical impulses. If you can translate those pulses to something a computer could process, you would be able to upload yourself to a computer, and become immortal to a degree," Cora said.

"No, I understand that—they've been working on the idea since before I was born. What I don't understand is how a project to upload the pixies turned into the murder machine that just attacked us."

"Oh, right," Cora said, chagrined. She then continued with Nyx's words. "The first pixies uploaded themselves, and everything went according to plan. They were able to interface with the dreadnought systems, and actually became independent entities when they began building mechanical bodies.

"Then after a few thousand years, one of the first pixies to be uploaded snapped. He had been driven mad by his confinement to the core, and decided that no one should ever have to go through what he was. So, he built an army of robots and commanded them to stop the project.

"There was a war, and the pixies were not able to stand against the endless swarm of robotic invaders. Then another uploaded pixie snapped and joined his comrade in the robot-making; this pixie had been a programmer in his former life, and he improved the design.

"And so the first A.I. was born. The A.I. took to heart the orders to stop pixies from creating more cores, and decided the best way to keep them from ever uploading a consciousness again was to destroy the entire race."

"Holy shit. It's like that old time-traveling robot war movie with the bodybuilder," Boon exclaimed.

Sara and the familiars looked at her with blank looks.

"What? I like old movies."

"Anyway," Sara said, rolling her eyes. "What happened next?"

Cora continued. "The war intensified, and the pixies were losing. They took their last chance and loaded up every dreadnought they had and took off across the blackness of intergalactic space. They theorized that the Vitas would begin searching for them, starting with the closest galaxies first, so they took a multi-generational trip, not stopping 'til they were far enough away that they could breathe easy. The

Milky Way became their new home, and they have been here since."

"And how long ago was that?" Sara asked, raising an eyebrow at Nyx.

There was a pause.

"That can't be right," Cora said almost to herself, then relayed, "Nyx says they came here over nine hundred million years ago. That's before complex life emerged on Earth."

"You're saying the dreadnoughts are older than that? How can something last that long?" Boon asked, shaking her head.

"Nyx says the ships continually repair themselves with the same nanobot system we have on the *Raven*. Over time, the entire ship is replaced, part by part, so in a sense, it's not the same ship."

Sara put her head in her hand, and set her coffee on the desk. "My head hurts. Why is this the first I'm hearing that the pixies are actually extragalactic? You didn't think that was maybe important to share when Boon and I came to visit you?" she asked Nyx.

The fox shrugged her tiny shoulders, and Cora said, "It's not common knowledge among the pixies. Only the Keepers of the Record were entrusted with the knowledge of our origin."

"Okay, but—" Sara started, then the ship lurched to the side, sending her coffee cup careening off the desk. She felt an enormous amount of Aether pulling from her well as she tried to maintain the ship's shielding.

"Captain, we are under attack!" Mezner reported over Sara's comm.

"I'm on my way," she said, jumping from her seat and taking two large steps to the ready room's door.

She motioned for Alister to follow, but he was already leaping through the air, aiming for her shoulder.

CHAPTER 23

Sara ran to the command ring and powered it up while Grimms gave her a sit rep.

"It warped in and immediately began firing. It's using some sort of energy weapon, but nothing we've seen," he said, as the ship rocked from another barrage.

Sara grunted as her Aether well was strained once again. She could see that their shields had burned down to an angry orange glow in several spots. The Vitas ship was spinning and dodging in a highly aggressive and random manner. Its relatively small size belied the power of its weapons.

"Hon, give me a lock and hit it with a barrage from the gauss cannons. Cora, can you hit it with the Aether cannons? We need to soften it up for Hon," Sara said, marking the dodging ship in her display with difficulty.

"Charging Aether cannons," Cora reported.

"Connors, give me some evasive maneuvers. No sense sitting here and giving it an easy target."

"Aye, ma'am," Connors said, his fingers flying over the controls.

The *Raven* shot forward, then juked to starboard at nearly

ninety degrees. The small ship adjusted its own maneuvers, and a dance began between the relentless heat of the two suns.

"Firing," Cora called, as one line of blue Aetheric power stabbed out, followed by a second.

"Both shots went wide," Mezner reported.

The *Raven* shuddered slightly, and a volley of three slugs leapt from one of the gauss turrets, but the small Vitas ship changed directions almost instantly, avoiding the shots. It let out a quick stream of particle beams that slammed into the *Raven*'s shields, and burned them down faster than Sara could feed them Aether.

The last two beams seared into the armored hull, making the ship jump under her feet. She grabbed hold of the command ring, and was able to keep upright.

"Damage report," Grimms yelled over the alarms.

"We have a hull breach on deck two. The bulkhead's closed, and the nanobots have been deployed," Mezner said.

Cora fired the Aether cannons again, but this time, she used short bursts and tried to lead the other ship, hoping it would run into the beams. She sent out six bursts, each only a fraction of a second in duration; all but the last one were dodged. The final shot grazed the Vitas ship, but did little to no damage that they could see.

Hon followed the Aether shots with another volley. This time, instead of firing one after the other, he shot all three at once, and spread them in a triangular pattern like a shotgun blast.

The Vitas were fast, but the ship couldn't quite get clear of the wider pattern Hon had put out, and one of the slugs clipped the bow, sending a spray of super-heated hull splashing into the blackness of space.

The small ship, however, didn't seem to notice, and continued to fire at them relentlessly.

Another barrage of particle beams blasted into Sara's newly reformed shield and tore it apart with unnerving ease. The *Raven* bucked, and a groan of stressed metal rang throughout the ship.

The little ship was all over them, only a few hundred meters out, which made tracking difficult for the big gauss and Aether cannons. The battle had only been going for ten seconds, and already the Vitas had scored several hits.

"Why are the PDCs not firing?" Sara asked, realizing the buzzing sound of their close defense weapons was absent.

"The sensors are having trouble picking out the enemy ship from the background radiation, ma'am. We only have a firing solution because you are able to manually select it," Hon reported, sending out a third shot with the gauss cannons, this time using two of the tri barrel turrets in the shotgun strategy.

The Vitas either got lucky in its sudden change in direction, or it saw the shot coming. Either way, the gauss rounds went wide, and the Vitas came in close to rake at the ship once again with its unbelievably powerful particle beams.

Sara gritted her teeth and dumped as much Aether as she could into the shields, making them glow brightly with golden light as the Vitas's beams slammed into the *Raven* for the third time. The shields dimmed with each blast, but Sara kept pushing as her well began to dry.

She gritted her teeth and grunted, "Cora, get us out of here."

"I need a destination," she said quickly.

"Just go. It doesn't need to be accurate," Sara urged, as her eye began to twitch under the constant barrage from the small vessel. It was as if it could sense that she was struggling, and pressed its attack even more.

"Okay, hang on, everyone," Cora advised.

The shots from the ship were too powerful, and coming

one on top of the other in a relentless drive to punch through Sara's barrier. The blasts were dealing more damage than she could compensate for, and the shields began to fail.

"Three," Cora began counting, and Sara nearly shouted with frustration. She had wanted Cora to jump the ship, not warp away again.

The shield was orange, turning to red fast.

"Two."

Sara began to feel light-headed from the strain, and she could feel with each blast that the shield was going to fail at any moment.

Then, to her horror, a hole burned through.

"One," Cora said, but it was too late.

A beam punched through and lanced into the *Raven*, sending a shudder through the ship. The lights began to flicker, but the pounding had stopped, and Sara could feel that all the Aether she was still pouring into the shields were actually strengthening them, not just prolonging their beating.

She blinked a few times, trying to determine where the other ship had gone, then she noticed the two suns no longer loomed in the holo projector. The projection was familiar, however.

"Are we back in the Teifen system?" she asked aloud, pulling her Aether back, but leaving the regenerated shields in place.

"Yes. I wasn't sure it would work without an exact location, so I used our last position in this system as a guide point," Cora said excitedly.

"What did you do?" Sara asked, still not sure how they were so far from their original position.

"It was a trick the core showed me. It combines the warp spellform and the jump spellform. Basically, it lets me make a warp thread and then jump through it, instead of traveling along it."

"You're saying you can jump us instantly anywhere we can warp to?" Sara asked to clarify.

"Not anywhere. Even with my larger Aether well, I just don't have the power to jump us extreme distances. What we just did was a bit like burning all the fuel in the tank on one fast, short trip, instead of the fuel efficient method of cruising along in warp," Cora responded.

"How was that ship tracking us? We changed direction halfway through the journey, that should have thrown it off," Sara asked the bridge at large.

"I'm not sure, ma'am," Connors said, looking up from his console. "As far as we and the Elif know, there is no way to trace a warp thread. We just know that the thread can only travel in a straight line."

"Actually, I think I may be able to change trajectory slightly while in warp, but it would take a lot of power," Cora said, then seemed to realize this was not the time to theorize about her new powers. "But Connors is right. As far as we know, there is no way to trace a warp thread."

Sara made a fist and slapped it into her open palm, making Alister grip her shoulder tighter. "Well, it looks like these Vitas have figured it out, which means we need to get out of here either by using gravitic drives, or jumping out of the system before warping away. Otherwise, we can never go home, because that damn ship is going to follow us forever."

"Whatever we're going to do, we are going to have to wait," Cora said, her voice becoming concerned. "The ship took quite a bit of damage right as we jumped, losing a number of the amplifiers on the hull. I can't jump us until those are repaired, and I can't cloak us, either. We have flight controls, but the finer adjustments on the gravitic drives are fried."

"Not to mention the two holes in our hull," Grimms said, looking at the damage report. "The nanobots will take a few hours to repair everything. And before you ask, if we repair the amplifiers first, we would have jump and cloak capabilities in forty minutes. However, with the hull breaches, our structural integrity is down—if we get hit in one or two strategic places, the ship will collapse under the stress of maneuvering. Honestly, it was two of the worst places for us to get hit."

Sara considered that for a second. "You think they knew where to hit us? That they were trying to cut us up?"

Grimms frowned. "I wasn't thinking that, because the precision it would take is beyond what I thought possible, but now that you say it..." He trailed off, raising an eyebrow at the damage report in his hands. "It's possible."

"What if we don't repair the breach completely, but instead just reinforce the ship's frame, then focus on the amplifiers?" Sara asked, trying to find the compromise.

"We can have a rough framework up in twenty minutes, and we can actually use crew to set the pieces, so the nanobots can focus on the amplifiers instead of building the struts from scratch," Grimms said, a plan formulating as he said it. "We can have the work done in an hour or less," he said, looking to Sara for her approval.

She gave him a nod. "Do it. Connors, take us in close to one of the larger pieces of debris. Let's see if we can't use it as a barrier between us and that little bastard. If we can keep them on the far side of it, that should buy us some time."

"Aye, ma'am," Connors said, setting a course for a large chunk of what was once a Teifen destroyer.

"I need ideas, people. How do we fight this thing?" Sara asked, opening the floor for discussion.

Hon cleared his throat. "I might have something, ma'am."

CHAPTER 24

Sara kept having to remind herself to breathe as she watched the surrounding space for any sign of the Vitas ship.

I have never felt that kind of power. It had an odd flavor, as if the damage the particle beam did to the shields was higher than what it did to the ship itself. And our Aetheric cannon didn't seem to faze their ship much at all, Sara thought as she bit her lip and searched the debris-strewn space around them. *Could they have the tech to dampen the effects of Aether? How are they able to travel faster than light without it?*

"Ma'am, the supports are in place, and the nanobots are moving in to finish up the job. The crew should be out of there in ten minutes or less," Grimms reported from beside the holo table.

"Thank you, Commander," Sara said, coming out of her thoughts. "How are the amplifiers coming along?"

"Another thirty minutes, and we will have full functionality, ma'am."

We're not out of the woods just yet, but I can at least see some light through the canopy. Sara nodded and nervously cracked her knuckles. "Have we gotten word from the *Cata-gain*?" she asked Mezner.

"No, ma'am. They should be getting our message any time, now. It will be another twenty minutes before we hear back from them, though," the ensign said with a shake of her head.

Sara blew out a breath, once again catching herself holding it in nervousness. She decided to mentally go over their plan of attack one more time.

The *Raven* was currently tucked behind the aft end of a destroyed Teifen carrier. They were keeping themselves on the opposite side of the huge piece of starship from where they had warp-jumped into the system. Sara's thinking was that if the Vitas were following their warp thread, they should come in on the same trajectory. This time, she had ordered the sensors to be on full blast, and Cora was washing the area with Aetheric waves to detect everything within a light year. They wanted to gather as much information as possible; who knew what advantage it might bring in the future.

The plan was simple. As soon as they saw the Vitas warp in, the *Raven* would jump in behind it and let loose a volley of gauss rounds, then immediately jump back behind the destroyer's wreckage. They would keep jumping in and out of the battle, hopefully keeping the enemy off balance.

They had noticed that the Vitas didn't seem to have any weapons besides their light-based beams, and hoped to use their jump ability to keep the enemy at a distance, where their light-speed weapons would be easier to dodge.

That was the plan, anyway. Sara didn't have much time to second guess her decisions.

"I have a positive ID, ma'am. They came in on the same coordinates as us, plus or minus seventy-five meters," Mezner reported.

Sara jumped into action. Sending a bit more power to the shields, she swiped a position behind the small ship. "Cora, jump."

The view changed from the hunk of slowly spinning metal and composite of the carrier to the small, oddly shaped aft section of the Vitas craft.

"Hon," the captain said, but she didn't need to tell him twice, as he let loose with twelve gauss rounds at point-blank range. "Jump," she commanded her sister again, and the spinning piece of debris returned to dominate their view.

Grimms gave a thin smile, leaning over the holo table. "At least one direct hit, ma'am. The Vitas are spinning with the impact. They appear to have some substantial damage to their engine array."

"Good, let's do it again," she said firmly, her confidence coming back.

They jumped, and the small ship appeared just as Hon let loose with another volley. This time, the Vitas ship spun on its axis so fast that Sara thought it was from the impact. However, when the slugs continued past the untouched ship, she could see that it had spun in order to dodge their incoming fire.

She could see the blaster cannons covering the ship begin to glow with building energy for a counterattack, but Cora jumped them away before it could get the shots off. On the holo display, she watched the spray of particle beams fly off into the void.

"What the hell? How did they know we were there?" she asked with a frown.

"I think it learned from our last attack, ma'am," Hon said, checking to make sure the cannons were reloading.

"They're headed this way," Mezner reported.

On the holo display, Sara saw a barrage of blasts coming toward the hunk of destroyer they were hiding behind. The

Vitas were still a few light seconds away, so the fireworks didn't start until they were nearly a quarter of the way to the *Raven*'s hiding spot. Then the hunk of starship in front of them began to spin and glow with the particle beam impacts; it was obvious that it was not going to last very long.

"Jump here," Sara said much more calmly than she felt as she marked a spot on her display.

Cora jumped them immediately, and the view changed again as they popped up behind a second, smaller section of derelict ship. They had jumped to a spot behind the Vitas, forcing them to slow down and turn to come at them again, hopefully buying some time.

"Hon, load up the gauss cannons with the warhead slugs. I have another idea."

Sara mentally asked Alister for a spellform of special design, and the cat raised his eyebrows as he understood what she wanted to do.

"It'll work," she told him. "It doesn't need to hold the blast, just get it started," she coaxed.

He tilted his head then gave a nod.

She could see that the Vitas ship had spun on its axis again. It quickly overcame its lost momentum and started accelerating toward the *Raven*. Even though there were several light seconds between them, the Vitas began firing bolts to take out their cover.

Sara marked the spot she wanted.

"Jump," she said, then, while keeping their ship's shields in her mind, began powering the second spellform Alister gave her.

As soon as they appeared behind the Vitas, it began to spin around to face them.

"Fire!" Sara ordered, powering up the new form.

Twelve highly explosive slugs shot out at the Vitas, and,

like she had predicted, the ship dodged slightly, but only enough to not be hit directly.

However, behind the enemy ship, a thin shield came glowing to life. It was shaped like a large, shallow bowl, and the open top was facing the *Raven* and the incoming slugs.

Sara only sent minimal power into the shield shape, but even then, the draw on her well was nearly overwhelming.

As the slugs approached the Vitas ship, it opened fire with everything it had. Light speed was slow when compared to the vastness of space, but it was still faster than gauss rounds, and the *Raven* needed to hold position while Sara's plan played out.

At nearly the same time, the enemy particle beams slammed into the *Raven*, and the gauss slugs exploded against the bowl-shaped shield, redirecting the blast back at the Vitas and enveloping it in fire, plasma, and shrapnel.

The two shields Sara was powering both took tremendous hits, but she needed both to survive, so she slammed everything she had into them.

The *Raven* was peppered with hundreds of blasts, and the shields quickly burned down to an angry red, finally failing toward the aft section. Several particle beams blasted through the hull, and one lucky shot slammed through the engine room, puncturing two of the reactors.

The ship shuddered and groaned, while electrical systems overloaded and blew fuses throughout the major systems.

Sara caught a glimpse of the Vitas ship spinning out of the blast, and was satisfied to see that the engines were dark, and there was a cloud of debris floating around the craft. It looked dead, but before she could confirm that, the view screen and her viewing bubble both went dark.

CHAPTER 25

THE *RAVEN* LISTED to the side, her starboard gravity manipulators damaged beyond use until the nanites could do their work. Power was out in the fore sections of the ship, including the bridge, which was running on battery backup for the time being. The only light came from the various consoles and the holo projector in the center of the room.

"Ma'am, we only have enough back-up power for one volley of gauss rounds," Hon reported.

"Life support is out on decks three and four. We still have not received word from the *Catagain*, ma'am," Mezner added.

Sara wiped a trickle of blood from the place on her brow where she had hit her head on the control ring in the last bombardment. She blinked a few times to clear her vision, and saw Grimms raise an eyebrow in concern.

"I'm okay. Just need a second," she said to him, turning to the holo projector to take in the situation.

Their last attack had done as much or more damage to the alien ship as it had done to them. The ugly thing spun slowly on its vertical axis, and a small cloud of debris was forming around the dark ship. There were no signs of venting gas, which surprised her, considering the state it seemed to be in. The *Raven* had lost pressure in at least two places, the last she checked.

"Mezner, what are the bits I'm seeing gathering around the aliens? Parts of their ship? They seem too uniform." She zoomed the projection in, noting the similarities in a lot of the spinning pieces that were spreading from the damaged ship.

Mezner began flipping through readouts, taking a close look before saying, "The objects have nearly identical mass and shape, but I'm not picking up any lifeforms in them, if they are escape pods of some kind."

"They could be weapons," Grimms noted.

"They could be, but why not shoot them *at* us? Cora, what are you seeing?" Sara asked the open air.

There was no reply.

"Cora?" she asked again, slightly panicky.

Still nothing.

She punched in a channel on her command ring. "Caroline? Teichek, do you read me? What's wrong with Cora?"

There was a brief moment of silence, then Caroline Green came on the line. Sara could hear alarms in the background, and people moving about. "Sorry, ma'am. It's pretty hectic down here. What can I do for you?"

"Why am I not getting a response from Cora?" she asked.

"Uh, let me check on something," Caroline said, then muted the comm.

Sara waited, and watched the spreading debris with growing concern. The fact that so many of the objects were the same was a sign it was some sort of maneuver, but she couldn't determine the goal.

Caroline came back on the line, her voice filled with concern that had not been there before. "I'm sorry, ma'am.

In the confusion, I failed to notice that Cora is in some kind of maintenance cycle. I think the ship is prioritizing her repair. That's the only thing I can guess."

"How long will she be out?" Sara asked, becoming more and more convinced the objects were not benign.

"Ma'am, I don't know. It's similar to when we first installed the core, but there is no reason the system should be rebooting. She just seems to be preoccupied."

"Is she in danger?" Grimms asked quickly, drawing a look from Sara.

"Uh, no, sir. She's just in a maintenance cycle," Caroline said. "If I had to guess, I would say she's doing better than when we were in battle. Her heart rate is lower, and her cortisol levels have come way down."

Grimms gave Sara a chagrined look, and she smiled slightly in reassurance. "I need you to wake her up," she told Caroline. "The battle may not be over, and she's more than half our defenses."

"I'll do what I can, ma'am, but I'm not even sure what's wrong at the moment."

Teichek came on the line, "Ma'am, I think this is a defense mechanism. The core is still online and monitoring all systems, and Cora's Aether is still flowing through the system. I don't think there is too much to worry about," he said in a maddeningly calm voice.

"I need you to do whatever you can to wake her up," Sara repeated. "The Vitas could attack at any moment, and we are sitting ducks with her out of the fight." Her knuckles were turning white as she gripped the command ring. "Run whatever tests you need too. Find out what happened and fix it."

"Yes, ma'am. We'll do what we can, but it may take a little while. The system we're using is still experimental at best," Caroline said.

"Great," Sara grumbled to herself, then said, "Let me know as soon as she comes out of it."

"Yes, ma'am."

Sara looked over her shoulder and saw that Nyx was out as well, curled in Grimms' chair where he had left her.

Shit. Where are you, sis? What can I do without you right now? She leaned over the command ring to get a better view of the holo table. "Grimms, what do you think?"

He stroked his white beard. "I think there's not a whole lot we can do about it, if it's an attack. The PDCs are out, the shield amplifiers are all blown 'til we can get new fuses in them—which Chief Sabine is giving me a twenty-minute ETA on," he said, checking his tablet. "I can have the troops set for battle, but if those projectiles are some kind of weapon, we don't know what the effects will be."

Sara pursed her lips and reached up to where Alister perched on her shoulder, looking over the holo images with her, and scratched him on the chin.

"What do you think?" she asked him quietly.

Her familiar gave a growl and bared his teeth at the floating objects.

"I concur," she said, making her decision. "Hon, send the last of our gauss rounds into the belly of that ship. We can't afford to wait and see who regains power first."

"That will be it, ma'am. We won't be able to recharge the cannons until the reactors are restarted," Grimms cautioned her.

She considered the consequences while Hon slowly found his firing solution, intentionally giving her time to think. After a moment, she nodded. "Good point, Commander. Hon, send one round at a time, so we don't overdo it."

"Aye, ma'am," he acknowledged, finishing his solution. "Firing."

A yellow line snapped out of the holo projection of their

ship and streaked toward the alien ship at an incredible speed. A bloom of fire indicated a hit, but when the image cleared, the ship was still intact and spinning lazily.

"What happened? Did we get a hit? The ship doesn't look any more damaged than it already did." Sara leaned in and squinted at the small projection.

"Checking," Mezner said. "It seems that one of the objects encircling the ship was in the flight path of the round, ma'am"

Hon looked up from his console. "Ma'am, I accounted for the objects' projected paths. It should have been a clean shot."

"Shit," Sara growled.

"Battlestations! Prepare for boarders," Grimms announced ship-wide over his comm.

The alarm began to wail as Mezner said, "I don't understand. There are no life signs on the objects."

"There were none on the ship, either. We're working on the theory that they are robots, not living beings. Hon, send two slugs, try and overwhelm them," Sara said, gripping the command ring with white knuckles and waiting for the move she knew was coming.

The remaining lights dimmed for a moment as two more shots leapt from the cannons.

"Impact," Hon announced in a bright voice then, when he saw the aftermath, replied in a more somber tone, "I'm sorry, ma'am. Both shots were intercepted."

"We have power surges in multiple objects. They are changing course, heading our way," Mezner said with shock. "They will be here in less than two minutes."

"All personnel, prepare for boarders. Suit up in shield helmets and battle armor if able." Sara smashed a fist onto the table. "Grimms, you have the con. I'm going to join the

Marines. If that ships prowess were any indication, the troops are going to need all the help they can get."

"Aye, ma'am," he said, a grim look on his face.

Making sure her shield collar was in place, Sara swept from the bridge, a growing cloud of anger and crackling energy following after.

"I almost feel bad for the invaders," Hon said when the door slid shut behind the captain.

"Don't. They're invading her home. They've brought this on themselves," Grimms said, looking at the unconscious form of Nyx as she lay curled in his chair, her small, cream-colored body barely moving with each breath. "I just hope we survive her onslaught."

CHAPTER 26

A CLANGING SOUND rang through the deck. Then another. Soon, it sounded like a heavy rain on a tin roof, so many of the things were latching on to the hull. Sara sprinted toward the cargo bay, trying to get to her armor, but she was sure she was too late.

"Alister, I'm going to need a shield that stays close, preferably right on top of me; these corridors are close, and I don't want to be blocking the Marines' shots with my shield."

The small, black cat was hunkered down on her shoulder, the gripping pads of his battlesuit holding tight. He sent her a 'so-so' feeling, letting her know that he would do his best, but that it wouldn't be as form-fitting as her armor. She got a mental picture of a tight oval shield and nodded.

"It'll have to do. Maybe we won't need it."

Alister growled low, and she gave a chuckle. "Yeah, you're right. We're going to need it."

She was grateful she had taken the time to get Alister and Nyx in their battlesuits while they were waiting for the repairs. And she was doubly happy they had developed the shield helmets for the small animals; it was one less thing she needed to worry about.

"How are we looking, Baxter?" Sara asked over the comm. At the same time she sent a feeling of worry laced with indignation about the invaders.

.A feeling of agreement and reassurance flooded her before Baxter responded. "We're on deck two, just outside the main airlock. It looks like the invaders are going to come in through there," Baxter said. His voice was calm, but she could tell he was running.

Shit, that's on the opposite side of the ship. I really am going to have to forgo my armor. She let out a huff. "Copy that, Sergeant. I'm on my way. ETA, two minutes."

She turned and took a flight of stairs down one level and began running in the opposite direction she had been traveling in. Then the ship shook, and there was a ripping sound that seemed to come from everywhere. Her hair whipped in the sudden wind when the blast door in front of her slammed shut, cutting her off from the sudden decompression. She ran into the steel door, stopping herself with both hands.

"Baxter, report!"

"They breached the airlock. I'm still en route, I'll be there in a second," he said, now slightly out of breath as he pushed himself harder.

She could feel the panic bleeding off of him. His men were engaging an enemy, and he was not there.

"Be careful, love," she said on a private channel.

"I always am," he lied.

There was a panic-filled moment when she realized she couldn't get to him. If there was a breach, she and everyone else would be cut off until the ship could be depressurized and the blast doors reopened, and that could take several minutes.

Several minutes was a lifetime in the middle of a battle.

She punched the heavy metal door in frustration, and pain shot up her arm. She growled at her inability to get across her own ship.

I wish I could fly there. She cocked her head as a thought pushed itself to the fore of her mind. *Hey, idiot, you can fly there. You're a War Mage.* "I'm coming in behind them. Give me one minute, and for fuck's sake, keep me updated!" she shouted into her comm as she bounded up the stairs she had just descended, and headed for the cargo bay once again.

She felt like she was taking forever as she ran as hard as she could through the corridors, bathed in the otherworldly red hue of the battlestations alert. She passed crewmembers and checked to see that they all had their shield collars on and were armed. Many threw her salutes as she passed, but just as many were far too busy and nervous to even notice their captain passing at a full sprint.

By the time she reached the cargo bay doors, the corridors had started the process of decompressing. When the doors slid open, her shield collar activated, covering her head and sealing the battlesuit to provide a breathable atmosphere.

She glanced at her shoulder to make sure Alister's new collar had activated along with hers. He gave her a slight nod as they burst through the doors and into the empty cargo bay. She briefly considered taking the two minutes to don her armor, but decided she couldn't leave her men to fight this unknown enemy alone. Instead, she picked up speed as she sprinted for the plasma shield barrier between her and open space.

She leapt the last few meters, flattening out like a super-hero as she plunged through the buzzing field. The sudden silence of open space was unnerving, but nothing she hadn't encountered many times before.

She turned around with a complicated movement she

had learned while doing zero-g maneuvers in the academy, and could see the *Raven* falling away from her. The battle damage was far worse when viewed from the outside; large chunks of the hull had been split open where the armor had been burned or stripped away, and sparks and gases poured from the aft section, where a direct hit had, luckily, only ruptured the fuel tanks for the fusion reactors, and not the reactors themselves.

God, this is going to take forever to fix. We might even have to decommission the girl, she thought darkly before turning her attention to the problem at hand.

She was on the opposite side of the ship as the attackers and their ship, but the slow revolution of the dead *Raven* was bringing the aliens into view. Even in the blackness of space, she could see the light of the system's sun glinting off the thousands of small, metal objects that were streaming toward her.

Her jaw set, and a calmness came over her at the thought of the destruction she was about to rain down on these bastards. Using a shield spell from Alister, she pushed the two of them around the *Raven* and into the direct path of the objects.

When the pair came over the ship's horizon, Sara could see the oblong objects slotting open. At first she thought they were coming apart, but she soon realized the humanoid robots had been folded down into a compact shape, but were opening up spread-eagle as they moved within a couple hundred meters of the *Raven*'s hull, preparing to hit the surface and grab hold, digging into the hardened armor plating.

She brought Alister and herself to a stop and assessed the situation. A long stream of the compact robots was flowing toward the *Raven,* stretching out for over a kilometer from the Vitas ship. She did a quick estimate and guessed that there were over five hundred of them, though only a fraction of that number had already made it to the ship.

Still, she knew her people would be overrun if they had to fight all of them.

I need to thin the ranks before they can get here, she realized, and she requested a spellform from Alister. The three dimensional spellform appeared in her mind, and she fed it Aether without even checking to see if it was correct.

Alister was so much better at spellforms than she ever had been that checking his work would be like trying to find the error in a mathematician's calculation when she only knew basic algebra.

A shield formed above her, and she glanced up at it as it grew thicker. It was constructed like a cone, with the tip blunted. It was five meters wide at the base and came to a rounded point that was about one meter across. It reminded her of a pellet from the air rifle she and Cora had when they were kids.

The robot army had not seemed to notice her floating above their target, but Sara was sure that would change in just a moment.

She sent a mental command to Alister, and he began to morph the spellform as she continued to feed it Aether. With surprising speed, the construct shot away from them and headed directly for the loose line of robots. She had aimed for the section right behind where they were unfolding and attaching to the ship, hoping that in their compacted forms, they would have less maneuverability.

The shield slammed into the first bot, and Sara felt a tug on her Aether well; it was taking an enormous amount of power to keep the shield intact. The first bot was broken open, and sparks jumped from its damaged parts as it flew off into the blackness of space.

Sara smiled. It was working.

Then the second and third bot hit the shield, and she grunted at the construction's sudden loss of Aether. They were thrown free just as the first had been, but the cost on her power was astounding.

Are they burning through my shield? That shouldn't happen, unless they're way heavier than they look, she thought, but she dismissed that idea when she saw that the shield itself was not taking much damage.

On every impact, it was flaring, but not so much that it was changing color. But *something* was draining her Aether away when her spell touched the bots. This was confirmed when the shield blasted into four bots at once, and she nearly passed out from the exertion. The bots were somehow siphoning off the Aether.

There is no way I can stop them all, if it takes this much power to hit them, she thought.

When the next impact took its toll, she let the spellform drop. The golden pellet dissolved into nothingness before another bot could hit it.

She had blasted eight of the bastards, and it had taken almost half her Aether to do it. *So that's not the way to win this battle...*

She looked around for something to throw with a spellform, thinking that if there was something hitting the bots that was not Aether-based, maybe she could mitigate the drain, but she couldn't find anything within grabbing distance. Most of the debris from the *Raven* was small and had traveled too far away when it was blasted off, and she didn't want to try and grab anything from the Vitas ship, if it was just going to drain her like the bots did.

With frustration, she decided she needed to get back inside the *Raven* and help her men. Even if they ended up fighting all five hundred bots, in a stand-up fight, she thought she could take that many enemies.

At least she hoped so.

She powered a new spell, and she and Alister were pushed to the airlock. She could see bots climbing in like four-legged spiders, but some of them were being blasted back out of the hole in sprays of rifle fire.

"Baxter, what's the sit rep?" she asked, trying to figure out the best way to get into the ship.

"We've lost twelve people, but the tide seems to be slowing," he said, and Sara could hear him breathing hard.

"That's only going to last for a few seconds. I took out the next eight in line, but I can't keep it up. I need to get in there," she said, thinking of what she could do to get past the constant spray of metal slugs.

A spellform appeared in her head, and she took a quick look at it. She rolled her eyes at her own stupidity.

Alister was showing her the spellform that Cora had used to teleport, back on Earth. Sara had forgotten that Nyx showed him and Silva how to do it.

"I'm coming in, Baxter. Have the men fall back from the airlock opening," she ordered, and prepared herself.

"We're clear, but there are several of those things climbing through," he responded.

"That's fine. They won't be there for long," she said to him, then added, "I hope," under her breath.

Then she powered the form in her mind.

CHAPTER 27

"I'm getting power signatures throughout the alien vessel, Commander," Mezner reported, her voice hoarse from stress.

Grimms gritted his teeth. *The last thing we need is for that asshole to come back online while we're sitting dead in the water.* "Is it repairing itself, or just rebooting some system?"

The ensign took a minute to reply. "It looks like they have a repair system comparable to the *Raven*, sir."

"Shit. How are our repairs coming?" he asked, staring down at the slowly spinning holo image of the Vitas ship.

"Unknown, sir. With Cora down, we can only estimate, but I would say we're more than an hour from being up," Mezner said, then leaned in to her console. "Sir! The enemy is sending out a signal. It looks like a communication, but it's not any coding I recognize."

"It's broadcasting? Give me a scan of the system, use whatever power you need. We need to see if there is another one of these ships close enough to get that communication," Grimms said, his stomach dropping at the thought of another of these ships coming after them.

"Aye, sir. Scanning now," she said, getting to work.

"Sir, I'm getting an anomaly several thousand kilometers behind the Vitas ship. It looks like a gravity well is forming," Hon reported, slightly panicked.

"A gravity well? Like another ship?" Grimms asked for clarification.

"No, sir. More like a large asteroid, but it's growing in intensity," Hon said, his eyes wide. "Oh, shit."

The ship lurched to the side slightly as it began to pull toward the anomaly.

"It's growing exponentially, sir. We're being sucked in," Hon shouted.

"Connors, do we have anything in the drives?" Grimms asked, already knowing the answer.

"No, sir. Gravitic drives are still offline," Connors said, trying them anyway and getting no response.

"Sir, the gravity field is collapsing in on itself," Hon said in disbelief. "It's forming a black hole."

"Shit! I need options people, anything," Grimms barked out, gripping the holo table.

Before anyone could respond, the ship leveled out.

"It's gone, sir. It just collapsed and disappeared," Hon said, looking up from his console, wide-eyed.

"The transmission has stopped, sir. I... I think they just sent a message through a wormhole," Mezner said with wonder.

"They used a wormhole to send a message? How did they form it?" Grimms asked.

Connors spoke up. "It would be an effective form of FTL communication, sir."

"I understand that, but I want to know how they formed it at all," Grimms said with frustration.

"I don't know, sir. The Vitas ship showed a spike in power, but I don't see how it was enough to do that," Mezner said.

Grimms growled and nearly spat in frustration. "So we should assume that they have contacted their fleet, and there are reinforcements coming. If anything, they will know the *Raven* can stand against them and what our capabilities are."

"Sir, the Vitas ship's weapons are showing power fluctuations. I think they are attempting to repair them," Mezner said.

"How many shots do we have left, Hon?"

Hon double-checked. "Nine, sir."

"Find a firing solution, but hold," Grimms ordered. "Let's hope our engines come online before their guns do."

"It's going to be close, sir," Mezner said.

"It always is."

CHAPTER 28

Sara fed the spellform with Aether, then she disappeared from the universe.

She had been a controller before she was a commander, and knew the spells used in a warp maneuver like the back of her hand. The jump spell was similar, but changed one major factor of travel.

In a warp, the ship never left the universe it was currently in; it merely traveled through an impossibly thin thread of Aether while encircled in another bubble of Aether. That bubble still traversed the same distance as traditional drives would take, but it did so in a compressed format that allowed the ship to sort of trick reality into thinking it was well within its physical rights.

Jumping, on the other hand, was another animal altogether.

The ship—or in this case, the person—is still wrapped in a bubble of Aether, but instead of traveling through a thread, the bubble is sucked directly *into* the Aether, that place below space-time, and then shoved out another tiny hole in space-time and back into reality.

Because the Aether has no dimensions that humans can understand, the distance traveled is very slight. It happens so fast that it seems instantaneous, but it still takes a few picoseconds to get from one place to the next. That distinction is important, because it means that the jumping object is not disappearing and reappearing, but is actually being moved. And when it reappears, it is actually expanding extremely quickly from a pinprick of reality.

Normally this wouldn't matter, because any sane person would only jump to an unoccupied spot. However, Sara's sanity was questionable at best, so when she decided to jump into battle with a gang of angry robots who were boarding her ship, she jumped into their midst.

Actually, she decided to jump into one robot, just to see what would happen.

A tiny hole formed in the torso of a robot that was powering up one of its arm cannons. That hole was quickly filled with a bubble of pure Aether that expanded rapidly; the bubble itself was being fed by the Aether it was coming from, and did not lack the power a shield would have under the same circumstances. The bubble expanded so rapidly that the robot's components didn't even have time to melt from the pressure, instead converting directly into plasma, which then burned away more of the bot as it came apart at the molecular level.

In less time than light took to travel a millimeter, the bot had disintegrated into a cloud of loose atoms, and Sara stood in its place. Half the bodies of the bots to either side of her received the same treatment, while the other half of their metallic frames slammed into the bulkhead so hard they shattered like glass.

She turned to see the airlock, filled with the crawling bots, blown clear from the ship as the shockwave traveled through the bulkhead and flooring. If there had still been atmosphere, Sara was sure the accompanying ripping sounds would have driven her to her knees. The entire small room was ripped free of the *Raven*, sent barreling into the stream of incoming bots, knocking them to the side and damaging several.

She now stood on the torn edge of her ship, thankful that the internal gravity was still working, and found herself on the opposite side of a twenty-strong group of two-and-a-half-meter-tall robots, as her Marines all stared in shock at her entrance.

"Keep firing, I have my shields," Sara shouted at them over the open comm. Then she powered the tight shield Alister had shown her on their way to the cargo bay.

The corridor lit up with high velocity metal slugs, and she ducked low to keep from taking too much fire from her own men.

The bots seemed confused at her sudden appearance, but quickly shifted their attack to accommodate her. The five in the back of the group turned with incredible speed and lunged for her, while the remaining machines pressed their attack on Baxter and the Marines.

Sara noted that each of the bots' forearms had small cannons on them, and they were beginning to glow with energy. In addition to the cannons, each arm ended in a hand with three long, stiletto-pointed fingers in a triangular formation.

These digits on the five bots closest to her glinted in the dim light as they came for her face.

She didn't hesitate, lashing out with a force blast, which she focused into a horizontal blade to slash all five enemies across the connector at the bottom of their torsos; it looked like a weak point.

The force blade sank into the first two, cutting a few

centimeters, but then winked out, as if it had run out of power.

"Shit, I forgot," Sara growled to herself as she poured more power into her shield.

The shield glowed brightly for an instant before bright flashes came from the barrels of two of the bots, and the claws of the other three raked across her shield right above her face.

The blasts were smaller versions of the particle beam the main ship used, and they burned her shield down to an orange glow. The claws, however, raked across the shield with considerable force, and as soon as they hit, Sara felt the power leaving her shield, and she had to struggle to keep it going.

One of the bots in front of her slumped to the side, half of its head missing from concentrated rifle fire from behind. She took the opening to roll to the side and get out of the bot's reach.

She had to be careful not to roll off the edge of the deck and into open space.

She came up on one knee and looked for anything she might use as a weapon. She spotted a panel on the wall hanging by a single bolt, the other three having broken loose amidst her arrival. She sent a mental command to Alister, who was still clinging to her shoulder, and he complied, offering her the desired form.

She powered the spell, and a hand-like appendage formed out of golden shields. She used it to grab the panel and rip it from the wall, bringing it down like an axe blade on the closest bot. She gritted her teeth with effort as the panel hit the bot in the shoulder and sliced completely through its torso in a diagonal line of sparks and shaved metal.

The top half of the bot fell to the deck, followed by the

legs, both dark and unmoving. Now that she had a weapon, she finally felt like she might have a chance in this fight.

She turned the panel so the flat edge was facing the remaining three bots, and shoved it toward them with all the strength she could muster.

The bots leapt at her, claws extended, but they never touched her. The panel slammed into the first, who was pushed into the second and then the third. The whole jumble of writhing bots was flung out into the black.

Sara lost the panel, as it moved its targets away with incredible speed, but she quickly found another to rip loose from the corridor wall.

Then she turned to face the remaining horde. Letting out a growling scream of rage and battle lust, she sent the panel into the group like she was cutting weeds with a machete. Bots began to fall to her unrelenting assault, arms and legs cleaved from their bodies, and torsos split in half.

The Marines were making progress, but the arm cannons were doing a number on them. Through the bots, Sara could make out Baxter in his armor, throwing up shields to protect his men as they pounded the enemy with rifle slugs. He seemed to be holding out better than Deej, who was so focused on shielding that he was not even attempting to use his rifle.

Sara also picked out the prone bodies of several Marines and a few crewmen. The sight of her people dead in the corridor fueled her need to drive these soulless machines from her ship.

There were only a dozen robots left, but they were concentrating fire on Deej's shields and burning through them at an incredible rate. She wanted to put up her own shield to protect her men, but every time she cut one of the attackers down, another turned to engage her.

She gave Deej another glance and saw that his current

shield was a burnt orange, quickly turning red, but before she could act, another bot turned and lunged for her. Its claws raked her shield, and she felt her Aether well drain just a little bit more. She jumped back to get out of its grasp while she maneuvered the panel into position to cut it down.

The panel dislodged from the back of another bot and streaked across the vacuum toward her attacker, but the bot sidestepped the projectile at the last second, and the panel shot through the gap between them and out into space. Sara had put a lot of energy into the move, so it took her a second to realize she had missed. She registered that she didn't have time to bring the panel back before she would be attacked again, and abandoned her weapon to forever spin off through the galaxy.

A second bot had turned to her to lunge with the first.

She mentally requested a new spellform, and Alister instantly complied. She quickly fed the new form with Aether, and felt a pull on her mind that was different from the shield spell. The spellform was a constructive spell, in the molding family. Her Aether gathered in a pool under the airborne bots, and quickly began to change the structure of the deck, coaxing it into a new shape.

She fed the spell with more power, trying to speed up the process. She had almost decided to try a new tactic, when the deck plates thinned at the edges of the Aether pool, and a spike of steel shot up to the ceiling, impaling the two incoming bots through the torso.

Sara grinned as they struggled and attempted to free themselves. Then she ripped another panel from the wall and decapitated them both in one sweeping blow.

She stepped around the newly formed pillars and saw that Deej was down on his knees, his shield about to burn out. Five of the remaining bots were focusing their fire, and Sara knew he would not be able to stop the blasts.

She began to cast a shield, when a particle beam tore through the open space and slammed into a golden shield that had been erected in front of Deej's failing one.

Boon pushed her way to the front of the Marines and gave Sara a nod. "Sorry I'm late, Captain. We had to wait for the decompression procedure," she said, eyeing the remaining bots. Then she looked past Sara, and her eyes grew large. Since she was wearing only a battlesuit—like Sara, not having had the time to retrieve her armor—her expression was plainly visible.

Turning around to see what had caught Boon's attention, Sara gasped in shock. It looked like her batting away of the few bots on her way in had not bought her much time at all; a large group had bunched up to fly in and attack in force.

The Marines were still cutting away at the bots, and Baxter was holding steady with his shields, but Sara would soon be trapped between two enemy forces, and her Aether well was nearly three quarters empty.

"Don't use direct spells on them, Boon. They have some ability that lets them absorb the Aether away from you," she said, preparing to fight the oncoming horde.

Sara felt the deck vibrate and jump beneath her feet, making her look over her shoulder. Boon had used the same morphing spell she had used, spearing eight of the bots on one thick column. Instead of using the deck plates however, Boon had used the corridor wall, and her spike crossed the corridor at chest-height. The remaining two bots were cut down by rifle fire, but not before another Marine was hit in the chest by a particle beam.

"Baxter, get your men back and heal up who you can. Boon and I need some space to move; we don't want to hit any of you on accident," Sara ordered, as the small, blonde woman ducked under the spike she had made and came to stand next to her captain.

Silva was in her battlesuit, and gave Sara and Alister a nod from her place beside Alicia.

"I've been using panels as axe blades, but anything will work if you put enough power behind it," Sara advised as she faced the oncoming bots.

"I feel like we should have that printed on shoulder patches," Boon joked.

Sara smiled. "It's my personal credo."

CHAPTER 29

GRIMMS SHIFTED his attention between the massing robots outside the ship and the power readings on the Vitas ship. The building attack worried him, but he figured there were two War Mages to handle that.

The major problem was Cora being out.

He was worried that she had been damaged in some way, and he wouldn't see her ever again. There was also the problem that if she was out for good, "ever again" was going to be less than five minutes.

"Sir, the attackers are moving in. I'm getting reports that the Marines are pulling back at the captain's request, and that they are taking the wounded to the medical bay. We are in the process of restoring pressure there," Mezner relayed.

"Good. Hon, is there any way we can send a gauss round into that cluster of robots?" Grimms asked, worried that the attack would overwhelm Sara and Boon.

"I can't get an angle, sir. They're too close to the ship," Hon said with a frown.

"Sir, the Vitas are powering up their weapons. It looks like they finished their repairs," Mezner panicked.

"Shit," Grimms growled. "Hon, lock on. We need to do whatever damage we—"

"Grimms?" Cora said from the speakers. She seemed a little dazed to his ears.

"Cora! We need to jump now!" he shouted, relief and dread flooding him from both sides.

"Wha—oh, shit! Jumping," Cora said, coming to rather quickly.

"They're firing," Mezner said, her hand white-knuckled on the console's edge.

The ship rocked slightly from an impact, then their position was adjusted on the holo table, and Grimms could see that they had jumped, but not very far.

"We're only a few kilometers away, what happened?" Grimms asked.

"The amplifiers are still damaged. I can only run so much power through them, or they'll blow out again," Cora reported, sounding much more put-together than when she had first woken up. "I can maybe get one more jump out of them at this distance, but then they'll be toast."

"The Vitas are still not able to activate their engines, but their rotation will bring us in range in a few minutes," Hon said, looking up from his console.

Grimms checked on the gathered attackers and saw that only a portion of them were still floating in space where they had been just a moment before. Which meant that some of them were on the ship.

"How are those engine repairs going, Cora?"

"It's going to be another ten to twenty minutes," she estimated.

"Prepare to jump again in three minutes. We will need to get as close as possible to minimize the robots' chances of blocking our shots. Hon, as soon as we complete the jump, I want you to hit them with everything you have left," Grimms said, doing the risk analysis in his head.

"If we take out the ship, there are still the robots to deal with," Mezner reminded him.

"One thing at a time, Mezner. One thing at a time."

THE LOOSE CLOUD of bots rushed in, closing the gap between them and the *Raven* at astonishing speed. Sara and Boon both grabbed hold of some floating debris and hurled it at the grouped enemy with force spells.

The chunks from the *Raven* hurtled through the gap, and most of the bots changed direction to avoid a collision, but they were too close, and the War Mages had flung the pieces with ferocity.

Several of the bots exploded in showers of sparks and pulverized metal scraps, but the horde kept coming.

Then the ship jumped, changing the view of space and only taking the closest bots with them in the bubble. There were still thirty or more enemies, but that number was better than the hundred that had been there a second before.

The bots unfolded and dove at them with their arms extended. Sixty small arm cannons began to glow with pent-up energy as they prepared to fire all at once.

"Take cover," Sara shouted as she shoved Boon to the opposite side of the gaping hole in the ship.

The blasts filled the area they had just occupied, turning a large portion of the deck into vapor and slag. The *Raven* rocked from the explosion, and Sara was forced to throw a shield up from where she had landed on the corridor's floor, just to block the flying debris.

Her shield was peppered, the large stuff missing her as she crawled to her feet.

"You okay?" she asked.

"Yeah, thanks for the assist," Boon said.

"No problem. Be sure to get something to use to bash these assholes a new one," Sara said, wedging a shield behind a loose panel to rip it from the wall.

Boon followed suit, and swung her panel back and forth to practice before looking at the closing horde. "Bring it, losers!" she shouted, lowering her stance.

Sara gave an evil grin, lowering her own stance, and glanced to her shoulder to make sure Alister was ready. The small, black cat gave a nod, then focused on the bots.

They didn't have long to wait, as the bots were moving at a good speed. Sara had a last second idea, and Alister provided the spellform she requested. With a burst of Aether, she began a morph spell on the hull of the *Raven*, right above the hole where the airlock had once been, where the armor was still thick with material to work with.

There was a pregnant second in which Sara was not sure the spell would work fast enough. She almost gave up on it, until she felt the material morphing under her Aether's pressure.

A spike of the hard, armored material shot out from the hull, splitting every ten feet into two spikes, which split again and again. The fractal-like structure grew like a plant on steroids in fast forward. Within seconds, there were thirty or more spikes spearing through the incoming bots, sending several into evasive maneuvers, but slicing through many of them, thinning the numbers and slowing the rest.

"Great work, Sara. I wish I wou—Gah!" Boon lurched forward, spinning her back to the incoming enemy to look behind them.

Sara glanced over her shoulder and saw three of the bots she had recently cut down coming after them. One had grabbed hold of Boon. Luckily, her shield was powered, and she hadn't taken any damage other than the drain on her Aether well.

"They're repairing themselves," Boon said with dread, still in the bot's grasp.

Then the horde hit the deck, sending a shudder through the ship.

"THEY'RE COMING AROUND, sir. They will be in range in thirty seconds," Hon said, his finger poised over the fire control.

"Cora, are you ready for the jump?" Grimms asked, a frown on his face.

"As ready as I can be. I had the repair bots focused on the amplifiers for the last two minutes, so there's a chance we won't blow everything out in the next jump, but it's going to be close."

"Let's hope our luck changes on this one," Grimms said with forced joviality, even though he was preparing for the worst.

"Twenty seconds."

The Vitas ship rolled slowly, its large array of forward guns glinting in the dim light of the sun.

"Hon, be ready," the commander said, completely focused on the holo table.

"Ten seconds."

Grimms could see the enemy's weapons glowing as the ends of the barrels came into view. "Get ready," he said, leaning in and watching the timer that Mezner had put into the hologram. He saw several of the small orbiting robots shoot in to attach to the Vitas's hull, and his stomach dropped.

"Jump now!"

The enemy ship spun the last few degrees quickly, using the robots' thrusters as a makeshift maneuvering jet, and let loose with a large number of particle cannons. Luckily, Grimms had seen the move coming, and the *Raven* was no longer there.

As the beams passed through empty space, the *Raven* appeared on the opposite side, only five hundred meters from the Vitas's ship. They were almost inside the orbit of bots patrolling their mother ship.

"Fire!" Grimms shouted, pounding a fist to the table.

The remaining nine gauss cannons fired in rapid succession, each slug following the path of the previous one by a microsecond.

The patrolling bots reacted instantaneously, igniting their thrusters to intercept the fire. To Grimms' disbelief, the first six shots were deflected by bots crashing into them. He also noted that the bots who were attached to the hull were pushing their ship out of the way.

Not fast enough.

However, the kill shot was not going to happen like Hon had planned.

The first of the remaining three slugs hit hard, ripping through the Vitas's armor, but at a glancing angle that didn't penetrate deep enough to cause much damage. The second and third slugs, while cutting furrows in the armor as well, did even less damage.

Essentially, they had missed.

"I'm not showing any fluctuations in their power, sir. It doesn't look like we did anything but superficial damage," Mezner confirmed, her voice quiet to match the mood on the bridge.

"We will be in range in forty-five seconds, if they continue at the same rate," Hon reported. "I don't have enough power for another shot, sir."

"Cora, can we jump?" Grimms asked, gritting his teeth and trying to think of a strategy. They had jumped in close to make sure their shots hit. It had been a gamble, and it had not paid off.

"I'm sorry, Commander," Cora said. "Too many of the amplifiers burnt out. It's going to take several minutes to get the parts replaced. I can fire the Aether cannons, but the servos on the turret are damaged, so we would need to line up perfectly to hit anything, and we still don't have gravitic drives."

"Thirty seconds," Mezner reported.

"What about emergency decompression? We could use the air in the ship to push us out of the way," Connors suggested.

"The ship is already decompressed so we can take care of the breaches," Cora reminded him.

"Twenty seconds."

"Can Captain Sara move us?" Hon asked.

"Not in the next fifteen seconds," Cora said.

Grimms gritted his teeth. "There has to be something."

"Commander, I'm getting a warp signature," Mezner said, swiping the information to the holo table.

"It has to be huge for us to get a reading," Cora noted.

Grimms was watching the Vitas ship and still trying to figure out what to do, so he missed the first of the Teifen ships jumping in.

The holo table exploded in red icons as the leading edge of the Teifen fleet jumped into their ruined system. Teifen destroyers immediately washed the *Raven* in Aetheric scans, and turned toward the combating ships. They were only a few hundred kilometers out, and the distance was closing quickly.

"The Vitas are using the bots to turn toward the Teifen. They're ignoring us for now," Mezner said.

"Let's hope the Teifen make the same choice," Grimms said, his mouth a tight line.

CHAPTER 30

Four two-meter-tall robots descended on Sara like ravenous dogs. Their claws snatched and tore at her shields, nearly draining her well. She tried to jump back, but was tripped up by a half-repaired foe she had sliced down earlier, and she tumbled to the floor. The four pursuers piled on top of her.

"Sara!" Boon shouted before slicing a robot in half at the waist, and turning to see several more bots pressing in on her.

She focused down on the morph spell, shooting spikes from the walls and floor in a twisted flurry, spearing several enemies and blocking the passage.

Sara screamed in response with rage and frustration as she ripped a section away from the wall and swept it over her body in a violent motion. The hulking chunk of corridor smashed into the four bots, throwing them clear of her and into the far wall. Sara pressed the torn wreckage harder, now that she was not being drained from the bots' touch, and smashed the section into their crumpled forms. She gave her makeshift club a twist and was satisfied to see sparks and metal parts explode from behind it.

"How many more are there?" she asked, stumbling to her feet with Boon's help. Even Alister and Silva looked tired from the prolonged battle.

"It's hard to tell. They keep repairing themselves," Boon huffed, taking the lull in the battle to catch her breath.

They watched as the spikes blocking the path were bent or blasted out of the way by the persistent invaders. Through the mass of robotic bodies, Sara could still see out into open space. The Vitas ship had reappeared, and was quickly assaulted by a barrage from the *Raven*. Even though she saw three of the gauss rounds hit, she knew that they had not been enough to disable the alien ship. Now it looked like her ship was dead in the water, and the Vitas were coming around for another shot.

"Captain, we have a situation," Grimms said over her comm.

"Yeah, no shit," she snapped, sending a freshly torn wall panel into the crowd of bots, slicing several open and shoving them back into their fellows.

"A new situation. The Teifen are arriving. They seem to be stalling the Vitas's attack on us," he said.

The corridor suddenly lit up with rifle fire from the far end, cutting down the back ranks of the Vitas bots.

"Baxter?" Sara asked over the open channel.

"Yes, ma'am. We circled around after dropping off the wounded. Looks like there's a bit of a party going on. Mind if we take this dance?"

The sound of his voice made her want to weep with relief. She and Boon were being slowly run over. They needed the space to fight and not hit their own men, but the Vitas's ability to absorb large quantities of Aether had hindered their attacks more than she had thought possible.

"You are always welcome to these dances, Baxter. Can

you keep them occupied for a second?" she asked, taking a step back to let her well recharge a little.

"Take as long as you need, Captain. We resupplied on the way over, so there are plenty of slugs to go around," he assured her with a smile.

"Grimms, what are the Teifen doing now?"

"They are burning hard right for us. The Vitas are still unable to maneuver well, but they are swinging around toward the Teifen. I think they are going to engage them, ma'am."

Sara frowned. They needed to convince the Teifen that the *Raven* was not their enemy, was maybe even an ally. "Grimms, I want you to send them all the raw data we have on the Vitas. Our battle footage, their capabilities, everything," Sara said, taking a chance.

"Ma'am, they'll see that we are defenseless. Any advantage we have would be spent," he reasoned.

"We're already at their mercy. Do it. It's the only chance we have of maybe making it out of this thing alive. I don't believe the Teifen are who we think they are," she said, hoping that her hunch about the order of the universe was not wrong.

There was a moment of silence, then Grimms said, "Sent."

Sara turned to the opening in the *Raven*'s hull and, looking past the raging robots, focused on the Vitas ship. She made a fist and pounded it into her open palm. "Come on. Do it," she said quietly.

A bot lunged for her, still blocked by Boon's spikes, but it didn't progress much more than a meter before Boon tore it in half. Sara hardly even noticed as she stared at the Vitas ship.

Then she saw one of the orbiting robots explode as it intercepted a gauss round. Then another, and another.

Within the blink of an eye, the void filled with projectiles moving too fast to see, but their destruction was unmistakable. The defensive bots were doing a good job of intercepting incoming fire, but they were soon overwhelmed, and the Vitas ship began taking direct hits. There must have been hundreds, if not thousands, of slugs fired. Chunks of the enemy ship were torn free, then those chunks were pulverized by follow-up fire. Within seconds, the Vitas ship was nothing more than dust and fist-sized debris.

Every bot on the *Raven* stood up tall, and the lights that glowed in their internals went out. Several of them tumbled to the ground, or were shot open with continued rifle fire, but it was obvious that the bots had been deactivated.

"Hold," Baxter shouted over the comm.

The fire ceased, and the corridor went dark.

"Ma'am. The Teifen are hailing us," Grimms said into her comm.

"I'll be right there, Grimms," Sara said, then with a nod to Boon, turned and began running for the bridge.

CHAPTER 31

SARA BURST ONTO THE BRIDGE, breathing heavy from her run and previous fight. Alister jumped from her shoulder to the captain's chair as she passed it, and sat at attention. Nyx, now awake, gave him a nod as he settled in.

"Sit rep?" Sara asked, stepping up to the holo table.

There were several hundred Teifen warships in the system now, including a large, heavily battle-scarred cruiser at the center of the cluster. More and more Teifen ships were arriving by the second.

"They began warping in a few minutes ago, then turned directly for us and the Vitas. It looked like we were going to be targeted as well, until we sent the battle information," Grimms said with a nod at her decision. "That was the right call, Captain. As soon as they got a picture of what was happening, they focused on the Vitas. Fifty or more ships began chain firing gauss rounds at the enemy until they pulverized them."

"As soon as the ship was down, the bots quit working," Sara said. "Boon's clearing them out now."

"Cora came out of her maintenance cycle right before the

Vitas were able to fire on us. If I had to guess, I would say the core knew we needed her, and released her," Grimms said, giving her a knowing glance.

"We are still being hailed, ma'am. Should I reject the call?" Mezner asked, her voice tinged with worry.

"Give me a second, ensign," Sara said, holding a finger up to the nervous woman. "Cora, what kind of time frame are we looking at before we have the amplifiers working?"

"Ten minutes," she replied. "All three reactors are coming online in the next three minutes. We'll have weapons and gravitic drives, but no way to shield or jump. I can probably pull off one more jump, but it will completely destroy the progress we've made on repairs."

"What about warp?"

"We can go to warp, but I can't guarantee the amplifiers will be able to hold the bubble, and if it collapses, we'll be crushed."

Sara took a deep breath. They were trapped for at least ten minutes. They might be able to fight in three, but they would need to do so without shields. She looked at the holo table and the ever-growing number of Teifen warships, and knew that fighting would be a death sentence for her and the crew.

"Open the channel, Mezner."

"Aye, ma'am," she acknowledged, accepting the hail. "We only have audio; the video system is still down."

Sara gave the apologetic ensign a nod, then greeted, "This is the *Raven*, I am Captain Sonders. I apologize for the lack of video, but we are having a few technical problems. To whom am I speaking?" She stood up straight and smoothed the front of her battlesuit, knocking free some debris she had picked up from the fight.

"I would say 'technical problems' are an understatement, Captain Sonders," a deep male voice replied. The words were joking, but his tone was serious, confusing Sara a little, without visual cues to read. After a moment, he continued, "I am Grand Admiral Bok, of His Majesty's fleet."

"It's a pleasure to meet you, Grand Admiral, and I thank you for the assistance with the Vitas," Sara said, hoping her pleasantries would forestall any attacks.

"I see in the report you sent us that you call the enemy by that name—Vitas. What do you know about them?" the admiral said conversationally.

"You have the report," she told him with a shrug. "That's about it. We jumped in, and the system was like you see it. We found no life signs system-wide, so we decided to do a tech scan, and that bastard came out of nowhere. You have all the information we have."

There were a few moments of silence as the admiral looked over the report; or at least, that was what Sara supposed he was doing.

Eventually he continued. "So, why do you call them the Vitas?"

Shit. Double shit. How the hell do I explain that without talking about the pixies?

She panicked, then cocked her head to the side and smiled. "We just picked a name. It was better than calling them 'That Ship'."

"Hmm," the admiral grunted. His voice was deep, and the grunt was gravelly, like he had been smoking cigarettes from the time he'd come out of the womb.

Sara's comm beeped, and Cora came on the private line. "Sixty seconds 'til we have reactors. Amplifiers are still eight minutes out."

"Admiral, what can you tell me about the attack on this system? Obviously you received word when it happened. And the fact that you abandoned your conquest of the Elif tells me that this place is important," Sara prompted, trying to buy time and hopefully get some information.

"This was an internal matter, and not of concern to you Elif. Count yourselves lucky that we have given back your capital," he said dismissively.

Sara leaned in to Grimms and whispered with surprise, "He doesn't know we're human. We can use this."

"Be careful, Captain," he said with a nod.

Sara cleared her throat. "This was the result of the Teifen fighting a two-fronted war. The Galvox ripped through this system and left nothing behind, and now there is a new player who exceeds all your capabilities. We can't afford to fight one another."

"Ma'am, we have visuals back online, if you want them," Mezner reported in her comm.

Sara held up a hand to forestall them. She wanted to wait until the *Raven* at least had some sort of defensive measures.

The Teifen admiral considered her words.

Just when Sara was about to speak again, her comm beeped, and Cora came on the line again. "Reactors are online, along with gravitic drives."

As she said it, the ship's lights came up, and the view screen came to life, showing the Teifen armada spread out in front of them. Sara felt the familiar hum of the reactors coming from the below the deck once again.

"Can you use the gravitic engines to cloak?" she asked quietly.

"I can," was all Cora said.

Finally. Something going our way.

The admiral started speaking again. "We see that you have power again. I advise you not to power your weapons, or we will be forced to fire upon you."

"No worries about that, Grand Admiral," Sara said sweetly. "I'm rather enjoying our conversation."

"That would be a first. The Elif usually find talking with me an unpleasant experience," he said dryly.

She smiled. "I would suspect that most of the time you talk with the Elif, it is not after they've helped you out. Me and my ship have done you a service, and I feel that you are an honorable—" she almost said 'man', but changed it at the last second, "commander. You would not attack your saviors."

A rumbling laugh came through the speakers. "Saviors? You seem to be under the impression that without us, you would have prevailed, little Elif. Need I remind you that it was our cannons that ripped these Vitas from the sky, while you sat there helpless?"

Sara muted the grand admiral, and began giving orders. "Cora, I'm going to need cloak in a second. Connors, start us on an evasive pattern of maneuvers as soon as we drop off their sensors." She turned back to the monitor and unmuted the channel. "Grand Admiral, I am fully aware of what has taken place over the last hour, but I get the feeling you do not. Have you fully read what we did during the battle? If you have, let me ask you a question: have you ever seen an Elif ship do the things in that report? Have you ever seen a ship design like the *Raven* before?" she said, stalling for time. She really needed those amplifiers to be up and running.

There was a long pause as the grand admiral considered the situation. Time stretched to the point that Sara began to get nervous, but right before she gave the orders to cloak, he came back on the line.

"I assume that you are about to tell me you are not Elif. What, then? Human?" he laughed, and Sara knew she had him.

"Mezner give me visuals. Cora and Connors, execute maneuvers," she ordered, leaning forward with a smile on her face.

CHAPTER 32

THE VIEW SCREEN switched from the intimidating view of the Teifen armada to the bridge of their flagship. A tall, handsome Teifen stood in the center of the bridge, his head down as he looked over the report the *Raven* had sent. He seemed to be oblivious to the fact that visuals had been restored, but when the crew of his ship began to gasp in surprise, he quickly looked up.

The Grand Admiral was the spitting image of the classic devil. He had red skin with small horns on his forehead that blended with his slicked back, jet black hair. His eyes were red and capped with thin, expressive eyebrows.

It took him a second to register why his people were gasping, then his eyes widened, and he lowered his tablet.

"Humans? What trickery is this?" he demanded.

"Grand Admiral, their ship just dropped off our scans," a large male Teifen with curling horns reported in near panic.

The admiral turned to the crewman. "Find them! Bring shields up to full."

"Grand Admiral, I apologize. I am Sara Sonders, Captain

of the *Raven,* and my first priority is to protect my people. We are still here, and I want nothing more than for us to talk. I give my word, we will not attack unless attacked first." She wore a slight smirk on her face. She realized she shouldn't be smirking, but seeing the devil surprised was pretty satisfying. "I need you to look at that report closely. The damage potential the Vitas have is far beyond anything we have ever seen in this galaxy. My ship and I were barely able to keep up with them."

Admiral Bok glanced down at the tablet in his hands, then back at the viewing screen. He was adapting well to the fact that he was speaking to a human, but his crew was still in shock.

"Captain, I must admit, when I first glanced at this, I thought the numbers were fabricated to make you look better than you were. I wanted to talk to the Elif captain who was so brash, he would lie about his actions to me. But now I must wonder if it is a different lie. How is it that there are humans roaming around the galaxy, and we are unaware of your path of destruction?"

"I assume you were under the command of the governor in this region?" Sara asked, tilting her head quizzically.

Bok became tight-lipped, and a look of disapproval came over his face before he gave a nod. "I am. What do you know of him?"

It seems the Grand Admiral doesn't like his leader all that much, she noted before continuing, "I know that he was a right bastard, and tried to exterminate my people. I defended my planet, he was unsuccessful, and died in his attempt." Her eyes became hard.

She had no idea what was happening in the Teifen ranks with the disappearance of their governor. To tell the truth, she had not even considered that they might believe he was still alive. It wasn't like there were any survivors from the battle to report back. There were survivors from the escape pods, but they were being kept in suspended animation as POWs.

From the Teifen's perspective, their governor had gone off with the remainder of the fleet and had not come back. Maybe they thought he was still out there.

Sara considered her next move. She needed to keep the Teifen from attacking, but more importantly, she needed to make them understand the threat the Vitas posed. This new enemy was more than either of their races could handle, and they needed to be addressed before Vitas ships came swarming through the Milky Way and it was too late.

She took a calming breath then turned back to the troubled Admiral Bok. "Grand Admiral, I see that you are having a difficult time believing me about the demise of your governor. I would like to make clear what happened, so that you have no illusions that we are as capable as I say we are and, in turn, see what that means about the Vitas."

She turned to Mezner. "Ensign, send a recording of the final confrontation between us and the governor's dreadnought. Begin the file after we warped in."

Grimms' eyes went wide for just a second, but he gave Sara a nod. It was the right call.

"Sending the file now, ma'am," Mezner said.

"Grand Admiral, please view the file. We will wait," Sara said, casually taking a step back and picking Alister up as she sat in her captain's chair.

As she began petting the black cat, she realized she must look like a villain from an old TV show, slowly stroking her cat with a tight smile on her face.

Eh, fuck it. Bok never watched Inspector Gadget. I can look all villain-y if I want too; he won't get the reference. I hope.

The grand admiral played the video on their main viewing screen, and his entire bridge crew was riveted the moment it began. Mezner put up a small window at the bottom corner of their own screen and mirrored the file's playback, so they could see what the Teifen were seeing.

The video picked up after the Teifen dreadnought warped away from the battle around Earth, so there was no indication of where the Sol System was. The dreadnought was in bad shape. Crackling sparks danced in the open holes that had been blasted in its hull. It was obvious that the ship was not functioning at any sort of battle-ready capacity, but it still filled the sky with its massive size.

The view was from the *Raven*. After a few seconds, it zoomed in on a lone figure streaking through the open space between ships: it was Sara in her armor, with Alister on her shoulder.

Sara watched the version of herself in the vid stop above the spine of the dreadnought and extend her hands toward the hull of the ship. Then she began to rip a giant hole in the spine of the city ship, using spells of immense power.

The Teifen watching gasped in shock, some even making what she thought might be religious warding symbols, not unlike a Catholic performing the sign of the cross. That piqued her curiosity.

She had heard nothing of their religion, so to see them performing warding symbols was fascinating. She decided to look into that aspect of Teifen culture when she had the time; it may give her a clue about how to deal with them in the future.

The vid continued, but Sara stopped paying attention. She had watched it several times in the weeks since as a reminder of what she was capable of.

Instead, she pulled up the damage report and began to

monitor how far along the nanobots were. Cora, watching the events on the bridge like always, beeped into her twin's comm.

Sara connected Grimms to the conversation before answering. "How are we doing, Cora?"

"Five minutes until the amplifiers are repaired. Good call on giving them a fifteen-minute video," she said mischievously.

Sara had to smile. "Thanks. I figured why not kill two birds with one stone?" She lowered her voice. "What do you think of the grand admiral?"

There was a quiet moment as Cora considered her words. Grimms walked over and, lifting Nyx from his chair, sat down and placed the fox on his lap. Nyx, for her part, settled into his lap like it was her favorite place in the world. Considering Cora's feelings toward the commander, it probably was.

The vid was showing the *Raven* swooping around to pluck the troops from the gaping hole in the belly of the dreadnought when Cora finally spoke up.

"I get the feeling that Bok is not of the same mindset as his governor was. It's the small things, like the fact that he abandoned the Elif system to try and protect his people here, and the look he gave when you first asked if he was under the governor's command. He did not look pleased at that notion."

Grimms cleared his throat. "I agree with Cora. I have been going over the reports they sent us in preparation of the mission to take back Effrit and Suttri. Once the governor left, there were only ground troops in the Elif system, and it was several hours before this fleet arrived to contain the situation. From the few reports that got out of Effrit during that time, the attackers became much less aggressive in their tactics, some reports even suggesting that the Teifen were pulling back to already occupied locations. When we warped into the system, the scans showed that there were far less casualties than we estimated, and hardly any structures had been taken out beyond the initial attack."

Sara glanced at the screen; the vid had progressed to the point where the passengers were disembarking from the *Raven*. She paid close attention to Bok's face when the captives came into view. She didn't know if it was her mind playing tricks on her out of hope, but it looked as if the captain and several of the crew were disgusted at the ravaged state of the Elif being ushered to safety.

"Two minutes 'til amplifiers are fully functional," Cora reported.

"I think we need to change the narrative of this war," Sara mused, absentmindedly stroking Alister.

"How so?" her sister asked.

"I'm becoming more and more convinced that the Teifen are not what the Elif would have us believe. Time and again, the actions of a few high-level Teifen are touted as the intent of their entire race, but what if it is just the governors and other Teifen higher-ups that crave war and domination? There have been numerous examples of human governments that were officially bastards, but the people under those governments were no different than you or me."

Grimms shifted in his seat and frowned. "True, but we can't make decisions for our entire race."

Sara bit her lip. That was exactly what she was hoping to do. She needed to implement some kind of ceasefire until the Vitas were taken care of, or the humans, the Elif, and the Teifen would all be wiped out.

The Teifen had been managing the Galvox for thousands of years, but now it seemed their enemy had an ace up their sleeve: an alien super-being.

Sara came to a decision. She was First Mage. Her priority was the protection of humanity, no matter what that brought down on her. She was already in hot water over the incident at the Elif embassy; this would make that look like a drop in the ocean.

But if it works...

CHAPTER 33

"The amplifiers are online. I'm starting repairs to the hull and other systems," Cora reported after two minutes of silence.

Sara gave a nod and, moving Alister to the seat, she stood, taking her place in the command ring. She didn't power it up, however. Instead, she waited for the vid to finish and for Grand Admiral Bok to process what he was seeing.

The wait was excruciating, now that she had made up her mind. But she took the time to observe the Teifen crew's reaction to what they were witnessing. Granted, most of the exciting stuff had taken place *inside* the dreadnought, but seeing the *Raven* dismantling the Teifen's largest and most formidable ship was effective enough.

The final minute of the vid was playing, in which Sara, Boon, Baxter, and Gonders were shrouded in a shield bubble, shooting out of the gaping hole Sara had ripped into the dreadnought. This was the most important part of the video, in Sara's mind. This was the show of power that would either make the Teifen understand, or drive them to attack. She was betting that there was little love lost over their governor's demise.

The blue sphere of Aether quickly expanded from the dreadnought's hull. Growing rapidly, it consumed everything it touched. When it looked like the sphere was about to overtake Sara and the others, it stopped, hovering for a second before it collapsed at an incredible rate.

Sara felt like there should have been a thunderclap to accompany the visual. *Too bad there's no sound in space.*

The sphere winked out of existence, leaving nothing but empty space in its wake. The dreadnought was gone, sucked into the Aether as if it had never existed at all.

She watched the flicker of a smile cross Grand Admiral Bok's face, then he focused on her as the video ended. He was quiet as he studied her with stern eyes.

Sara, for her part, kept her face blank, but not hostile. She knew the *Raven* had some advantage, now that her systems were repaired, but the Teifen fleet was still large enough that they could overwhelm her if they tried.

The Teifen bridge crew was pale, or what passed for pale, with their motley colors of skin. Some even stared off in shock and wonder at the power displayed.

Sara decided she would take the lead in this negotiation. She cocked her head at that thought. *I suppose that's what this is now. A negotiation.* She took a breath as she organized her approach. "Grand Admiral Bok, you seem to be an individual of considerable words and actions. You obviously care for your people more than the conquests of your empire, as witnessed by your abandonment of Effrit. I applaud that sort of thinking, because it is similar to my own. No government's conquest outweighs the safety of its people."

The admiral gave a curt nod. "I agree."

"You have seen what we are capable of. This small ship was able to dominate and ultimately destroy a dreadnought. I have no illusions that your entire fleet could not destroy us, but at what cost? Not to mention that there are more ships just like ours back home that would take up the fight in our absence.

"Luckily, that scenario can be avoided completely," she told him nonchalantly. "We have no quarrel with you. Not personally. The Elif have," she shrugged slightly, "shall we say, misled us. But we have an agreement with them, and we stand by our word. I would like to make an agreement with you, as well, Grand Admiral. If you would be willing."

Bok took a step back as she finished, lowering himself into his captain's chair and crossing his leg, as if he were settling in for a friendly conversation. His face was neutral, but Sara felt like relief was etched into his expression as well.

He's going to make a deal. She smiled.

"For generations, we Teifen have been taught that humans were monsters, that they would come and force compliance at the end of a rifle barrel. Ours was a peace made from fear of retaliation. If a society had a different set of morals than their human overlords, they were forced to abandon them and conform, and if they did not, they were punished.

"Billions died of starvation when trade was cut off from planets that had angered their human rulers. Cultures were wiped out when their religious practices were not seen as moral or in line with human beliefs. There was a whole galaxy to explore and travel across, but we were not free. We were subjects of a race that held us in check with fear."

Shit. It sounds like we were right bastards. No wonder they tried to exterminate us.

Bok continued. "We were forced to take action. A group of Teifen decided they could not be kept under the yoke of human oppression, and they fought back. They organized into twenty clans, but were not strong enough on their own to obtain the freedom we Teifen desired. Humanity systematically obliterated the clans 'til there were only ten left. Those ten joined together and became the empire we have today. Together, they were able to fight humanity to a stalemate.

"But that wasn't good enough. We needed to be free of you. Do you know the only way to be forever free from an attacker?" he asked, tilting his head in question.

This was not going the way Sara had hoped. "You need to eliminate them," she conceded.

"Correct. We asked the Elif to help. They were scared, and wholly under humanity's thumb. However, there was a small group who decided to help. They joined us and created a pathogen that would destroy humanity wherever it touched them in the galaxy. So we did what we thought best and used it. It worked better than we could have dreamed; we were free," he said, looking down into his lap. He folded his hands and looked Sara in the eye. "For a time, anyway."

Sara was now enthralled in the conversation. This was more information on ancient humans than anyone in recent history had heard before. At least, that any humans had heard.

"What do you mean by 'for a time'?" she asked.

He gave a quick, sad smile. "Do you understand what it takes to kill a whole race of people?"

Sara considered that and nodded. "Unfortunately, I think I do. There is a philosopher from my world that gave our people a warning. He said, 'beware when fighting monsters that you do not become the monster yourself', or something close to it. He was speaking of art and culture at the time, but I think it applies here."

Bok nodded in assent. "An apt saying. And one, I believe, that underlines my thinking on this matter. Those ten clan leaders, who later became the governors of the empire, were transformed into the monsters your philosopher warned of. We shrugged off one form of oppression for another, a worse form of oppression. A self-imposed oppression."

Sara glanced at the crew behind Bok, and was surprised to see that they were just fine with his thinking this way of their leadership. *What he is saying is tantamount to treason.* She looked over her shoulder at Grimms, who had an eyebrow raised, obviously as shocked by the Teifen's words as she was.

She turned back to the grand admiral. "Why are you telling me this? Wouldn't we already know this tale?"

Bok flashed his teeth in a tight smile. "That's the thing, Captain Sonders. I don't think you would know all of this. I think you and your people are not the same humans we have been told about for all these millennia. Those humans would have ravaged us the first chance they had. Now, you have the advantage, but here we are, still talking. We don't have you on sensors. You could destroy my ship before we even knew what was happening, if that video is true; which I believe it is."

Sara smirked, she couldn't help it. "A softer, kinder humanity?"

Bok smirked himself. "Kinder, perhaps. Not softer. In all the histories, there was never an account of the kind of destructive power you showed us in that video. If anything, you are more powerful than your predecessors.

"I want to make an arrangement with you, War Mage."

Sara smiled. "I am willing to speak with my people on your behalf."

He shook his head. "No. I do not know your people, but I do know you. I will make my arrangement with you.

"I am the Grand Admiral of this sector. With the governor now dead, I am also the governing body. For as long as I am in control of this sector, I promise not to attack you or your allies, the Elif, unless attacked first. There is more than enough that needs my attention with the pressing attacks of the Galvox; from the reports I am receiving throughout the empire, the attacks are happening everywhere. If what you say about the Vitas is true, and they have joined forces with the Galvox, then that would explain the Galvox's sudden domination in the rest of the empire. As far as I am concerned, the war with the Elif is over."

Sara gave a half smile. This next part was going to determine if it was a good deal or not. "And what do you want from us in this agreement?"

"A favor," he said simply. "It will not entail you betraying your people or attacking your allies. All I ask is that you be willing to fight to save innocent lives if at all possible."

Holy shit, that's just vague enough to be an actual deal with the devil, Sara thought, looking at the admiral's red skin and tiny horns. She glanced over her shoulder at Grimms. He was tight-lipped, and gave her a shrug; this was her call.

If I agree, the war is over. But it sounds like the war is over anyway, with the Galvox attacking their flank. However, I can guarantee *there won't be any more attacks if I take the deal.*

"Will you return all the slaves you've taken from the Elif?" she asked, suddenly remembering the captives boarding the *Raven* during the video.

He gave a frown of disgust. "I do not condone the taking of slaves; that was the governor's hobby... The people under my command know such actions would lead to their death. Slavery is a symptom of the monsters the governors have become. *I* will do as you ask. In addition, there are several planets being contested on the Teifen-Elif boarder; we will abandon those as a sign of goodwill."

So now it's the end of the war and the liberation of several planets... this keeps getting better.

"Okay, Grand Admiral. You have a deal."

Bok gave his first warm smile. "Good. Let your people know of this agreement. We will hold our end as long as they do the same."

"I think they will be more than happy to hear that, Grand Admiral Bok," Sara said with a nod of her head.

"I hope they are. Communications will be sent to the Elif outlining this treaty. I will speak with you soon, War Mage Sonders," he said, then tilted his head in consideration. "I hope I am right about humanity abandoning their monstrous persona, for all our sakes."

The call was cut, returning the image on the screen to the view of the Teifen armada. Sara noted that there were still ships warping in at a steady rate. The full armada was numbered in the several thousand by this point.

She didn't say a word. Instead, she brought up her viewing bubble and selected the Effrit system. "Cora, let's have maximum warp. We need to let the Elif know what just happened."

"Aye, ma'am. Warp in three, two, one."

The image of thousands of Teifen ships shrank down to a pinprick, and slowly began to expand.

"I guess we won the war?" Connors said to the silent bridge.

"For now. Unfortunately, we just learned who the real enemy was in this ancient war," Sara said, frowning in worry.

"The Vitas?" Mezner guessed.

The captain shook her head. "Humanity."

CHAPTER 34

SARA FLOPPED onto her back on her bed and let out a long sigh. Alister hopped up beside her and sat down next to her head. He looked at her with a raised eyebrow, but she didn't move. She was too tired. After they had gone to warp, she had helped Boon, Baxter, and his men toss the broken and disabled bots out through the hole in the hull. The metal bodies flashed and sparked when they hit the warp bubble before being sucked out into the Aether. They had kept one bot, and locked it down with strapping material in case it came back to life.

After that, they'd begun to work on repairing the holes in the ship. They brought large printed pieces of hull and spot welded them in place, letting the nanobots do the fine work. In the span of a few hours, they had the *Raven* back into some semblance of fighting shape, but there was still a long way to go.

Alister reached out a paw and tapped Sara on the forehead, making her eyes snap open. "Huh? What is it, Alister?"

"Merow," he said, cocking his head to the side.

She twisted to the side so she was looking at him, and raised an eyebrow. "What does that mean?"

The little black cat rolled his eyes, then lifted a paw and opened his mouth. He mimed stuffing something into his gaping maw.

"Oh, right, sorry. I wasn't thinking of food," she said, as her stomach rumbled and growled, calling her a liar. She smirked. "I'll have something brought up. I'm far too tired to stumble down to the cafeteria."

Alister shrugged as if to say, *'Whatever, as long as there's food',* and yawned.

This made Sara yawn, which made Alister yawn again.

"Sop hooing at," she said through her second yawn. She then smacked her lips and blinked away the sleep before getting out of bed and sending a message to the cooks.

"It will be up in just a few minutes, ma'am," the cheerful private on the other end of the comm told her.

"Thank you," Sara replied before closing the channel and undoing the neck closure of her battlesuit. She pulled the garment open and began shimmying out of it. When she finally kicked the suit off her bare feet and shuffled to the closet, she noticed Alister trying to remove his own suit.

"Here, let me get that for you," she said, coming and sitting naked on the bed.

He lifted his chin like a child having his shirt buttoned, and she undid the clasp there, letting the material relax enough that she could pull it off him. He popped out of the black material and shook himself from head to toe, nearly falling over in his attempt to get his fur to lay the right way. Small clumps stood on end from when they had pulled the suit on in a rush during their initial flight from the Vitas.

"Sorry about that. I'll try and be more careful with your fur in the future," she said, doing her best to help him lay it down flat again.

He shrugged again. "Merp."

"Yeah, I know it was a tense time, but I still need to look out for you," she apologized again.

He reached out a paw and put it on her bare leg. "Merow," he said, confirming it was no big deal.

"Thanks, buddy."

There was a knock at her door, "Come in," she called out.

The door slid open right about the time she remembered she was still naked.

"Oh, shit," she heard a female voice say.

Why do I keep doing this? Clothes, Sara. People wear clothes.

She turned to see Boon standing with two trays of food balanced in her hands. Silva was on her shoulder, her wide-eyed expression a mirror of Boon's. Sara then made eye contact with the private who happened to be passing by her open door. The private, for his part, turned red and looked away immediately.

Great, add one more to the 'I've Seen the Captain Naked' club.

"Shut the door!" she barked to the wide-eyed Boon.

Poor Boon didn't know what to do, and started for the table to put the trays down, but turned to the door after a step, her hands still full.

Eventually, Boon set one of the trays on the ground and slapped the button to close the door. By that time, three more people had passed by, and every one of them had turned bright red before pretending they hadn't seen anything.

"Uh, sorry? Why did you tell me to come in if you were naked?" Boon said rather loudly as she faced the door and looked up at the ceiling.

Sara sighed then began to laugh. "Sorry, Alicia. I'm so tired I'm not thinking straight. Give me a second," she said, pushing herself off the bed and opening her closet. She pulled on a pair of yoga pants and a large sweatshirt. "Okay, you can look. I'm decent."

"You might be clothed, but I doubt you're decent," Boon quipped, stooping to retrieve the second tray.

"Har har. How did you open the door with your hands full in the first place?" Sara asked, shuffling to the table.

"I used a spell to push the button with a shield," she replied, setting down one of the full trays on Sara's side of the table.

"Why didn't you do that to close it?"

"Because you were buck ass naked, and I panicked," she said haughtily.

Sara laughed and pulled a chair out for Alister, who ignored this and jumped directly on the table. He was face-deep in a bowl of beef stew before she could say anything.

Alicia took the seat opposite Sara, and Silva snaked down her arm to the tabletop and started in on her own bowl of stew.

"Well, that was a hell of a day," Boon said, as if they were an old married couple talking about work.

Sara smiled. "Yeah. Didn't think first contact was going to be a thing when I woke up this morning."

"Not to mention *aggressive* first contact," Boon said, taking a bite of her roll.

Sara just nodded and took a bite herself. As soon as the first bite was down, she realized how hungry she was and shoveled a few more bites in before saying anything more.

"How's Gonders?" she asked after a time. "I know she was down in the fighting, but I didn't see her."

Boon shrugged. "She's okay. They kept her in the medical bay after Baxter healed her. I think they just wanted her to get some rest. Regrowing an arm takes a lot out of you, even if Aether is used to do it."

Sara stopped eating, the spoon hovering halfway between the bowl and her mouth. For the first time, she saw the worry etched deep in Boon's face.

I'm an asshole. I didn't even know Gonders had been hit. My friend is scared, and I hadn't even taken the time to look over the wounded report. When am I going to grow the fuck up, and do my job right?

"Are you okay?" Boon asked, breaking Sara out of her self-loathing.

"Oh, yeah. Sorry. I just realized I hadn't known Gonders was that bad off. I feel like shit for not saying something earlier," Sara said, putting the spoon back in the bowl untouched. She hung her head and took a shallow breath.

"What's wrong?" Boon asked, concern thick in her voice.

Her concern made Sara feel even worse, and Alister stopped eating when he felt her emotions kick into overdrive. A tear rolled down her nose and hung there a beat before dropping into her lap. She sniffed in surprise, wiping at her wet eyes with the back of her hand.

"Captain, what's wrong? Are you hurt?" Boon tried again.

"I don't know what I'm doing, Alicia. I thought this would be easier than it is, but it just keeps piling up. First I find an old spell that shouldn't have worked, then we get shipped off to a colony that's under attack, and I nearly kill my own people when I can't control my powers. We think the Teifen are the enemy, but now it looks like they're not. The Elif are lying to us, and our own government has me on a shit-list for confronting that little asshole of a prince—who, it turns out, *did* betray us, but they don't care about that. Oh, no, the only thing that matters is that I scared the little shit into talking. We have to keep the pixies secret, even compelled by magic to do so, so now we can't explain anything important to our own people about the Vitas and why they're here, even though we know quite a bit. And now I've gone and made a deal with the devil. 'A favor', he says. What the fuck does that mean? Who does he think he is, Don Corleone?

"And to top it all off, my friend's girlfriend lost her arm in a battle on my ship, and I didn't even take the time to look at the damn casualty list to see who was on it. I'm a terrible captain. I put us in danger more than I need to just because I have some justice complex I don't even understand."

She was crying hard enough that her nose began to run. Snatching a napkin off the tray, she loudly blew her nose.

"And now I'm sitting here crying like an idiot," she said, wiping her nose again with a sniff.

A small hand snaked across the table and took Sara's free hand. She looked up and saw Boon smiling at her like she was made of fireworks.

"Sara, you're the best captain I've ever known. All those things you just listed off? Those are the reasons I *want* to follow you. You do what's right, not what your superiors tell you to do."

Sara snorted. "Great, now I'm also a bad example of the chain of command."

Boon laughed. "No, you're a great example of rising to the challenge. You just won back several planets that the Elif have been fighting over for years. You guaranteed their entire race's safety from the Teifen with a ten-minute conversation. You are a badass. A genuine, take-no-names, fuck-your-laws, I'm-going-to-do-what's-right badass.

"But what makes you a true hero to me? You took me, your cabin girl, and made me one of the most powerful mages in the galaxy. You introduced me to my friend Silva. And you helped me find something great with an amazing woman.

"I know you don't read all your reports... You're too busy saving our asses."

Sara gave a laugh, shooting some snot out of her nose. She quickly wiped her face with the napkin and laughed again, this time along with Boon.

"Thanks. I think I needed that," she said, her eyes red, but head clear.

Boon shook her head. "I didn't do anything. Just said what we all know. The pressure on you is incredible. We keep finding ourselves in the middle of everything, and you keep bringing us out on top. I will do whatever I can to help. You can count on it."

The door slid open, and Baxter came rushing in. He was naked except for a small hand towel he had pressed to his junk, and his body was half-covered in soap bubbles.

"Are you okay? I felt a spike in your emotions. Did something happen?" he asked, brandishing a back scrubber like a bristly sword.

Sara and Boon, wide-eyed at his sudden entrance, burst into laughter.

Baxter's concern immediately turned to annoyance as he lowered the scrub brush. "Ha ha, sorry I was so concerned for your safety," he sulked. This made the two women laugh even harder. He rolled his eyes, then stomped to Sara's bathroom. "I'm going to finish my shower," he grumbled before hitting the button to close the door behind him, cutting of the women's view of his naked butt.

It took the two several minutes to laugh off the tension of the previous conversation, but eventually they were both wiping their eyes, calming down.

Boon looked at the closed door of the bathroom and said, "He really does love you."

"Why do you say that?" Sara asked.

"Because the shower room is two decks below us."

CHAPTER 35

THE VIEW SCREEN flashed with Aetheric light as the *Raven* dropped out of warp. Scans of the Elif's home system flooded in and showed a much different picture than Sara had seen when they left to follow the Teifen fleet the day before.

She could see that the fighting had stopped, even though Teifen ships were still warping out. The Elif had created a sort of corridor for the transport ships to travel down so they could be monitored for any sign of aggression.

"Well, this looks promising," Sara said, and Grimms nodded along with her assessment.

He turned to Mezner. "Have the communications mage on duty send out the packets. And see if you can't find out why the *Catagain* never bothered to get back to us when we sent out the distress signal."

"Aye, sir. The packets are being sent now," Mezner said, holding a finger to her comm. "Ma'am, we're being hailed by the Elif flagship. Admiral Zett is calling personally. Oh! I'm also being hailed by the *Catagain*."

Sara sighed. "Put the admiral through, and tell the *Cata-*

gain they are going to have to wait their turn." She brushed a stray hair back from her forehead and nodded to Mezner.

The view screen switched to the view of Admiral Zett, his crisp, white uniform nearly glowing in the lights of the flagship's bridge. His face was tight, as if he were barely holding back rage.

"Admiral Zett. It is a pleasure to see you again. I see the battle is over?" Sara said pleasantly.

She swore Zett nearly rolled his eyes. "As if you didn't know that would be the case. It seems while we were here taking back my homeworld, you went off and made a deal with the Teifen. A few hours ago, I received a ceasefire from the grand admiral himself," he said with a slightly clenched jaw.

"That sounds like a good thing, Admiral. Why am I getting the feeling that you are upset with me?" Sara asked, plastering a smile on her face.

"You do not have the authority to negotiate on behalf of the Elif empire. You go too far, Mage. There is a way things are done, and they do not include you, unless you are ordered to do your part," he growled.

"So you would have rather fought this battle to the bitter end, losing countless Elif lives in the process, because... why?" Sara asked, feigning confusion. She was goading the admiral, and she knew she should stop, but she couldn't seem to help herself.

He blinked slowly and over-enunciated his words, as if he were talking to a particularly dense child. "If there were to be negotiations with the Teifen, it is my job to make sure my people gain the advantage in any agreement. You do not have the authority to make claims on behalf of my race. I am sure you left more on the table that could have been taken from them."

Sara closed her eyes and took a calming breath before

continuing. "Admiral, while I understand your concern at not getting more from the ceasefire, I assure you that you got more than you were going to if you kept shooting at them."

"I guess we will never know now, will we?" he said haughtily.

"What leverage do you think you could have brought that would have gained you more than an end to the war, and the security of several contested planets?"

Admiral Zett set his jaw. "We had the Teifen on the run. They knew we were coming, and had begun fleeing before our might. Obviously they fear annihilation in our vengeance."

Sara bobbed her head and held up a hand to forestall the admiral. "Ah. I see, we finally get to the root of the issue. Vengeance. You're upset that I was able to end this conflict before you could kill more of them, is that right?"

"How dare you. I am an admiral of His Majesty's Navy. Vengeance is below me. This is an issue of you presuming to know our emperor's will, and making deals with the enemy behind our backs. This is treason," he roared, his face contorted with rage.

Sara stared back at the admiral, stone faced. She let the moment drag out for several seconds, watching as he slowly realized how angry he was, then waited longer, until he fully felt the embarrassment of his outburst.

I am done with this clown. They can speak of orders and rank 'til they are blue in the face for all I care. I am a War Mage of the first order, and I have nothing but their best interests at heart. If they can't see that, they can all go to Hell.

Before he could speak again, but not before he was fully composed, Sara began talking in a low, even voice.

"Admiral Zett. I used words to save millions, if not billions, of your people, and you stand there telling me I am a traitor? I didn't force a ceasefire at the end of a rifle barrel. I didn't mass an attack on a world filled with civilians as an example of my might. I used words and reason.

"There is a threat out there in the form of an aggressive alien species we call the Vitas. They don't care about your rank, or your orders, or your feelings. They are not motivated by politics, or emperors, or vengeance. They are programmed to destroy, and they will stop at nothing until they have accomplished their goal.

"I have sent you a recording of the battle the *Raven* just fought against one of their ships. In it, you will see that we barely made it out alive. Knowing what you know of our capabilities, tell me, Admiral: what chance do you think you and the rest of the galaxy stand if you are continually fighting amongst yourselves?"

Zett blinked slowly, and took a calming breath. "I will review your report, but know that I am lodging a formal complaint with your commanding officers. You are an out of control fire, tearing through the galaxy, and eventually, you will burn the hand that tends you.

"I am giving you one hour to leave my system. Never return. Is that understood?" he asked.

I tried. At least the civilians don't have to pay for this fool's arrogance with their lives. Sara sighed. "I understand you, Admiral," she said, cutting off the communication. "More than you realize."

The thick silence on the bridge lasted for several seconds before Mezner spoke up. "Ma'am? We still have the *Catagain* on the line. Do you want me to put them through, or tell them we will contact them later?"

Poor Mezner, Sara thought, giving the blonde woman a smile. "No, it's fine. Just give me a minute, okay?"

"Yes, ma'am," she conceded, relief in her voice.

Grimms stepped up next to her. "You all right, Captain?" he asked quietly.

She gave him a nod and a smile. "Just fine, Commander. How long 'til we hear back from the UHFC?"

He looked down at his tablet. "If they don't take too long getting the message to Admiral Franklin, and they understand the instructions Cora sent for the communications feature of the core they have, it should be twenty minutes or so."

Sara nodded.

They had decided that the instant communication feature of the core was too vital not to tell Command about. Honestly, Sara wondered why she hadn't done it sooner. It would have taken the techs on Earth years to figure out all the capabilities of the cores, unless they had by chance decided to hook up the one old core they had from colony 788 to a controller—but that core was being used as a data mine, so they would not risk installing it on a warship.

Cora had access to the only 'experienced' core in the galaxy, and they were finding it to be a huge advantage, much like starting up a computer with all the software already running, instead of a fresh, out-of-the-box model, like the ones they were creating back on Earth.

"Mezner, you can put the *Catagain* through now," Sara said, smiling at her communications officer.

"Aye, ma'am. On screen now."

A dour looking Reese turned to stare daggers at Sara. "What the hell do you think you're doing? Admiral Zett is in a rage over this deal you made behind our backs. He is contacting the UHFC and threatening to withdraw Elif support over your treachery," he nearly spat.

Sara held up a hand, stopping the tirade in its tracks. "Can it, Rodgers. I've already spoken to the admiral and sent my reports to Command. Throwing around words like 'treason' could cause you more trouble than it's worth."

"Oh? And what would *you* call making backroom deals with the enemy?" he asked smugly.

"I would call it 'peace talks'. Politicians have been doing them for years." Sara raised an eyebrow. "What's with all the hostility, Rodgers?"

Reese sniffed and stood tall. "I was told to watch you. You have a history of sticking your nose where it doesn't belong, and the Admirals Council has concerns. I would say this constitutes sticking your nose where it doesn't belong, wouldn't you, Captain?"

Sara began to laugh; she couldn't help herself. This whole situation had gone from a tragedy to a comedy.

Reese Rodgers didn't think it was a laughing matter at all, however. "What is the matter with you? Don't you see that your actions are putting humanity in danger? If we lose the support of the Elif——"

"What?" Sara cut him off. "If we lose the support of the Elif, what? What changes? Did you see a fleet of *Elif* come to defend Earth when the governor's dreadnought showed up? Did you hear the warnings of imminent attack that the Elif prince gave us? No? Oh, that's right, they left us high and dry. The only reason Earth is not a burnt-out shell of a planet is because I scared that little shit into telling us he had sold us out to our enemies. This ship went toe to toe with a dread-nought and won because we had to.

"If the Elif can't see that we just handed them a victory they could only dream of, then they're too stupid to be of any help to us!" Sara felt her eyes bulging with rage.

The bridges of the *Raven* and *Catagain* were both silent in the wake of her verdict.

Reese stared at her as if she had just grown a second head, and it had begun singing. "Admiral Smith was right; you're like a wild animal. You need to be put down," he said, shaking his head sadly.

Sara felt a spike of panic at his words and cut off the communication with the swipe of a hand.

"Cora, jump us here now!" Sara shouted, marking a location at random on the holo display.

"Jumping," Cora said, and the view suddenly changed to empty space.

"Mezner, did the *Catagain* try to send us a message right before we jumped?" Sara asked, a gut feeling shouting to check, but hoping she was wrong.

"Yes, ma'am. It was cut off, though," she reported.

To everyone's surprise, it was Grimms who shouted, "Fuck!"

CHAPTER 36

"Baxter, there is a bomb or some other device on this ship, and we need to find it now," Sara said into her comm.

The bridge was still reeling from Grimms' sudden outburst, but the captain was right there with him.

"A bomb? From the Vitas attack?" he asked in confusion.

"No, it looks like it was slipped aboard by our own people." She took a breath to calm herself. "I think I've been pushing some folks a little harder than they'd like."

When Baxter came back on the line, he was breathing a little heavier from running. "Enough that they would kill their War Mage? You turned the tide. You should be a hero to them."

"With the new War Mages being trained and instilled with an undying loyalty to the Admirals, I'm becoming more of a liability. They think they can't control me."

There was a few seconds of silence before Baxter said, "Well, they can't. That's kind of what makes you effective."

Sara smiled, despite the circumstances. "While I would agree with you, there are some who are stuck in the old ways of politics where their word is law."

"Huh, and here I thought *your* word was law," he joked, but it stung her a little.

Shit, is that the way my people see me? As if I think I'm above the law?

"Baxter," Cora cut in, "whatever the device is, it had to have been loaded onto the ship when we resupplied. I'm sending you a copy of the manifest now. Get your people searching through everything. We don't even know what they sent us."

Alister began pacing back and forth on her chair. "Merow," he growled.

Sara leaned down and raised an eyebrow. "You know where it is?"

"Merp," he said excitedly.

"Is it in a storage locker?" she guessed, knowing he could only communicate 'yes' or 'no'.

However, instead of answering, he sat down and closed his eyes, becoming perfectly still. Nyx hopped over from Grimms' chair and stared at Alister intently. Obviously he was trying to communicate, but Sara couldn't hear anything.

Suddenly a memory flashed in her mind. The perspective was off, so it took her a second to realize the view was from her own shoulder. It was only a split-second flash, but she immediately recognized the room.

"The cargo bay?"

"Merp!" he exulted, jumping up and down.

She wracked her brain, trying to remember anything unusual that happened in the cargo bay. Then it hit her.

"The extra crate of warheads!" she exclaimed, and Alister nearly did a flip in his excitement. She again spoke into her comm. "Baxter, inside Dropship Three, there's a cargo crate strapped down in the hold. It contains what we thought was an extra shipment of warheads. Do not open it; they could have triggered it to go off when opened."

"Aye, Captain. What do you want us to do with it?" he asked, huffing into the comm.

"Throw it out the bay door," she said, as if that were the obvious option.

"Captain, if we just throw it out, we won't know if that was actually the bomb, or if we threw out a perfectly good case of warheads," Grimms reasoned.

"Shit. You're right. We need to open that case," Sara said, trying to come up with a plan.

"Why don't we just X-ray it?" Baxter asked, his voice calmer now.

He must have reached the cargo bay, she thought. Then she rolled her eyes. "Yeah, that's a way better plan."

"I'll have Gonders bring me a medical scanner. Last I spoke to her, she was getting a little antsy to get out of the med lab, anyway," Baxter said, and his line went quiet as he called Gonders.

Sara began tapping her lip and she closed her eyes in thought. *Maybe it's just a misunderstanding. Grimms and I have been looking for the devil in the bushes a little too hard... Maybe we're just jumping to conclusions.*

"I found the crate," Baxter reported, coming back on the line. "It looks pretty standard to me. Give me a few minutes, Gonders is on her way."

Grimms muted his comm and turned to Sara. "We need to know how deep this goes."

She muted her comm as well. "What do you mean? How deep what goes?"

"The plot to have us blow up in an 'accident', or during the battle to take back the Elif home system. We need to find out who's involved. Is it multiple people, or just Admiral Smith?" he explained, raising an eyebrow.

Sara smiled, teeth and all. She couldn't help it.

Grimms gave her a sideways look. "Captain? Did I say something funny?"

She shook her head. "No. Sorry, I just never considered that it wasn't the entirety of the UHFC after me. I suppose I should put a little more trust in my own people."

"Captain," he began, trying to sound reasonable, "the vast majority of Earth and her people see you as a hero. They don't care that you're bucking the system. They care that, because of you, Earth was not destroyed in the Teifen attack. You're famous, ma'am. If whoever is behind this can't make it look like an accident, they're not going to try it. There would be riots in the streets if you were assassinated. You did sort of save the human race, and the people know who you are now."

" 'Assassinated'? Don't you think that's a bit overdramatic?" Sara asked.

Grimms shook his head. "Not at all. That's exactly what this is: an assassination attempt. We just happened to figure it out first."

Sara bit her lip and frowned. "Am I really that much of a threat?"

Grimms frowned. "To some. But those people are not thinking of the big picture. All change comes with discomfort. Some people can handle that better than others."

The main view screen flipped over to Baxter's helmet cam, giving them a view of the crate in question.

"I'm patching in Sergeant Major Baxter's feed, ma'am," Mezner said, stating the obvious.

"Thank you, Mezner. Baxter, we have your camera feed up here. Has Gonders arrived yet?" Sara asked.

Before he could answer, Gonders ascended the ramp of the dropship, a small device in her hand. She was in black medical scrubs, probably taken in lieu of the patient's gown she should have been wearing, and it was obvious that she was favoring her left arm.

"Howdy, Gonders. How's the arm?" Baxter said, reaching out for the scanner.

Gonders raised a pretty eyebrow. " 'Howdy'?"

Baxter gave a short laugh. "Yeah, I tend to get a little country when I'm nervous."

"Seriously? That might be the weirdest nervous tic I've ever heard of," Gonders said, leaning on the bulkhead behind the crate.

"Uh, you may want to clear the area. This could go off any time," Baxter said.

This is like watching a bad police show, Sara thought, then laughed as she imagined Baxter delivering his tag line of 'Howdy, put your hands up'.

Grimms gave another raised eyebrow at her laugh, but turned back to the action before she could explain.

"If this goes off, will it destroy the ship?" Gonders asked calmly.

"Hell yeah it will. This is an entire crate of warheads."

She gave a shrug. "Then it doesn't matter where I stand."

There was a tense moment, then Baxter's camera began to bounce up and down, and a deep laugh could be heard. They watched as the camera stilled, and he began cycling through the scanner's menu, looking for the X-ray setting. The scanner didn't actually use X-rays—instead relying on better and safer tech—but some terms just stick.

Flipping on the device, Baxter began slowly sweeping the scanner over the crate. It took several minutes, but eventually he found what they were looking for.

"Captain, I found the device. It looks like they replaced one of the warheads at the bottom with a comm relay. It looks like they also have the crate's lid triggered to blow. This is it. What do you want me to do with it?" he asked, disappointment thick in his voice.

Sara felt the same way, and from the look on Gonders' face, she was right there with them.

"Get it off my ship. Throw it out the bay door, and we'll hit it with a gauss round."

"Aye, ma'am." He stood and went about looking for a hand cart. He found one strapped to the wall. "Gonders, give me a hand," he said, tilting one side of the crate up and sliding the lip of the cart under it.

Gonders came around and took the cart's handle, as Baxter pushed the opposite side up, levering the crate onto the two wheels. They carefully made their way down the dropship's ramp and turned to the bay doors.

"Hey, hit the switch," Baxter called out to a marine standing close to the door's controls.

The marine punched in the code, and the huge double doors began sliding open, a plasma shield filling the open space and holding the atmosphere in.

"Here, I'll take it, Gonders. You don't have your armor on," he pointed out as he took her place at the handles.

As soon as he had control of the cart, he began to pick up speed. After a few quick steps, he was jogging toward the opening, the cart rolling with ease on the level bay floor. He continued running, right up until the crate and cart both rolled off the deck and out into open space.

Baxter stopped with a bone-jarring jerk. Sara smiled when she realized he had activated his mag boots to keep from following the deadly cargo over the edge.

"Package away, Captain," he reported with relief.

"Connors, put some distance between us and that crate. Hon, fire when we're clear," Sara ordered.

"Aye, ma'am," Connors and Hon chorused.

The ship strafed to the side, quickly putting several kilometers between it and the warheads.

"Firing," Hon announced, as one of the big cannons rumbled.

Instantly, the crate exploded in a white-hot flash, as thirty-nine warheads went off at once. The fading plasma ball was a stark reminder of what could have become of the *Raven*.

After a few minutes, Cora beeped into Sara's comm. "Admiral Franklin just contacted us through the core. Looks like they figured out how to use the thing. Where do you want me to pipe the call?"

Sara considered talking to the admiral in private, but, just having escaped their first assassination attempt, she figured the crew should hear the conversation. If for nothing else than to be reassured that there was at least one admiral on their side.

At least, she *hoped* he was still on their side.

"Put it on the main viewing screen, Cora."

The image of Admiral Franklin in all his gray-haired majesty filled the screen. "Captain Sonders, this is marvelous. Do you know how long we have been trying to break the code of instant communication over vast distances?" he asked, a big smile on his face.

Sara couldn't help but smile in return. "I'm glad you approve, Admiral. However, the congratulatory talk will have to wait. I think we need to have a frank conversation, sir."

The admiral, cuing in on Sara's mood, became serious. "After reading the reports you sent, I have to agree."

"This is not about the reports, sir. This is a different matter altogether," Sara said with hard eyes.

Admiral Franklin raised a bushy eyebrow. "What could possibly be more important than discussing the end of a long and bloody conflict?"

"Let's start with the bomb on my ship."

CHAPTER 37

"ARE YOU READY?" Gonders asked as she fed the shield spellform in the magical practice room's wall.

Boon adjusted the Aetheric dampener on her head and gave a short nod. "Ready. How about you, Silva?"

The white ferret gave a short nod from her shoulder and chattered in the affirmative.

"Okay, this time I want you to be more aware of your surroundings. If you get shot in the butt one more time, I'm going to spank you," Gonders said in a serious tone.

Boon had to laugh. "If you really want me to watch my back, you wouldn't reward me for failure," she teased, flashing a mischievous smile.

Gonders smiled back. "Okay, how about if you get shot in the butt I *won't* spank you?"

"Now that's some motivation."

Gonders gave a short laugh, but when she spoke again, her voice was all business. "Don't forget what I taught you. Spells are all good and dandy, but your weapons are just as effective in a lot of situations. You and Sara rely on your spellforms far too much, and it taxes you needlessly."

Boon pulled her pistol from the leg holster she had strapped to her battlesuit. "Yeah, yeah," she said with an eyeroll. "Start the program, already."

"Good luck, babe," Gonders said, pushing a button on the wall display.

The blank walls of the practice room faded away, and Boon found herself in a modern urban environment. She stood in a tight alleyway between two metal and glass skyscrapers. The base of the buildings that made up the walls of the alley was a dull gray concrete, with the occasional splash of color where it was spray painted with graffiti. There was a row of dumpsters along one wall, and a delivery truck parked in the middle of the alley, blocking her view of the street beyond.

She turned slowly, looking for any signs of attack, but found nothing. The filtered sounds of the city made a sort of white noise that masked any small movements she would normally be able to hear, so she was relying on her eyes to alert her to danger.

Several minutes passed without anything except the normal sounds of a city beyond the confines of the urban valley Boon found herself in. She knew Gonders was trying to lull her into a false sense of security. Even though she knew what Gonders was doing, the inaction and constant alertness were beginning to wear her down.

Even Silva was beginning to relax as the minutes passed.

Boon turned in a slow circle, her pistol held at the ready as she glanced into every shadow like it was full of monsters.

Another minute passed, and Boon blew out a frustrated breath. "Come on, babe. I thought I was supposed to be doing some combat training? This is boring."

Gonders' voice came out of nowhere. "Combat doesn't abide by your timeline. It happens when it happens. You just need to be ready."

Boon gritted her teeth. "I understand that, but we only have the room for another——"

She cut off when the sound of running footsteps caught her attention. She spun toward the truck, her pistol aimed at the gap between the vehicle and wall. A figure burst out of the gap at a full sprint, and Boon nearly pulled the trigger before realizing it was a civilian.

"Goddammit, Gonders!" Boon yelled, lowering the pistol.

As soon as her guard was down, the shit hit the fan.

She caught movement above her. She raised the pistol and ducked, all in one fluid motion. A Vitas robot was leaping over the parked truck, its arm cannons charging as they aimed right at her face. She pulled the trigger, sending a three-round burst into the thing's chest and head. The hyper-sonic pellets ripped through the bot's thin, metal skin, sending up sparks. Despite the damage, the bot was still coming, and those arm cannons were still aimed at her.

Silva filled her mind with the requested spellform at the speed of thought, and Boon shot a burst of Aether into it. Instead of trying to shield herself, she cast a force spell across her own body that shoved her back several meters. The particle cannons ripped up chunks of concrete where she had just been standing.

Boon squeezed the trigger of her pistol several more times, and three rounds ripped through the bot, shredding its torso and right arm. The bot spun from the multiple impacts and toppled to the ground, though Boon could see that it was still moving.

On instinct, she powered another spell. A flat shield formed under her feet and quickly lifted her three meters off the ground.

She smiled when a second bot dove through the empty space she had just occupied. She fired shots down over the edge of her shield platform, peppering the bot from above. She must have hit something vital, because it seized up and toppled forward. Its momentum sent it crashing into the one on the ground, and they both skidded under the front end of the truck, becoming lodged under the bumper.

Boon quickly scanned the area and saw three more bots rushing the alley from the street beyond. She powered a second spell, and the concrete wall closest to the charging bots morphed from a flat surface to a spike of stone that speared the lead bot through the hips. The spike ripped out most of its lower torso as well, but the top half of the bot continued forward, ripping the legs free, and took aim at her as it skidded on its stomach, uncaring that it was half the bot it used to be.

The two coming in behind the leader vaulted the concrete spike and sent two particle beams each at her. She powered a shield to deflect the shots, then, letting the platform she stood on wink out, she dropped the three meters to the ground and sent several bursts into the gap between the truck and the wall, cutting down the lead bot.

She powered a shield and grabbed hold of one of the dumpsters, sending it flying across the alley right in front of the truck. The second bot didn't see the dumpster coming until it had cleared the gap, but by then it was too late. The steel box hit the bot at several hundred meters per second, lifting the attacker off its feet and smashing it into the opposite wall. The dumpster was mostly crushed, but it had hit hard enough that the bot was buried several centimeters into the concrete, stuck.

Using another force spell, Boon vaulted over the truck and began pelting the half bot with pistol fire while she was still in the air. She landed, skidding a short distance, and kept the pistol trained on the now unmoving torso.

She smiled and pumped a fist into the air. "Take that, you sons—"

She was cut off as a particle beam shot out from under the truck, knocking her off her feet and onto her stomach. That gave her a perfect view of the first bot—crammed under the front end of the truck, but still very much functional—as it shot a second beam right into her face.

The holo projection stopped just before the beam made contact, fading away.

Boon dropped her head to the deck with a *thump*. "Fuck."

"That was pretty good, but you need to remember who's still in the fight. It only counts as a win if you can walk away," Gonders said, coming over and dropping into a cross-legged position beside the defeated Boon.

"I know. I totally forgot about that first one. Shit, I was so close," she said into the floor.

Silva came and stood on her shoulder blades and nuzzled the back of her head in sympathy. Gonders reached out and smacked Boon hard on the butt, making the blonde woman jump.

"Hey! What was that for?" she shouted, reaching around to rub the sore spot.

Gonders shrugged innocently. "Consolation prize."

Boon stared at her like she was crazy for a second before both women burst into laughter. Silva leapt off her mage and into Gonders' lap, as Boon rolled over and sat up.

Wiping a tear from her eye, Boon smiled. "I'm glad you think I deserved it, but I need to get better. I can't go out there unprepared, I'll just end up getting Silva or myself hurt."

Gonders cocked her head. "You are getting better. These bots are way faster and tougher than the Teifen program, and a few weeks ago, you could barely handle that."

Boon shrugged and nodded. "You're right. I just feel like it's taking forever. You could beat the pants off me in a fight."

Gonders laughed. "Babe, it took years of training for me to get where I am. This stuff takes time and practice. And if you think I can beat you in a fight, you have some serious delusions going on in that pretty little head of yours. You're a *War Mage*. I watched you and Sara destroy an entire dreadnought with your powers—compared to that, I don't even hold a candle."

Boon pursed her lips in thought. "Speaking of dreadnoughts, I've been thinking."

Gonders raised an eyebrow. "Okay, I guess we're talking about that now?"

Boon chuckled. "Sorry, it's just been on my mind lately. I want to know what you think."

"Okay, what's up?" Gonders asked, rubbing Silva's chin and making kissy faces at the ferret, who cooed with delight at the attention.

"Well, there's a dreadnought just sitting at the bottom of the Atlantic; it seems like a huge waste of a resource. We should be trying to figure out how to use it. I know Sara wants to keep it secret for now, but we should still be getting it ready."

Gonders nodded. "I agree. It could be a huge *boon* to our operation," she said straight-faced.

Boon rolled her eyes. "Ugh, you think I haven't heard that one a thousand times?"

Gonders laughed. "Sorry, but I'm serious. Having a dreadnought could be the deciding factor in a lot of battles. You saw what the Teifen dreadnought could do, and I bet our version could blow the pants off theirs. There's only one problem," she said hesitantly, giving Boon a knowing look. "We don't have anyone to fly it."

"Actually, I think we might." Boon looked down at Silva.

The ferret took a second to realize the two women were looking at her.

"Errr?" Silva said, wide-eyed.

CHAPTER 38

"I understand your concerns, Captain," Admiral Franklin assured her.

Sara had sent him the recording of her conversation with Reese Rodgers, in which mention was made of Admiral Smith. Franklin was particularly concerned about the rigged crate of warheads.

He went on. "There are some who are threatened when their authority is questioned. Unfortunately, I believe Admiral Smith is one of these people. However, I never thought she would try something like this."

Sara liked the old admiral. He had been serving in the military since before the Elif had arrived on Earth, and his attitude was that of someone who looked at the results rather than the method. He had been instrumental in the *Raven* running the operation to retrieve the Elif emperor from the dreadnought, and had defended Sara personally during her hearing for the Elif embassy incident.

Sometimes she wondered if he was the last sane commander she had.

He sat at his desk in his office in Hawaii, the morning

sun streaming in through the window behind him. He had a concerned look on his face as he drummed his fingers on the desk, deep in thought.

After a minute's consideration, he spoke again. "I have a few people who owe me favors. Let me work on getting to the bottom of this, rooting out the problem from the source. It might take me a few weeks, but with the Teifen and Elif conflict at a standstill—thanks to your actions, I might add —we have some breathing room.

"With the arrival of these Vitas, I think it's more impor- tant than ever that we find any other human civilizations out there. I'm under no illusion that we have the manpower to fight this new enemy, even with the new War Mages coming into the fold."

"How many mages have been able to take on familiars?" Sara asked, curious to know how far along they were.

"Six pairs so far, though the Rodgers twins are the only others in the field. Of the remaining five pairs, four only finished the spell in the last two days. I want to give them some time to work with the Alant program you sent us." He furrowed his brow for a second. "Where did you get that, anyway? I was looking over the original report you sent along after delivering it, and there is no mention of its actual origin."

Sara had prepared this lie in advance, even sending follow-up documentation to back it. "We retrieved it from Cora's core. There were some files behind a firewall that took us some time to get to. I've sent subsequent reports since its delivery."

She felt bad for lying to the admiral, but there was some part of her that could not let the truth about the dread- nought get out. She decided to delve deeper into those feel- ings when she had the time.

"I'll have to take a look at those; I was unaware you had

sent follow-ups," he said, making a note. "Regardless, I'm going to send you out to continue your mission to find and contact any other human civilizations. These Vitas are going to be a problem, but even worse are the Galvox."

Sara cocked her head. "Why are the Galvox a bigger problem? From the reports I've read, they don't seem all that sophisticated in their battle tactics."

"Maybe not, but after reviewing your scans of the remains in the Teifen system, we know without a doubt that the Galvox and Vitas are working together. The battle damage showed that the Teifen ships were hit with both Galvox and Vitas weapons, but the Galvox were only hit with Teifen weapons. For whatever reason, the Galvox and Vitas have an alliance, and that could mean that the Vitas are organizing the Galvox into a more efficient fighting force," Admiral Franklin said. "With the vast numbers the Galvox can field, a little organization on their part could spell the destruction of the galaxy."

Sara nodded in assent. "And you think finding the ancient humans could turn the tide?"

"It couldn't hurt. Your reports from that planet you found show a fully developed, advanced civilization. Perhaps they continued with their Aetheric roots and have become even more powerful. We will never know if we don't go out and find them. Obviously they are not coming to us.

"In the meantime, your ship needs to be repaired, and we need to get that Vitas robot to a research facility for study," Franklin said, typing away at his keyboard as he talked. "My son is in charge of Reemass Station and the development of the colony on the planet there. Reemass was the first of three colonies set up for us by the Elif, so their facilities are furthest along and most equipped to study the robot. I'm sending him a message now to let him know that you are coming, and to ask that he keep the information quiet for now."

He hit the return key on his keyboard and turned back to the camera. "The orders have been sent. If you could do me a favor while you are there, it would be a great help to me and the Confederation."

"Name it, Admiral. Whatever you need," Sara said, and meant it. He had shown his loyalty to her, and she wanted to give back in whatever way she could.

"Could you set them up with a core and the ability for this instant communication? I know the core's creation is a secret the War Mages can't divulge, and we are concentrating on outfitting the fleet with them before we start to incorporate them elsewhere. But if you can provide Reemass with a core, they will be free to study it and, hopefully, can more quickly further our understanding of their capabilities." The admiral gave a warm smile. "And it would be nice to be able to speak with my grandchildren in real-time again."

Sara smiled. "It would be my pleasure, Admiral. Thank you for everything. Especially looking into the matter of Admiral Smith."

"Not at all. You have done more for humanity than anyone in history, my dear. You are a treasure to humankind, and I will fight to protect that treasure at all costs. Be safe, Captain. This planet is counting on you."

"Thank you, sir. We will do our best."

He smiled. "I know you will. Franklin out."

CHAPTER 39

"*RAVEN*, you have been cleared for docking bay two. Welcome to Reemass Station," the air traffic controller said in what Sara thought of as the 'classic air traffic controller' voice. She had to smile at his sing-song cadence.

"Connors, bring us in," she ordered, leaning back in her chair and taking in the view of planet Reemass and her orbital station.

The station, while roughly the same design as Xanadu, was comparatively smaller, but still large enough to house several thousand colonists as they prepared the planet for habitation. A large, donut-shaped cylinder was held to a central axis by four spokes, and spun in a lazy revolution to provide artificial gravity. Most space stations employed centripetal gravity to save on power usage, unlike most ships that had power to spare.

In contrast to Xanadu, Reemass Station was actually the counterweight to a space elevator. The long, thin cable was held taut by the weight of the station and the rotation of the planet below. This made the transfer of materials to the surface much cheaper in the long run.

Connors banked around the station, and Sara noted that they were the only warship that would be docked there. However, they had picked up friendly ID tags of four UHF ships patrolling the system when they arrived.

With practiced ease, Connors brought the *Raven* to rest in the docking clamps. There was a shudder as the magnetic clamps engaged, and a large green light flashed on the station's hull, indicating they had successfully docked.

Sara opened the ship-wide comm channel. "We have arrived at Reemass Station and will be docked for the next twenty-four hours. Shore leave has been approved for all crewmen, on a rotation. So check with your officers for your slot.

"I'm sure I don't have to say this, but I'm going to anyway: behave yourselves. And have some fun. It will be a while 'til we get back Earthside."

She shut of the comm channel and turned to Grimms. "You coming?"

"Actually, I think I'm going to get caught up on some reading, Captain," he said with a smile and a pat to Nyx's head.

She smiled back. "Suit yourself, Commander. I won't be long. I'm just going to drop off the robot, then probably sleep for the next twenty hours. The last few days have been..." she searched for the word. "Stressful."

"Don't worry, I'll hold down the ship while you're gone," he said with a salute.

She returned the salute and, picking up the black case she had prepared with Boon earlier, motioned for Alister to follow as she exited the bridge. She wound her way through the corridors, heading for the newly repaired airlock.

She turned to Alister. "You know, you can stay onboard if you want."

"Merp?" he asked.

"I mean, only if you want to. I'm not saying don't come. It's just going to be boring, is all," Sara said with a shrug.

Alister considered his options then cocked his head up at her. "Merow?"

She smiled. "Yeah, it's totally fine. We're just dropping off the robot and installing the core. It'll be an hour, tops."

"Erow?"

"That's a great idea. I'll meet you in Boon's quarters when I'm done," she agreed.

Alister gave a shrug, then at the next corridor, turned and gave her a 'Merp!' before taking off at a run toward the stairs.

Sara couldn't help but laugh at his excitement at not having to go on the delivery run.

"Cora, what do we need in way of repairs while we're here?" she asked over her comm.

"Honestly, nothing," her twin replied conversationally. "The nanobots are still working on a few systems, but nothing that won't be done in the next ten hours or so. What we do need are more raw materials for the nanobots and printers to work with. We lost a lot of supplies in the attack."

"Okay, I'll be sure you get what you need. Can you send a list to my tablet?"

"Already done," Cora said.

"Thanks."

Sara turned the last corner and saw Baxter, Gonders, Deej, and Oriel waiting for her. Between them was a crate strapped to a cart. All four marines were in full Aetheric armor and had rifles in their hands, except Deej, who instead of holding a rifle was pushing the cart.

"Captain," Baxter said with a nod of his helmet.

"A little overdressed?" Sara said, raising an eyebrow and switching the black case to her other hand.

"After fighting these things," he indicated the crate with the Vitas robot inside, "we're not taking any chances. Plus, I figured if the staff on Reemass sees how cautious we are, they might take extra care when messing with the bot's insides."

"Fair point. Shall we?" she asked, stepping into the airlock and keying the door open.

"Hey, where's Alister?" he asked as the door cycled.

"He went to hang out with Boon and Silva. I told him this was going to be boring and that he could stay if he wanted-ed," she said with a shrug.

It would take thirty seconds for the door to cycle; fifteen seconds in, Baxter said, "It's weird not seeing him on your shoulder."

"Yeah," Gonders agreed.

"It's almost like seeing you naked," Oriel deadpanned in her southern drawl. Then after a beat, she added, "Almost."

Sara furrowed her brow at the Marine, then turned slightly red when she realized that Oriel was one of the people that had passed by her door the day Boon was struggling to close it.

Further commentary was cut short when the airlock unbolted and swung open.

The docking bridge was far nicer than Sara had expected. Instead of metal deck plates, like on Xanadu, this bridge was carpeted and lined with windows that showed off the gleaming outside of the superstructure.

Waiting on the bridge were six people. Four looked to be techs of one kind or another, but the two men standing out in front were obviously in charge. The one to Sara's left stepped forward, his hand extended.

"Hello, I'm Director Franklin," he said, giving her a firm handshake.

Looking at him was like looking at a picture of the admiral in his younger days.

Franklin indicated the tall Asian man beside him, who stepped forward to shake hands next. "This is Dr. Sloan," he introduced. "He will be heading the research on the present you've brought us."

"It is a pleasure to meet you, Captain Sonders. A real pleasure," the young doctor said, pumping her hand so vigorously that his mop of black hair fell into his eyes. He didn't seem to notice, as he continued the handshake just a little too long to be comfortable.

"The pleasure is all mine, Dr. Sloan. I hope you can get some useful information out of our friend here," Sara said, finally able to pull her hand free and indicate the crate. "We will escort you to the holding facility. Please, lead the way."

Deej pushed the cart out onto the bridge, and the techs parted to let him pass. They started to lean in, obviously excited to get started, but Baxter, Gonders, and Oriel formed up around the crate, making the techs take a step back.

"We should probably wait until the specimen is secured before we go poking and prodding it," Sara said by way of apology.

The three of them began walking, with the Marines right behind, and the techs bringing up the rear. Sara observed their surroundings as they went. The station was beautiful; trees grew out of central planters, and an artificial sky made the large central corridor seem open and bright. They also passed numerous storefronts and eateries on their route.

They walked in companionable silence for a few moments, until the director spoke. "My father tells me this robot is part of a new species, is that right?" Franklin asked, seeming to hardly believe it.

Sara nodded. "That's right. We believe they are artificial in nature, and they seem to work from a central ship. The bot went dead after we destroyed its mother ship, but we really don't know anything about them, so we don't want to take any chances," she said, trying to reiterate how dangerous the thing was.

"Fascinating," Dr. Sloan said, shaking his head slightly.

"I've included the data from our battle, along with the video from each of the Marines that fought the boarding party. I thought maybe seeing them in action would clue you in to their inner workings."

"Oh, that is marvelous. Thank you, Captain Sonders, that will be most helpful," the doctor gushed.

He seemed slightly off, as if he knew the words to say, but not quite the intensity with which to say them. Sara chalked it up as a quirk, and gave the doctor a smile.

"My pleasure, doctor." She patted the case in her hand. "Director Franklin, where would you like the core set up?"

He looked down at the case. "I thought the lab would be the best palace for it."

She nodded, and they continued down the main corridor.

The station was populated, but not crowded by any means. They passed small groups of people going about their business, but for the most part, Sara struggled to find more than ten people within eyesight at any point in the journey to the labs.

"Where is everyone?" she eventually asked, when they passed a cafe that had one lone patron, sitting and reading her tablet alone.

Franklin looked over at the woman Sara was staring at and gave a chuckle. "On the planet. The vast majority of the population here is working on the construction projects on the surface. This is early afternoon for the station, so the halls feel a little empty. Come evening, this corridor will be quite crowded with people out for their evening meals." He indicated a side passage. "This way."

They wound their way deeper into the station until they finally came to a large set of blast doors. Dr. Sloan swiped his key card and placed his hand on a scanner. After a moment, the door hissed open.

The lab was huge. Its ceiling was a good three stories high, and the space was at least thirty meters to a side. Numerous workstations were placed at regular intervals, each with one or two people working at them. There were more people in this one room than she thought she had seen on their entire walk through Reemass Station.

Dr. Sloan led them to a large, vault-like door with thick glass windows in it. He pressed his hand to the reader on the wall and keyed in a code. There was the sound of bolts being retracted, then the door clicked ajar. Dr. Sloan pulled it open and directed them to put the crate on the steel table in the center of the room.

"This room is a Faraday cage, so it should isolate any signal from the robot, but just in case that doesn't work, the room is also a vault equipped with countermeasures." He indicated the corners of the ceiling.

Sara was surprised to see small turrets installed there, providing complete coverage of the room.

"I'm more at ease, knowing the bot can be contained, but I have to ask..." She rose an eyebrow. "Why do you have such an extensive setup in the first place?"

Director Franklin smiled. "All research facilities have a room like this."

"But why?" Sara insisted.

Dr. Sloan was the one to answer. "In case someone brings a deadly robot for us to study."

Franklin barked a laugh. "Actually, he's right. You never know what you'll need, so they just give us everything they can think of."

"What was kept in this room before we got here?" she asked, suspicious of the kinds of experiments that were actually happening in the facility.

"Until yesterday, we used it as the break room," Dr. Sloan said with a smile.

CHAPTER 40

Sara and Boon created a core while in transit to Reemass, and then it took less than ten minutes to set up. They were starting to understand that the cores only did what they were programmed to do. Cora had programmed this particular core with basic instructions and the instant communications feature. Her own differed slightly, in that its programs could execute pre-installed scripts, giving it the illusion of thinking. Just like a computer.

Where a core differed from a computer was it didn't require a coding language to program it. The cores, much like Aetherically adept humans, seemed to be able to understand any language. A mage in a tank system was programming the core attached to it simply by using the system. The core was able to observe and adapt to the user. Slowly, they would find a more efficient balance; the core would begin to take over the small things, like maintenance and reactor adjustments, leaving the mage to focus on the big picture stuff, like warping and sensors.

Cora had printed up a case for the core based on the design attached to her own tank, and installed a screen and keyboard that would allow the user to interface with the core more easily.

In the lab, Sara attached the box to the network, and booted up the core with a touch of her fingers. She then enclosed the core inside its own section of the case, which was then locked using the thumb scanner they had installed.

"You can't actually touch the core unless you're a twin mage. If anyone but a twin mage touches it, it will zap them hard enough to knock them unconscious," she told Dr. Sloan when he asked why she was locking it away.

"So we can never get to the core?" he asked, crestfallen.

Sara smiled at his sincerity. "No, but, with the core networked to your system, you will be able to use it without directly interacting with it."

He brightened at that and gave her another vigorous handshake. "Thank you, Captain Sonders."

"You can repay me by finding out everything you can about that robot in there," she said, nodding at the sealed room containing the Vitas.

"Oh, I will. Just you wait!" he said, then abruptly let go of her hand and walked away.

She squinted after him, as if trying to hear the different beat of his drum.

"Don't worry about Dr. Sloan. He's a genius, and like most geniuses, he's a little odd—but I wouldn't trade him for all the worlds," Director Franklin said, stepping up beside her.

"I'm not worried," she laughed, "just fascinated. How long do you think it will take him?"

They began to walk back toward the lab entrance as Franklin considered her question. "I would be surprised if you don't hear something from him in the next day or two. Three at the most. Once something catches his attention, he works on it until he understands it, and he works quite fast."

They exited the lab, and were soon back at the airlock to the *Raven*.

Sara extended a hand. "It was a pleasure, Director Franklin."

He shook the offered hand and said, "The pleasure was all mine. I'm having my people bring the raw materials to the *Raven*'s loading bay now. They should be done in an hour or two."

"I appreciate the quick service, Director," she said with a bow of her head.

"Not a problem." He turned and began walking back down toward the bridge.

"That went easier than I thought it would," Baxter admitted, watching the man retreat.

"You're bound to win some of 'em, Sarge," Oriel said with a musical laugh that was in stark contrast to her intimidating, black armor. "Speaking of winning some, when do we get shore leave?"

Baxter mimed looking at a watch. "Well, look at that. You've been on leave for the last hour."

"Well, shit. What am I doin' hanging out here with you?" she said with a smile. She gave Sara a sharp salute. "Ma'am."

Oriel and Deej stepped through the airlock and headed for the lockers to stow their gear, leaving Baxter and Gonders with Sara.

"Are you taking some shore, Gonders?" Sara asked as she stepped into the airlock, followed by the others.

"Maybe. It depends on what Boon wants to do. We might just stay in our room and watch a movie or something."

"Heh heh, 'or *something*,'" Sara said with as creepy a face as she could make.

Gonders physically recoiled. "Uh, what?"

Sara and Baxter both burst out laughing.

"Too easy, Gonders," Sara laughed. "Actually, I'll probably see you there. I need to pick up Alister."

"We'll see you as soon as we stow the armor," Baxter said, still chuckling. "Come on, Gonders," he said to the flabbergasted woman, and headed down the corridor.

After a beat, she saluted Sara and chased after her sergeant.

SARA STOPPED by her room and changed into what she now thought of as her 'lounging clothes', which were just a pair of black yoga pants she never seemed to do yoga in anymore, and a large gray sweatshirt that she could never seem to throw away, despite the worn out collar and several small holes. She grabbed a pair of ankle socks, but on second consideration, tossed them back into the drawer and flexed her toes a few times, enjoying the freedom. Stopping at her small wet bar, she filled a glass with ice and a few fingers of whiskey, then headed out her door and turned toward Boon's quarters.

She passed by a few crewmen along the way and gave them all a friendly wave, or exchanged brief pleasantries. Most were dressed in a similar fashion as she, seeing as they were technically on shore leave, even if they were not leaving the ship.

Sara came to Boon's door and, giving it a knock, got an immediate, 'Come in'. She pressed the button on the wall panel, and the door slid open.

"Oh, hey. I was wondering if you were going to show up," Boon said from across the room. She was sitting cross-legged on her bed and wearing her kitten pajamas.

Sara immediately noticed that Boon's toenails were bright red. She looked down at her own toes and frowned. *I should paint my toes,* she thought, looking back at Boon's shiny red ones. *It's so cute.*

Alister and Silva were curled together in a knot that looked like it would take a sailor two days to undo. To her surprise, Nyx was in the room as well, laying on the bed beside the other two pixies. However, she was not asleep, and seemed to be having a conversation with Boon.

"Hello, sister," Cora said through the speakers, and suddenly Nyx's presence made a whole lot more sense.

"Hey, what's going on in here? You guys having a sleepover?" Sara chuckled.

Boon rolled her eyes. "Does it look like we're having a sleepover?" she retorted in a sardonic voice.

"Uh, kinda," Sara said, not knowing if her friend was joking.

The blonde woman checked her surroundings again then shrugged. "Huh, I guess it does kind of look like that," she conceded. "Me, Cora, and Nyx were having a conversation, and the others fell asleep."

"Surprise, surprise," Sara said, rolling her eyes.

Boon's room was smaller than her own, and lacked a couch. There was a table, but it was only for two people, and just barely at that. Sara opted to sit on the double bed with the rest rather than take one of the hard plastic chairs tucked under the table.

She laid down on her side across the bed, behind Boon and the pixies, and propped her head up on one hand. She took a sip of her whiskey and smacked her lips.

"So, what are you all talking about?" she asked, after making herself at home.

"We were actually talking about the dreadnought and what to do with it," Cora said.

"Really? Have you got any ideas?" Sara asked excitedly, as she sat up cross-legged, like Boon, and scooted in closer.

Boon shrugged with exaggerated care and, in a voice that was two octaves higher than normal, said, "Uh, maybe?"

"Right now, it's barely an idea. More like the idea of an idea," Cora said, jumping in. "We were talking to Nyx about how the pixies originally flew the ship, and trying to come up with a way that we could maybe reoutfit it so they could do it again."

"Really? They could do that?" Sara asked, raising an eyebrow at Nyx.

"No, they can't," Boon said dejectedly.

"Nyx says the modifications happened so long ago that they have no record of how it was done," Cora said. "I mean, it was several hundred thousand years ago. We humans barely have five thousand years of history recorded."

Sara pursed her lips. "To be honest, I had this idea rolling around in the back of my mind, as well. It's too bad we can't get it to work."

Boon held up a finger. "We need to utilize the dread-nought. It's not doing us any good sitting at the bottom of the Atlantic. I think you should send me and Isabella on a shuttle back to Earth while we're here at the station. It might be the last chance we get for a while. Even if we can't figure out how to get the ship up and running, we can at least map it out, and maybe get some new ideas," Boon said with a shrug.

Sara considered the idea. Eventually, she nodded. "I like it. I mean, I don't like that I won't have you here if we get into a fight, but I think you're right. We need to move on the dreadnought, and I can't take the time to do it myself," she said with a smile. "Besides, it looks like we're going to be out roaming the galaxy on a wild goose chase for the foreseeable future anyway. We may as well be getting shit done back home while we're at it."

Boon's face split into a huge grin. "Izz is going to be super excited."

"Excited about what?" Gonders asked from the door. She was freshly showered, and still drying her long, black hair with a towel.

"Sara wants us to go work on the dreadnought!"

Gonders grinned. "That sounds like a real treat, being trapped in a ship a few thousand meters underwater."

Boon laughed. "Trust me. That ship is so big, you'll forget where it is the moment you see the central park inside."

Gonders flipped the towel onto her shoulder. "Okay. I trust you. When do we leave?"

"Sometime in the next twenty-two hours," Sara said, noticing Gonders' toes were painted as well.

What the hell? Even Gonders, the badass Marine specialist, found the time to paint her toes... Why am I suddenly so obsessed with painting my toes?

Baxter took that moment to stick his head in the door. "Hey, there you are. Are you hanging out in here, or were you coming back to your room?" he asked, giving Sara a smile. "I thought maybe we could have a drink..." He turned to Gonders and made the same face Sara had at the airlock. "Or *something*."

Gonders frowned at him, then looked at Sara. She was making the same creepy face as Baxter.

"You two are so weird," she said, backing away slowly.

Sara and Baxter burst into laughter.

CHAPTER 41

Sara stood on the bridge of the *Raven*, watching the cargo transport move away from Reemass Station. Boon and Gonders were onboard, and Sara wanted to see them off.

When she had contacted Director Franklin asking about transport back to Earth for two of her people, he informed her that there was a regular shuttle, and Sara had arranged for the two women to be on the ship. The trio had spent their remaining time together planning what needed to be done on the dreadnought. Nyx had even given them the name of a Keeper that would be able to help with the project, and brought up a few ideas she had.

After several pots of coffee, a good meal, and a short nap, they had packed up what belongings they had, and headed for the passenger shuttle. That was an hour ago. Sara was far more emotional about them leaving than she would have guessed. It seemed that over the last few months, Boon had gone from being just one of her crew to her close friend. Sara hadn't had many close friends growing up, other than her sister, and having one now and watching her leave was a bigger deal than she would have imagined.

The sleek passenger shuttle moved away from the system, gaining speed, until it reached safe warping distance. In the blink of an eye, it vanished.

Sara felt a tug in her gut when the ship slipped away, but she smiled knowing that Boon was off to do important work.

"Grimms, are we ready to get back out there?" she asked, a small smile still on her face.

"Aye, ma'am. The crew is all accounted for, and the raw materials have been loaded," he said, glancing down at his tablet. "The nanobots completed all repairs a few hours ago, and they have been resupplied as well. We're ready to start looking for our needle in a haystack, as it were."

Sara reached over to where Alister sat on the holo table next to her and scratched under his chin. He had been pretty upset about Silva leaving; though, Sara didn't know if that was because they were actually friends, or if he was just going to miss his hardcore napping partner, since she saw the two of them do little else together.

"Connors, take us out," Sara ordered.

"Aye, ma'am. Unlocking docking clamps now," he said, working his console.

The large, green light on Reemass Station turned red as a *ca-chunk* reverberated through the *Raven*'s hull.

"Docking clamps released," he said, easing the ship away from the station.

When they were a few dozen meters away, he swung the prow of the ship up and away, giving them a view of the green and blue planet below. Soon they were pointed out into open space, and he poured on the speed.

"What heading, ma'am?" he asked, glancing over his shoulder at Sara.

She raised an eyebrow. "Good question, Connors. I suppose we should start where we left off," she said, zooming in to the system where they had found the abandoned human planet.

She was deciding where to make her mark, when a hesitant Mezner said, "Uh, ma'am. I'm receiving an encrypted communication."

"Is it from the station?" Sara asked, immediately thinking Dr. Sloan had found something.

"No, ma'am. It's coming from out of system. They're using an Elif code, but it's an old one; it's on the 'do not use' list."

Sara frowned. "Could it be dangerous? Like a virus or something?"

Mezner shook her head. "With the core in use, any virus would be destroyed before it had a chance to do any damage. The code is one the Elif think the Teifen have gotten a hold of."

"The Teifen?" Sara echoed in surprise.

"Maybe it's our new friend, Grand Admiral Bok," Grimms suggested.

"Is it a video communication?" Sara asked.

Mezner leaned into her console and looked closely at the data. "It's a whole packet, ma'am. It looks like there are several files, including a map update and a video communication."

After a minute's consideration, Sara said, "Put it onscreen."

"Aye, ma'am."

The message was indeed from Grand Admiral Bok. He was sitting in what looked like an office—*probably his ready room,* Sara guessed. His hands were folded on the desktop, and he wore a slightly bored look, which she thought of as his 'resting devil face'.

"Captain Sonders, I hope this message finds you well," he began, and Sara raised an eyebrow at his friendly manner.

She had thought of the Teifen as a hyperaggressive race for so long, it was jarring to see one being pleasant.

"I realize it has only been a little over two days since we last spoke, but I am taking this opportunity to call in that favor you owe me."

"Great. This guy doesn't waste any time, does he?" Sara quipped with an eyeroll.

Bok continued. "The situation is even worse than I originally thought. My late governor, it seems, has been ignoring pleas for help from our Rim worlds. Several of the systems are now unresponsive, and I fear they have come to some grizzled end.

"My fleet is now fully engaged in several battles with the Galvox across several systems. Luckily, we have not encountered any of the Vitas thus far, but I fear they are not far behind their allies.

"My people have mapped out the regions that have gone dark, and included the information in this message. As you can see, it looks as though a force is moving in like a wave from the edge of our galaxy."

Sara waved to Mezner. "Show me the map he's talking about."

The holo table rearranged itself to show the section of space they were currently in, along the spiral arm. Several hundred systems lit up with names and other metadata for the occupied systems. There was a crescent shape along the edge where the names were grayed out, as if something had taken a bite out of the galaxy.

"I have no ships to spare to investigate what is happening out on the Rim, but I would like to help them if I can. In that regard, I am calling in my favor. I ask that you travel out to the system I fear is the next target, and see what can be done."

Bok leaned back in his chair, a grim expression on his red-skinned face. "I know that this is a rather quick turn of events, and our truce is far from stable, but I have no more options. I either ask this of you, or let my people die out there, alone, on the edge of the galaxy. So, here I am, choosing the one option that might make a difference."

The video ended, and Bok's image disappeared.

"Well, that was unexpected," Sara said, after a few seconds of silence.

"It could be a trap," Cora said, and Grimms nodded.

"It could be, but then again, he could just be a decent leader who wants to save as many people as he can," she countered with a frown.

"We could go into the system cloaked. See what's happening, and make our call once we have a better idea of his true intentions," Grimms said.

Sara's brows rose in surprise. "I never would have guessed you would want to do this, Commander. I like the cloaked idea. And who knows, maybe we'll find a human colony along the way."

"The odds of that are pretty slim," Cora said.

"It's not like we had much of a lead to begin with," the captain said with a shrug. She marked the system Bok had indicated with the swipe of a finger. "Mezner, send this packet to Admiral Franklin directly. Be sure to mark it for his eyes only. We don't need the rest of the UHFC knowing about our deal with the grand admiral, unless Franklin thinks they should."

"Aye, ma'am. Sending it down to the communications mage now," Mezner said.

"Cora, as soon as the message is away, engage warp," Sara said, stepping back to her captain's chair and sitting down.

Alister leapt from the holo table to her lap and settled in.

After a few quiet moments of Sara hoping she was making the right decision, Cora dropped them into a warp thread.

It was too late for her to change her mind.

CHAPTER 42

Gerrold Grenolt leaned back in his makeshift lounge chair—really just a pile of old clothes and discarded bedding—and took a sip of Regelian Red from the tin mug he had rummaged from a drawer in the engineering room. He gave a contented sigh as he gazed out into the vastness of space through the *Rizz*'s observation dome. Reaching up, he carefully slicked his black hair down between his long, thin horns.

Newer Elif warships had done away with the observation domes, calling them 'out of date' and 'an unnecessary weak point' in the design, but the *Rizz* was not one of those sleek new warships. No, the *Rizz* was a hunk of space junk so old there had been nothing but dust lining her halls when Gerrold had found her, floating between the stars.

It had taken him and his crew nearly two years to get the *Rizz* into her present condition. Now the *Rizz* only *looked* like a piece of space junk, but her guts had been completely revamped with the best components money could buy. At least, the best components money could buy out on the Rim.

In the pirating business, it helped to be underestimated.

Working in an Elif warship while being Teifen usually came with a whole slew of problems, but not the kind of problems most people would first assume. Mostly, the problems came from the fact that the average Teifen was a good head taller than your average Elif. The ship's low ceilings could become an issue for people like Hooper, Gerrold's closest friend and the cook/gunner on the *Rizz*. Gerrold was small in stature, at least for a Teifen, but Hooper stood well over two meters tall, with a belly to match.

Sitrix, Hooper's girlfriend, was the only other Teifen on board. She was an ex-harem girl from the regional governor's personal stock; she and Gerrold had become friends while he was a guard on the dreadnought, and they had escaped the governor's wonton cruelty together to strike out on their own.

She was their talker, their public figure, as it were. Sitrix was the one who took the goods they pirated and sold them at market. There was a huge advantage to having a beautiful, confident woman making the deals: people underestimated her, just like the *Rizz*.

The rest of the crew were all Elif, and for one reason or another, had decided their government could kiss their asses. Then they moved out to the Rim, where things like emperors and regional governors were a little less of a problem.

Gerrold had found his pilot and controller, a set of twins named Bestin and Restin who'd been trained by the Elif Royal Navy, in a bar trying to drink themselves to death. After buying the boys a few rounds, Gerrold finally got them to open up about what had driven them out to the Rim worlds. After much hemming and hawing, Bestin's story boiled down to them abandoning their post when they were ordered to fire on a Teifen civilian transport. He and his twin brother stole a shuttle out of their ship's bay that very hour.

And then there was Seena. *Oh, beautiful, dangerous, angry*

Seena. She had been a front-line mage in the Royal Marines 'til she was framed for a crime her superior committed. After all the years Gerrold had known her, she still wouldn't tell him the whole story, but like him, she had abandoned her post while still wearing her Aetheric armor. This made the two of them the 'away' team—the up close and personal side of pirating.

"Hey, whatcha doing?" a lovely female voice said, making him nearly spill his drink down the front of his jumpsuit.

Then there was the last and most terrifying member of his crew: Reggi.

Gerrold turned in his 'recliner' and held up the bottle of Regelian Red to show the short, slightly built woman coming up the stairs into the round glass dome.

"Hey, Reggi. Just taking a break and looking at the stars. Want a drink?"

Reggi shook her head, sending her brown bob bouncing. "You know I hate that stuff, it gives me the most brutal hangovers. I honestly don't know how you can stand it," she said, coming over and sitting on the floor beside him.

Reggi was a mage, a powerful one. That, however, was not what made her so terrifying; Gerrold and Seena were both mages, after all. What made Reggi such a terror was her heritage. Her human heritage.

"What do you think our chances are?" she asked after a few minutes of stargazing.

Gerrold blew out a breath. "Well, we just have to hold until the planet's evacuated, and last I saw, they were getting pretty close. Every ship not capable of fighting is shuttling people to New Hope. The rest of us are just waiting 'til that's done, then getting the hell out of here. So I guess the question is how long is the evacuation going to take? Because I don't plan on sticking around any longer than we have to."

Reggi laughed. "You really are a pirate, through and through. Don't you want to stop the attacks?"

"Hey, little missy, don't you go disparaging our calling. We might be pirates, but we're commissioned pirates. I still give a shit about our home out here on the Rim. Why do you think I risk our butts going out and robbing the core worlds, just to come back and give most of the prizes away?"

She gave him a sideways look. "Because our privateering contract says we have to give up half."

Gerrold waved a hand dismissively. "Aw, shut up. What do you know? You've only been part of the crew for a few months. Once you've been doing this for a few years, we'll talk. There's a loyalty out here you just don't understand yet," he said, taking a sip of the red liqueur before continuing. "We survive so we can fight another day. What good would it do us to stand and fight an enemy to the death, when we can just let 'em pass us by?"

"Yeah, but they're not passing us by, Gerrold. They're wiping out whole star systems and not slowing down," she said, waving a hand at the expanse of stars. "Back home, we draw a line in the sand, and anyone who crosses that line doesn't survive. Sure, a lot of my people die, but everyone else back home is safe."

" 'Everyone else back home' has War Mages. I don't know if you've noticed, Reggi, but there aren't a lot of those 'round these parts," he said, turning to her in frustration.

But she wasn't paying any attention to him. Instead, she was squinting at something outside the dome. "What is that?" she asked, pointing out into the black.

He squinted. "I don't see anything... Oh, shit!" he exclaimed as something passed in front of a star, blocking the light for a split second.

He began rummaging through the pile of clothes and bedding, eventually having to get up and dismantle the pile entirely to find what he was looking for. The room's electronic scope fell out of the leg of a pair of pants he picked up, and he snatched it off the ground.

Turning to the glass, he tried to pick out the anomaly again, but he had lost it in his search for the scope.

"Where did it go?" he asked, and Reggi, never having taken her eyes off of it, stepped up next to him and pointed.

He needed to squat down to sight along her arm, and he eventually saw another star blink as whatever it was passed in front of it. He held up the scope and began focusing it. The short, black tube made whirring noises, as the servos moved the internal lenses back and forth as he searched the area.

He glanced over a section of space and almost swept past it, but something made him take a second look. He watched the area for a few long seconds. Right as he was about to continue on, one of the stars in the scope moved and warped.

He zoomed in and pushed a button, trying to place a tracking mark on the object. Though the software was not able to lock on to anything, he was still able to get a close-up view.

"Ho. Lee. Shit," he said slowly.

"What is it?" Reggi asked, leaning forward and squinting harder. "I can't really see it, only the stars around it being warped."

"It looks like a black hole," he said, and meant it. It was like there was a blank space that the light was bending around. He zoomed in further. "Wait, I think I see…"

There was an outline of something, just for a second, as a light flashed behind it. But now the center of the anomaly looked as black as the rest of the space around it.

"Bestin," Gerrold said over his comm, "I'm tracking something with the spotting scope in the observation dome. I'm sending you the feed now. Can you pick it up on sensors?"

There was a second's silence, and Gerrold thought maybe Bestin had taken his earpiece out again. Just when he was about to call Restin instead, Bestin answered.

"Hey there, Cap. I don't have anything on sensors that shouldn't be there," he said casually. "I'm patching in the signal from the scope now."

Another long pause followed, during which the anomaly passed in front of several stars, warping or blocking their light completely.

"Uh, what am I supposed to be seeing here?" Bestin asked.

Gerrold growled. "What do mean? Don't you see the thing warping light as it passes in front of the stars? It's right in the center of the scope."

Another long pause. "I'm sorry, Cap, but there's nothing there. All I see is you slowly sweeping across the starfield. There's nothing else to see," Bestin said, confused.

"Reggi, go up there and make sure Bestin's not just being an idiot," he said out the side of his mouth. Then over the comm, he said, "Reggi's coming up. She's already seen it, and I swear to the Ten Lords, Bestin, if you're drunk, I'll rip your nuts off."

Now Bestin sounded defensive. "She can come and look all she wants, Cap. There's nothing on the fucking screen."

Gerrold took a few calming breaths, trying not to lose his shit as he gave Reggi time to get to the bridge. Luckily, it was only one floor down and a quick run, even for the short-legged woman.

"He's right, Gerrold, there's nothing on the screen. It look like normal space from here," Reggi confirmed, slightly out of breath from her run.

"What the hell?" he said quietly to himself. Then louder, he said, "Set a course using the scope's direction. I'll stay here and keep the object in view."

"You got it, Cap," Bestin said.

The *Rizz* began picking up speed, making it all the harder to track the anomaly, so Gerrold zoomed out a few clicks. Once he had a wider view, it became fairly easy to track.

"Got you now," he said, staring through the scope. "Whatever you are."

CHAPTER 43

"IT'S BEEN TWELVE HOURS, and the stream of ships hasn't stopped. They have to be abandoning the planet," Sara said, watching the tiny holographic line of mismatched ships warping in and making for the only habitable planet in the system. Another stream of ships was leaving at the same time.

She and Grimms were leaning on the holo table, each with a cup of coffee in their hands. They had been observing the space surrounding the Teifen planet of Ostrik for nearly a day, when transports suddenly started showing up en masse and picking people up. From the light Aetheric scans Cora had done when they arrived, the population was estimated to be just under a hundred million.

Sara took special note that the inhabitants of the planet were both Elif and Teifen. It seemed that the hard lines each empire had drawn were a little fuzzy this far out. She wondered if the Grand Admiral was aware that his people were living in a mixed society.

"At the rate they're moving, it will still be another couple of days before they get everyone off-planet," Grimms said, taking a sip of his coffee.

"It looks like they know their system is a target. I'm guessing Bok sent word," Sara said, then turned to her gunner. "Hon, what are the latest numbers on their defensive ships? Are you still having trouble getting a clear picture?"

"Yes, ma'am. The number changes constantly as data arrives, but the latest count is just over a thousand ships. Though they're pretty spread out—I think this is more a militia, and less a navy."

"Have we figured out if they are using cloaking technology? I don't understand how our passive sensors can be giving us false information like this." She shook her head and looked at the small, green icons spread around the system that represented combat-capable ships in the area.

"If they are using cloak tech, it's obviously not a hundred percent effective. Though it would make it difficult to gain target locks," Hon mused. "I'm sorry, ma'am. Without doing a large scale Aetheric scan, we won't know exactly what's out there."

"I don't want to do that just yet. Granted, the more time that passes, the more I think this is just what it looks like—a system about to be attacked by a stronger enemy."

Grimms took another sip of his coffee. "Is it time to make contact?"

She frowned. "These people aren't unaware of humanity's return to the stars. I don't want to freak them out too much. To be honest, this is a call for the brass," she said. "Mezner, contact Admiral Franklin via the core, and put it onscreen, please."

"Aye, ma'am," Mezner said. After a few seconds, the ensign looked up from her console. "Actually, ma'am, we're getting a communication from Director Franklin over the core right now. Would you like me to have him wait while you contact his father?"

Sara looked at Grimms and raised an eyebrow. "No, put

him through."

Director Franklin appeared onscreen, sitting in an office. He had a decidedly unsettled look about him.

"Director Franklin, how nice to see you. What can I do for you?" she asked politely.

"Captain, I apologize for the unscheduled call, but have you spoken with my father recently?"

Sara cocked he head, "I was actually just about to call him. Why, did something happen?"

Franklin began to wring his hands. "I was on a call with him, the first time I've spoken to him in real-time in months. We were chatting about the kids, nothing important, when I heard someone yelling in his office. He looked up, and the call was cut off. I haven't been able to reach him since."

"Mezner, get the Admiral on the line," Sara said, then turned back to the director. "I'm sure he's fine. I'll contact you as soon as I hear anything."

Director Franklin gave a nod. "Thank you, Captain. I'm hoping it's just a technical issue," he said, reaching forward to end the call. "Oh, I nearly forgot. Dr. Sloan wanted me to tell you that the bot's composition is taking him a little longer to pin down than he anticipated, but he will send you his findings as soon as he has it figured out."

"Thank you, director. We will be in contact soon." She ended the call and turned to Mezner. "Have you got the admiral?"

The woman shook her head. "I can't get a connection."

Cora spoke up at that. "The only way we wouldn't be able to connect to the core is if the computer it's installed in has been powered down."

"Well, shit," Sara grumbled to herself. Aloud, she said, "Keep trying to reach him. Maybe they're, I don't know, rebooting their system, or something."

"Aye, ma'am."

"Captain, I'm getting an odd reading," Hon said, sending the data to the holo table. "At first, I thought it was a small meteor and sent the trajectory data to Connors for a course adjustment, which he implemented a few minutes ago, but when I checked again, the meteor was still heading right for us. So I double-checked that we were on a new course, and we are. I'm now pretty sure it's not a meteor, ma'am. It definitely changed trajectory under its own power."

"A ship?" Sara asked, stepping into the command ring and powering it up. Alister perked up when he heard the ring power on, and hopped down from the captain's chair to join her.

"I don't think so. But all I have to go on are the passive scans, and according to them, it would be about the size of a basketball. It might be a drone, but I'm not getting any kind of electronic signature," Hon related.

Sara saw the object in question, as Hon provided a flashing icon on the holo table. Inside the viewing bubble, she turned in the direction the object was coming from and saw the same icon flashing on the bubble's inner surface. She reached out and selected the icon to enlarge her view of it.

"Hon, power up weapons. Cora, give me a full Aetheric scan of the system," she shouted, powering up the shields with a thought and a blast of Aether. "We have incoming."

"OH, SHIT. OH, SHIT!" Bestin yelled into the comm, making Gerrold cringe from the volume.

The *Rizz* went into a dive relative to the anomaly they had been tracking, and Gerrold was not able to keep it in his sights. However, the moment before Bestin began freaking out, Gerrold had seen what they were up against, as a golden wave of shielding rippled across its hull. He had to agree with Bestin's sentiment.

"Do you have it on scans?" he asked, dropping the scope back into the pile of dirty laundry and taking the stairs two at a time down to the bridge deck.

"I'm pretty sure the whole system has them on scans, Cap. That ship just lit up like a supernova. It pulsed an Aetheric blast of scans so strong, I felt the hairs on my arm stand up," Bestin said, his voice coming fast and breathy. "They've powered their weapons and shields. I'm powering up our main cannons now. Restin, get those shields going."

"Already on it," Restin said, as Gerrold burst through the bridge door and slipped into his chair, between the twins.

The *Rizz* was an old corvette class scout ship. It was technically a warship, but one of the lowest on the totem pole when it came to weaponry. It had two gauss cannons that fired thirty-kilo slugs, and four PDCs for point defense; that was about it. It was plenty of firepower for taking on merchant vessels or freighters, but even the shielding amplifiers were substandard.

Where this class of corvette shone, though, was in the engines. It had the gravitic drives of a ship three times its size, and relied on maneuverability to keep itself from being blown to space dust.

However, as soon as Gerrold saw the specs rolling in on the ship in front of them, he knew it was hopeless. Even with the stealth coating they had applied to the hull, they could only hide so much from a warship of that caliber, especially if the Aetheric scan the new ship had hit them with was as strong as Bestin said it was.

"What the hell design is that?" Restin demanded to know, glancing at the wire frame reconstruction of the ship on their small holo table, which was situated between the three seats and the small front view screen.

"I have no idea, but I'm not sticking around long enough to find out," Bestin said as he punched the drives to full.

The *Rizz* shot off like a gauss round, accelerating at nearly fifty *g*s and putting some distance between them and the alien vessel.

"Oh my god," Reggi said, leaning over Gerrold's shoulder to study the holo projection. "I recognize that design."

"Oh shit. They're chasing after us, Cap," Bestin said, juking the *Rizz* to the side, then rolling her the other way. "How the fuck are they keeping up with us? We can outrun nearly everything in production."

"They're hailing us, sir," Restin said, looking up from his console in the controller's seat.

"Put it onscreen," Gerrold said, sitting forward in his chair.

The *Rizz*'s bridge was small, really just big enough for the controller, pilot, and the captain. So with Reggi leaning over his chair and staring at the holo table, Gerrold was feeling a little cramped.

The small view screen flickered to a view of a rather large bridge that seemed almost too bright, with its white walls and consoles. He saw two humans standing in the center of the bridge, and three more sitting at individual stations around them. The two humans in the center were a man and a woman, and he had to admit they didn't look worried in the least.

Always a bad sign.

Gerrold glanced over his shoulder and saw that Reggi was staring at the screen, her face as pale as he had ever seen it.

"My name is Sara Sonders, and I'm the captain of this vessel, the *Raven*. If you wouldn't mind, I would like to have a word with you, Captain..." She let the question hang like a dead fish between them.

"Gerrold Grenolt, captain of the *Rizz*," he said, his mouth going dry.

Why the hell are there humans out here? Reggi said they never left their systems unless it was something really important. Could they be out looking for her?

"Would you mind if we stop this game of tag? I wouldn't want to wear you out," she said with a smile.

Gerrold was fascinated by the woman's hair; it was a bright, blood red. Even Teifen with red hair never had a color quite as vibrant as that. He took it to mean she was quite gifted with Aetheric power. Most truly powerful mages had a physical tell like that.

"Stop the ship, Bestin. We can't outrun them," Gerrold told the Elif twin mage.

After a moment's hesitation, he pulled the throttle back, and the ship stopped accelerating.

The woman flashed a warm smile. "Thank you so much, Captain Grenolt. First, I would like to say that we are here to help. Grand Admiral Bok asked us to see what we could do in the defense of this system..." She trailed off, looking over Gerrold's shoulder at Reggi. "Is that a human on your ship?" she asked, flabbergasted, her professional manner flying out the door.

Reggi stood stock-still, not making any move whatsoever.

"Uh, is that going to be a problem?" Gerrold asked, quickly trying to think of the best way out of this surreal situation.

A small, black animal jumped up onto the woman's shoulder as if it were a perch and stared at Reggi, its mouth open in shock.

At the sight of the animal, Reggi sucked in a breath, and began to shake.

"Oh god. She's a War Mage," Reggi whispered.

CHAPTER 44

"Captain Grenolt, where did you find a *human* willing to join your crew?" Sara asked, nodding toward the small, brown-haired woman over his shoulder. "She did join your crew willingly, correct?" she added, realizing the woman could very well be a captive.

Alister cocked his head to the side and said, "Merp?"

Grimms gave a grunt at Sara's side and met her eyes for a brief moment. He mouthed, 'Navy?'.

Sara shrugged.

The captain of the *Rizz* leaned back in his chair, still looking at the human over his shoulder. "This is Reggi," he said, indicating the woman. "We found her in the wreckage of her ship a few months ago. We offered to take her home, but she refused to tell us where her planet was."

Reggi had been frozen, up until this point, her mouth slightly open and her eyes bugging. However, Gerrold's words seemed to shake her free, and she stepped around his chair.

Pressing her palms together, she held her hands to her forehead, bowed at the waist, and said, "I apologize, War

Mage. I should have taken my life when I had the chance. I am weak, and have shamed our people. Please spare these who took me in, they did not know any better." She bowed even lower before continuing, "If it pleases you, I will gladly throw myself from the airlock."

"Uh, what?" Sara said, glancing at Grimms.

"Merp!" Alister said again.

Reggi began to stand at Sara's question, but stopped halfway and bowed again, not sure what to do, but obviously scared to do the wrong thing. "I apologize for not being clear, War Mage. What part would you like me to repeat?"

"I heard you, I just don't understand why you would throw yourself from the airlock," Sara said to the top of Reggi's head, then rolled her eyes. "Will you stand up, so we can have a conversation?"

Reggi visibly tensed. Stiff as a board, she slowly straightened to her full height. She kept her face down, however.

"Look at me, Reggi," Sara urged as gently as she could. The girl began to shake, but she did look up. "That's better." Sara gave her a little smile. "Now, tell me. Are you from Earth?"

"Earth?" Reggi asked, then shook her head, "No, War Mage. I've not even heard of such a place."

Sara raised both fists into the air and screamed in triumph. "What are the fucking odds?!" She turned to Grimms and slapped him about the shoulders. "You said it, but I was all, 'the odds are not in our favor' or something. Well, fuck me if I wasn't wrong." She put her arm around Grimms' shoulders and faced the viewing screen and the open-mouthed people staring at her. "Look at that, Grimms. A human not from Earth. We are actually ahead of the game for once!"

Grimms chuckled. "Yes, ma'am. It seems our luck is strong today."

"Excuse, me," Gerrold said, waving a hand to get Sara's attention. Reggi grabbed it and tried to stop him, her face a mask of terror. "Stop that, Reggi! Hey, Captain Sonders, can you please explain what the hell you are doing here? It's clear you have no clue who Reggi is, and you don't seem to want to attack us. You mentioned Grand Admiral Bok? How do you know him?"

Sara tried to calm down, but she was so excited, she had to take a second. "Sorry, Captain. We have been looking for someone like Reggi for a while now, and never thought we would find her out here.

"Bok and I made a deal recently: he would stop attacking the Elif if I would do him a favor. So here I am," she said, spreading her arms and smiling.

"He sent you here for what, exactly?" Gerrold asked, still not clear on what she was telling him.

"To fight, or help, or whatever needs to be done. To be honest, I don't really care. We found a human that's not from Earth, so as far as I'm concerned, the mission has already been a success."

Gerrold scooted forward and leaned an elbow on his knee. "I can't believe Admiral Bok actually sent someone. The governor has been ignoring the Rim for several hundred years."

"Well, the governor is dead now," Sara said with the slightest of smirks. "But I can tell you that Admiral Bok is trying to get you what protection he can. He's currently off fighting the Galvox, so he sent us."

"The governor's dead? How?" Gerrold asked.

"Uh, well. It's a pretty long story, but the ending goes something like, 'I killed him'," Sara said with a shrug.

"You killed the governor, and now the grand admiral is asking you for help instead of hunting you down?" Gerrold asked, leaning back in his chair. "This is one hell of a story."

"Not really. It seems to me that the governor didn't have a lot of love flowing his way. Admiral Bok was not a fan, and I'm assuming that you and your people aren't all that broken up about it," Sara said with another shrug. "But right now, I need to speak with Reggi. I need to get in contact with her people."

Reggi took a step back as if she were being asked to enter a burning building. "I don't understand, War Mage. What could I possibly have that you would want?"

Sara cocked her head to the side. "Are you okay? You seem to be frightened of me. Do you think I'm going to hurt you?"

Reggi put her hands up in a surrendering pose and took another step back. "I would never make assumptions, War Mage. I apologize."

"Hey, it's all right. I'm here to help," Sara soothed, realizing just how terrified the girl was. She decided to take the focus off Reggi to give her a chance to calm down. "Captain, can you fill me in on what it is your people are expecting, here? I can see the planet is being evacuated, so I assume you are anticipating an attack?"

Gerrold looked from Reggi to Sara and back again before clearing his throat and smoothing back his hair. "The Rim worlds have been under attack for months. It started with one system far out on the edge of the galaxy. It was a small colony; they had not started up their production facilities yet, so they were not in constant contact with the other world. We're not exactly sure when they were attacked, but a few months ago, someone noticed that no one had heard anything from them. A ship was sent out and was able to send back word that the colony was lost, with no survivors. But then that ship never returned.

"Then the second and third systems fell. They were able to get word out that it was a Galvox raid, but when we sent ships to help, the systems were already gone. Again, no survivors. We didn't know why the Galvox would be out here, since they would have to come out from the core and circle around the Teifen empire to get to us, but both systems reported sightings of a fleet of Galvox. We did find some of their ships in the wreckage, but far fewer than we'd expected.

"The planets were scorched clean, everything had been burned to the ground. We had not seen that kind of viciousness from the Galvox before, and it made us wonder if it was not some other race, using Galvox ships."

Sara nodded. "That's pretty much what's started happening in the inner systems. We do know that it is the Galvox, and not someone using their ships—however, they have a new ally: an alien race we are calling 'the Vitas'. They are very advanced, and have given us quite a run for our money."

Gerrold gave a nod. "So this is happening all over the place. At least now we know we were not just being ignored."

"There may have been a little of that going on under the governor, but it seems Admiral Bok really does want to help," Sara qualified, then leaned on the holo table. "How long until the planet is evacuated? And how do you know this system is next to be attacked?"

Gerrold checked his display on the arm of his captain's chair. "It looks like we still have a day and a half 'til the population is fully evacuated, but the main cities will be empty in the next seven hours or so. The rest of our people are in smaller towns and villages, spread throughout the countryside.

"As far as knowing this system is the next target? We don't. It's just our best guess. The trail of attacks is spreading in an arc from the edge of our territory, and this is the next closest system in line."

Sara considered his reasoning for a second. "I think I

should contact whoever is in charge and officially let them know we're here. We can maybe help out with—"

An alarm on the *Rizz* cut her off, and Mezner called out over it, "Ma'am, we have multiple warp threads opening up. I think it's the Galvox."

"You want to help, Captain Sonders? Now's your chance," Gerrold said, then dropped the call.

"Connors, get us there. Hon, you are free to fire. Set PDCs to full auto. Cora, charge the Aether cannons and prepare to jump," Sara ordered, watching the *Rizz* turn and accelerate toward the emerging Galvox ships.

"Let's see if we can tip the scale, but our first priority is making sure the *Rizz* survives. We need Reggi," Sara said, stepping into the command ring and powering it up.

Alister sat between her feet with a "Merp."

"That's right, buddy," Sara said, sending a flow of Aether into the shield form he had given her. Then she marked a location with the swipe of a finger.

"Cora, jump."

CHAPTER 45

By the time Cora jumped them into the fray, several hundred Galvox ships had flooded into the system. The small, fast Galvox ships were heavily armed, but had no shields to speak of. They relied on their ability to overwhelm the enemy and keep them off guard with swarming tactics. They lost as many ships as they took out, but there were far more Galvox than defenders.

Sara noted that the Rim worlders' ships were difficult to see on the holo display. Their signatures were small and flickered in and out. She reasoned they must have some sort of stealth coating, and made a note to ask them about it when this was over. Nothing the *Raven* had come across so far even came close to the effectiveness of the Rim's method, except Cora's ability to use the gravitic drives to mask them.

The Galvox were having trouble hitting their targets, but they made up for their inaccuracy by saturating the area with hundreds of gauss rounds. The defenders were a mix of armed freighters and personal yachts, with the occasional warship thrown into the mix. The ragtag fleet was surprisingly effective, despite their lack of firepower. When one ship fired, the Galvox would swarm and launch everything they had at the offending ship, more often than not hitting the target by sheer volume of ordnance.

The Rim Worlders had been spread throughout the system, not knowing where the attack would hit, and the unlucky dozen ships that happened to be close to the Galvox warp terminus were quickly being overwhelmed, but the rest of the defenders were warping across the system to join their fellows.

The *Raven* arrived on the scene before the *Rizz*, despite leaving after the pirate ship; it had jumped the several AU in the blink of an eye, rather than taken the long way around in warp.

As soon as the *Raven* appeared, her PDCs began to rumble and spit fire at every Galvox ship in range. A dozen or more of the lightly armored ships were torn to ragged pieces before the enemy even knew they were there.

Hon targeted individual ships with each of the gauss cannon slugs, before sending the turrets spinning to acquire new targets. He was tearing through the enemy with vicious accuracy, not even needing the explosive warheads.

The Galvox seemed to make a collective decision, and all focused on the human warship in their midst. They fired several hundred large slugs, but to their great surprise, the *Raven* did not stick around. Instead, in a flash of Aetheric light, it vanished. The slugs crossed the now empty space and slammed into Galvox ships on the other side, sending several craft down in flaming explosions of friendly fire.

Meanwhile, the *Raven* had reappeared insystem of the battle and let loose with her Aetheric cannons. Instead of focusing on punching through the shields of one ship, Cora swept the beam across the battlefield in short bursts, ripping chunks from the exposed Galvox ships.

As the enemy swung their ships around and began to fire,

Sara formed a long spike of a shield around the *Raven* and accelerated into the clustered ships like a lance, ripping several open as they slammed through the Galvox formation.

The entire time the battle raged, more and more Galvox were warping in. A large portion of them peeled off to fight the *Raven*'s deadly joust, but some pressed on to the planet and the other defenders.

The *Rizz* completed its warp to find the enemy being ripped to shreds by the *Raven,* and opted to leave that battle to the professionals. Instead, they angled to intercept the Galvox that were headed for the planet. Using their exceptional engines, they caught up to engage the Galvox from behind, taking out several ships before they began to take heat themselves. The *Rizz* juked and dodged, keeping out of the line of fire, but several of the defenders that had joined the battle with her were not so lucky.

Despite the beating the *Raven* was dealing out, the Galvox numbers kept growing, and soon the system was swarmed with thousands of the small, agile ships, which were raining down hell in groups of fifty or more.

The defenders were being overwhelmed, and soon, the evacuation transports were being targeted.

THE *RIZZ* WAS HIGHLIGHTED on Sara's display as the only green icon in the system. She kept an eye on them, while coordinating the destruction she and her crew were performing on the Galvox and their endless horde of ships.

"Cora, can you widen the beam on the Aetheric cannons? Maybe we can hit more of them at once," she suggested, trying to come up with a more effective way of dealing with the lightly armored enemy.

"That would be nice, but the focusing apparatus is not

that broad. I can maybe get a few more meters of width at most, but nothing like you're hoping," she reported.

Mezner spoke up. "Ma'am, I'm getting several incoming communications. It appears the *Catagain* is attempting to contact us."

Sara actually stopped and looked at the junior officer. "Are you serious? They must know we know they tried to kill us."

Mezner shrugged. "They keep trying. They are using the core *and* sending Aetheric comms packages."

Grimms cleared his throat. "We should give them our coordinates, ma'am."

"Are you serious?" she repeated, spinning around to see a nodding Grimms.

"We can't take enough of these Galvox out fast enough; the system is being overwhelmed. Even if the *Catagain* is coming to try and finish the job, they will have to fight off the Galvox first. We need the help," he stated simply.

Sara thought about it for a half a second before nodding. "Mezner, send the coordinates and warn them it's a battle-field. Share the friendlies' ship IDs we have. We don't want them attacking the wrong people."

"Aye, ma'am. Sending the information now."

"Cap, I don't know what the hell that ship is powered with, but it doesn't seem to obey our understanding of physics or Aetheric law," Bestin said excitedly.

They were doing a fair bit of damage themselves, but they needed to warp away now and again to recharge the capacitors for the two main cannons. Currently, they had warped out a few AU and were watching the battle unfold while their small reactors worked overtime.

"It's powered by a War Mage," Reggi said, her eyes transfixed on the green icon jumping around the battlefield. "The most terrible form of energy in the universe."

"I thought War Mages were humanity's leaders? Why all the hate?" Gerrold asked, knowing next to nothing about his human crew member's past or culture, besides what the stories said.

"Oh, they rule us, all right. With an iron fist. I don't know why this one is helping us, but you need to be wary; they are a ruthless bunch," Reggi said, baring her teeth.

"She seemed nice to me," Restin said, checking the capacitor readout.

"Yeah, I have to agree with Restin. She was hot," Bestin said with a grin.

Reggi looked at him, deadpan. "I've heard of War Mages peeling the skin off someone for disrespecting them. They would keep healing the victim, just to make it last longer. Do those sound like the actions of a 'nice' person?"

Restin gulped and shook his head. "Damn, Reggi, what kind of fucked up society are you people living in? Why not just overthrow the War Mages?"

The woman barked a laugh. "Why don't you go piss on a sun and put it out? That would be more effective than a rebellion against the War Mages. They are literally more powerful than entire armies."

Gerrold watched the *Raven* jump around and destroy another dozen Galvox attackers before he commented, "She's good, but still having trouble. I don't see an all-powerful being; all I see is an exceptional captain with a few tricks up her sleeve."

Reggi frowned. "To be honest, I thought she was holding back. But I don't understand why... War Mage Carnayan would have ripped them from the sky the moment they showed up."

"Who's that?" Gerrold asked, glancing over at her.

Her eyes flashed with fear. "He's the leader of my world. First Mage of Hestus, my home planet."

"Bad guy?"

"Very bad guy," she said with a shiver.

CHAPTER 46

"MA'AM, THEY JUST KEEP COMING," Mezner reported. "Their count is close to two thousand already. We have taken out nearly two hundred ourselves, and the defenders have taken out an additional five hundred, but I estimate it has cost them nearly a hundred ships to do so."

Hon cut in. "Ma'am, we are beginning to run low on PDC rounds. We will need to switch over to the warhead-equipped slugs soon, the standard slugs are down to twenty percent reserves. And the PDCs are down to forty percent."

"How is the *Rizz* doing? Are they still holding their own?" Sara asked, swiping new coordinates for Cora.

"They appear to be outside the battlefield, probably recharging systems. Those small ships are not built for sustained engagements," Grimms said, eying the flashing green icon.

"Ma'am, I'm picking up one, no, make that two, now *three* Vitas ships. They just warped in, I've highlighted them in yellow," Mezner shouted to ensure she was heard.

Sara quickly found the clustered ships and marked a spot directly on the starboard side of the closest ship. "Connors, give me the full hundred gs acceleration," she said while requesting a spellform from Alister.

The black cat gave a nod, and the form appeared in her mind. She poured Aether into it while the *Raven* jumped forward at incredible speeds.

The spellform was one she and Alister had worked on; it was for a modified spike shield, like she had used to punch into the Vitas dreadnought in the first engagement. The problem with ramming the Vitas was that whatever they were made of or coated in absorbed the Aetheric energy at an unbelievable rate.

Sara decided she needed to do the maximum amount of damage in the quickest fashion she could, so she designed a double shield. It was still a cone-shaped spike, but the edge of the cone was wavy, like the letter 'W' repeated over and over, resulting in an outer edge that was a series of raised ridges. Sara hoped the shape would keep a large portion of the shield's surface area clear of the Vitas's Aether-absorbing material. It was going to cost her a large amount of Aether, but hopefully it would be devastating to the Vitas. Just in case it didn't work quite as well as she hoped, she dumped a huge amount of her well into the second form.

The second shield was the standard one she kept up on the ship the entire battle. Normally she would not spend the power to keep both shields going, but she was afraid that even if the ship was split in half, it would still be able to get a few shots off, so she wanted to protect their asses as they passed through.

"Cora, jump!"

The *Raven* flashed through the Aether, spilling out into normal space only fifty meters from the Vitas ship's starboard side. Having accelerated for nearly five seconds before the jump, they were traveling at close to 5000 meters per second.

The shield pierced the Vitas' hull, the pressure of the

collision converting most of its mass to gas and plasma and plunging into the now soft material faster than anyone onboard could track. Within a second, they were five kilometers off the disintegrated ship's port side.

Sara found herself on her knees, Alister 'Merow'ing at her in panic from her shoulder. She shook her head and realized she had passed out for a second; the drain on her Aether well was far more than she had anticipated. She felt like she had used at least half of the Aether available to her.

"I don't think I can do that again," she admitted to Grimms as he helped her up.

The ship bucked, and she felt her well drain even more as the aft shields were pummeled with dozens of particle beams.

"The other two Vitas ships are firing on us, ma'am," Hon reported, opening fire with the *Raven*'s large cannons in response.

Sara leaned on the command ring, shaking her head, but was able to mark a jump location, "Cora!"

The ship jumped, saving them from continued hammering.

"I don't think that tactic would work again, even if you had the Aether to spare," Grimms said, returning to the holo table when she gave him a nod, and stood on her own. "They adapt quickly, and have response times much faster than ours."

The ship bucked again, and Sara could see that the Vitas had warped to their location and started hammering them again.

"Cora, jump here, then here, then here," Sara said, marking the next three locations. "Hon, give me explosive slugs and lock on to my mark. Don't fire 'til I tell you," she said, selecting one of the Vitas.

"Aye, ma'am," Hon acknowledged, going to work.

Her sister initiated the first jump, and Sara watched to see how long it took the Vitas to locate them.

"Fuck, that was fast," she growled.

The Vitas exited their warp, and Sara marked the spot, telling the computer to keep the location locked relative to the *Raven,* then had Cora jump again while she did her best to keep the shields powered amid the barrage of particle beams.

They vanished then reappeared, the mark glowing softly on her display, and Sara watched. Within half a second, the Vitas were warping toward them. The Vitas exited their warp, and Sara nearly shouted with joy. As she had suspected, the enemy had appeared directly in the marked spot.

As the first of the Vitas's particle beams slammed into the shields, Cora jumped again, and Sara yelled, "Fire!"

Hon let loose with all twelve barrels at Sara's marked location. The timing wasn't perfect, but it was close enough. The slugs streaked through the blackness, glowing lines on the holo table showing their progress.

The Vitas warped in, giving them only a fraction of a second to react to the incoming ordnance. Even in that short time, the targeted ship was able to dodge the majority of the slugs, but two slammed into its hull and detonated, ripping a large chunk from its port side and causing the ship to spin out of control. Even with the large amount of damage, the ship was still able to fire several of its particle beams with accuracy.

The *Raven* was pummeled, making Sara grunt as her well was drained even further to keep the shields up. The golden hue quickly turned a burnt orange, and Connors rolled the ship to expose a fresh section for the second round of incoming beams.

Sara marked another location and had Cora jump them away from the attacking ships. She was satisfied to see that the ship they had damaged was not able to follow its fellow. However, she could see that it was engaging ships within its range, and had some maneuverability. It seemed they had knocked out some of its weapons and its warp drive, but that was about it.

"Fire," she commanded Hon, and he let loose with another barrage, hoping to catch the second Vitas ship in the same trap.

To no one's great surprise, the Vitas did not follow its previous pattern and warp to the preselected location. Instead, the ship warped in behind them, only a few hundred meters away. Immediately, the *Raven* bucked as her stern was pummeled with beam blasts.

"Jump," Sara said, selecting a location nearly at random.

The Vitas arrived only a second later, once again blasting them from behind. Sara was having trouble maintaining the shielding in the aft of the ship, and selected another location, this one a few million kilometers away.

"Jump," she commanded, and the ship slipped through the Aether to arrive far out in the system.

"I can't keep up the current pace of all these jumps, eventually I'll be tapped. We need to come up with another strategy," Cora said in frustration.

"How long do we have before they get here?" Sara asked, watching as the Vitas went to warp.

"Maybe thirty seconds, ma'am," Mezner said.

Sara saw that the Vitas ship they had disabled was having difficulty hitting the defending ships. In fact, it didn't seem to be hitting anything; all the damage was coming from the masses of Galvox that were hunting down ships in packs.

"They can't see them," Sara said, almost to herself.

"Merp?" Alister asked from between her feet.

"The Vitas. They can't see the Rim worlders' ships. It's

that stealth coating they use," Sara said louder, catching Grimms' attention.

He leaned in and watched for a second. "You're right. They only target the ships we can clearly see, the ones without the stealth coating. I think they're blind to the others," he confirmed.

"That's why they joined forces with the Galvox. They need them to see the Rim world ships. Oh my god. That's why they're out here in the first place. They don't want them to become a threat later, so they're trying to take them out first," Sara said, the entire invasion suddenly making sense to her.

"Mezner, send a message to Grand Admiral Bok. Tell him about the stealth coating the Rim worlders are using and that we think the Vitas are out here to eliminate the threat. It's a weakness we have to exploit if we want to defeat them," she said, a plan forming in her mind.

She marked another set of locations. "Cora, we're going to do a short series of jumps as soon as the Vitas show up. We need to buy some time," she said, finding the ship she was looking for in the menagerie of attackers and defenders.

CHAPTER 47

"Cap, it's the *Raven*," Bestin said, flicking the controls and rolling the ship out of the line of fire of a dozen Galvox, who were unable to keep up with the quick maneuver. "They want us to meet them at the coordinates they've sent."

"We're a little busy, here," Gerrold said, using his chair display to look at the message. He scanned through the text quickly, getting the gist and cocking his head in consideration.

Bestin banked them around a group of Vitas, peppering their flanks with PDC fire and ripping the aft sections from two of them with the main cannons. They wove through the enemy like a sewing needle through cloth, leaving a path of burning and floundering Galvox in their wake.

The *Rizz* came around a particularly tight formation of Galvox only to find another pack of them heading directly for the ship. Bestin did his best, but was not able to pull up in time to avoid the hail of slugs headed their way.

Restin grunted as his shields were quickly burned to an angry red in the wake of three sequential impacts.

"We can't take this much longer, Cap. There's just too damn many of them," Restin said through gritted teeth.

"Warp here, brother," Bestin said, marking a location on the holo display.

"Belay that, warp here instead," Gerrold said, marking the coordinates the *Raven* had sent.

"Are you sure? You heard what Reggi said. You think you can trust the War Mage?" Bestin asked.

"Warping now, we can't stick around here," Restin said, gritting his teeth as another slug struck them a glancing blow.

The small view screen mashed down, then began expanding quickly.

"I guess we'll find out," Gerrold said with a frown.

———

"The *Rizz* just went to warp, ma'am. They should arrive at the coordinates in ten seconds," Mezner reported.

"Hon, get ready. Connors, we are going to have to draw the Vitas in. Be prepared for some of that fancy flying you do so well," Sara said from her viewing bubble in the command ring. "This is going to hurt, so let's make it count."

"Aye, ma'am," chorused throughout the bridge.

The Vitas appeared off to their starboard, and Cora jumped them the short distance to the preplanned coordinates, before the particle beams could rip through the still-recovering shields.

Sara watched as the Vitas ship almost immediately went to warp to follow. The *Raven* was jumping short distances of only a few thousand kilometers, letting Cora use a minimum of Aether. The distance was short enough, though, that it took longer to actually enter the warp thread than to travel down it. The few seconds they had before the Vitas warped in and began firing again was mostly taken with the mechanics of actually going to warp. This meant that the Vitas were only blind to what was happening while in the warp thread—too short a time to execute a surprise attack. If the *Raven* jumped further out, the Vitas would just warp in further away from them, and move via gravitic engines, allowing them time to see any incoming attacks.

The Vitas were nearly perfect opponents. They learned to avoid attacks after the first successful attempt, so Sara needed to come up with a new plan every time; they'd showed no true weaknesses.

But now they'd exposed a blind spot, literally, and Sara was planning on exploiting the hell out of it. She just needed to put her trust in a small ship full of pirates.

In truth, this was not one of her most risky plans. It just seemed that way to her because she wouldn't be the one pulling the trigger.

Trust. I really need to work on that, she thought, watching as the *Raven* made its last preprogrammed jump.

RESTIN WAS SHAKING HIS HEAD. "There is no way we can take that ship on, have you seen the struggle the *Raven* is having? We won't stand a chance."

"She says they can't see us due to our stealth coating. I've been watching the disabled Vitas ship; it never takes a shot at a stealthed ship. I think she's right," Gerrold said, hoping it was true.

"What do you think, Reggi?" Bestin asked. He seemed calmer than his brother, but was still rather tense.

Reggi was pale and had been since her conversation with the War Mage, but she had also been paying attention.

Reggi swallowed hard and watched the holo projector for

a few seconds before answering. "I think this War Mage is different. I don't know if it's because she's not as powerful as the War Mages I'm used to, or if she actually cares," she said, wringing her hands. "She's been fighting. Like *really* fighting, and taking damage to protect this system. I think she's telling us the truth. Or at least, the truth as far as she can see."

Gerrold nodded, "My thoughts exactly. Well, maybe not 'exactly', but pretty close." He flipped a switch on his command chair. "Hooper, Sitrix, prepare for rapid fire. We need to get as many shots off as we can, as quick as we can."

"Aye, Cap," Sitrix said.

They watched the *Raven* vanish and reappear a few hundred kilometers away from their position.

I need to figure out how they do that, when this is all over.

"Bestin, full speed ahead," Gerrold ordered, and the ship shot forward, taking a circular approach to the target area.

"There it is," Reggi said, pointing at the Vitas ship coming out of warp.

It was further away than Gerrold would have liked, but it was what it was.

"Hooper, Sitrix, wait 'til the last second. We need to get at least two shots off, but we can't fire too early, or they will see the slugs coming."

"Got it, Cap," Hooper boomed over the comm.

"We've got a squad of Galvox closing in," Bestin reported as the ship neared their target.

"Great, one more thing to worry about," Gerrold growled, glancing at the holo projector and seeing the squad closing in from the side. "Focus on the Vitas. Set the PDCs to full auto. Hopefully we can warp out before they get too close."

He knew this was a false hope. The enemy would be peppering the *Rizz*'s aft section before they could get their shots off.

"A SQUAD of Galvox are closing on the *Rizz*," Mezner reported.

Just then, the Vitas dropped out of warp and began firing. A dozen particle beams streaked through the black, fizzing and spitting power the whole way.

Sara had known they would need to take a few shots from the Vitas to give the *Rizz* enough time to take her shots, but now it looked like they would also need to provide cover.

"Connors, give me a heading to intercept those Galvox. We need to protect the *Rizz*," Sara said, gritting her teeth and dumping as much Aether as she could spare into the shields. "Hon, take shots as they present themselves."

"Aye, ma'am," he said, targeting and firing almost immediately.

The *Raven* shot off toward the *Rizz* and her closing enemies. Several Galvox exploded as twelve large slugs from the *Raven's* cannons smashed through their formation. The Vitas took the opportunity to focus fire on the *Raven's* aft section with concentrated fire, and the *Raven* shuddered as the particle beams blasted into her shielding.

Sara began to sweat with effort, and she dumped power into the defense at incredible rates, but it was not enough to keep up with the unrelenting barrage. With a scream of effort and pain, she felt the shields burn out and she fell to her knees.

The ship bucked and began to roll, as several particle beams ripped into its armor and eventually punched through the hull.

Hon never hesitated, continuing to fire on the Galvox—who, not expecting the ferocious attack, folded under the pressure—and those that could, scattered.

The pounding from the particle beams cut off nearly as

abruptly as it had started, and through bleary eyes, Sara could see the Vitas ship drifting with several holes through its hull. It wasn't dead, but its focus had been taken by the *Rizz*, which was coming back around for a second attack. The Vitas fired blindly, missing the *Rizz* by a huge margin.

Then it was the *Rizz*'s turn.

Her two cannons were smaller than those on the *Raven*, but they were still slinging chunks of solid steel at a considerable percentage of the speed of light. They punched through the Vitas, creating fountains of debris and plasma as they passed out the backside of the ship.

"Hon, let's help the *Rizz* out and send a volley of the warheads into that piece of shit," Sara said. She was still on her knees, but her head was clearing.

"Aye, ma'am," he said with a big smile.

Twelve warhead-equipped slugs shot out of the still glowing barrels of all three turrets, and a split-second later, they detonated inside the Vitas ship, turning the fearsome enemy into a cloud of superheated gas and irradiated chunks of debris.

CHAPTER 48

"WE NEED to take out the last Vitas ship before they can get back into fighting shape," Sara said, pulling herself to her feet with Grimms' help, as he reached into the command ring and gave her a hand.

Alister had moved to her shoulder, completely exhausted but still able to hang on as she rose.

She gave him a scratch. "Great work, Alister," she praised, butting heads with him affectionately.

"Ma'am, I'm not seeing the damaged Vitas ship on scans," Hon reported.

"I'm playing back the last five minutes," Mezner said, and the holo table projected a second image that was grayed out slightly, to differentiate between real-time and playback.

Sara found the Vitas ship where it had been sitting disabled the entire battle. The recording moved forward quickly, as Mezner scanned ahead. The ship suddenly spun on its axis and began heading toward the *Raven*, but stopped when the second Vitas ship was destroyed. It seemed to hesitate for a few seconds, then it turned and warped out of system.

"They ran?" Sara asked, her forehead wrinkling. "I have to say, I didn't see that coming."

"Ma'am, the Galvox are pulling out as well!" Mezner said, her face splitting into a huge grin.

Sara watched as the small ships began warping out in groups of fifty or more. They seemed to be taking the same direction as the Vitas, but she wouldn't know for sure until they analyzed the data more closely.

"How many of the Rim worlders survived the attack?" Sara asked, remembering why they were there to begin with.

"My quick estimate is that nearly seventy percent of them survived, though it looks like only the ships with the stealth coating managed to avoid destruction," Mezner said.

"We need to get together with the *Rizz*. Connors, give me—"

Mezner cut her off. "Ma'am, a ship has just warped in. It's sending UHFC codes," she said, scanning her console. "It's the *Catagain*, ma'am. They're hailing us."

"Get me in touch with the *Rizz* first. We can't let our prize slip away," Sara said, rolling her eyes at the lateness of their 'ally'.

"I have Captain Grenolt on the main screen, ma'am," Mezner said, as the view screen switched over from the starfield to the cramped bridge of the *Rizz*.

"Captain Sonders. I have to say, you really saved our skins on that last attack. I wasn't sure we were going to make it," he admitted, his forehead glistening with sweat.

"I dare say you wouldn't have. Those Galvox are aggressive, if nothing else," she said with a smile. "We need to meet and have a nice long conversation. I think there is a lot we can accomplish, if we put our heads together."

"I agree, Captain. I think we should take care of this newcomer first, though," Gerrold said, squinting down at his holo projector.

"Don't worry about them, they're here for me. Let me take care of this, and we can set up a meeting," she said, glancing down at the *Catagain*'s icon. The battleship was speeding toward them.

"Be careful. We'll be here when you're done," Gerrold assured her, then cut the channel.

"Ma'am, the *Catagain* is powering weapons and shields," Hon said, confused.

"Mezner, get those assholes on the line," Sara ordered, narrowing her eyes at the holo image.

The screen flipped over to the black-haired War Mage, as he paced back and forth on his large bridge. When he saw that the call was connected, he stomped to the center of the view.

"What the hell do you think you are doing out here in Teifen space, fighting other races' battles? Have you completely betrayed your people to work for the enemy?" he roared.

"I see you are late to the fight, Reese. Good work. It seems every time we need you, you aren't around; must be all the time you spend trying to smuggle explosives onto other people's ships," Sara said with a steely calm.

Reese seemed slightly taken aback, but his eyes betrayed him. He knew exactly what she was talking about.

"Ma'am, we're receiving a signal from the *Catagain*. It's the same one they used to try and detonate the bomb before." Mezner wasn't even trying to hide the contempt in her voice.

"Who told you to murder us?" Sara asked, not beating around the bush.

Reese took a step back. "I don't know what you're talking about. I have been sent here by the Admirals' Council to collect you and your ship."

" 'Collect' us? Are you saying we're under arrest? Because

the last I heard from the admirals, we were to continue the search for human colonies."

Reese barked a short laugh. "You mean Franklin's orders? Yes, the UHFC is aware that he basically issued a blank check for you to do whatever you wish without proper supervision."

"Proper supervision? Like we are children?" Sara raged.

"From where I stand, you're *worse* than children. At least a child responds to a firm hand; you just seem to push back harder," he said, a look of disgust on his face.

"Are you planning on carrying out Smith's orders, then? To fire on us when we resist? Or will you try to smuggle another bomb onboard? What's your plan here, *Captain*?" Sara asked, cocking her head.

Reese Rodgers smiled without any warmth. "You will come with us and cause us no problems, or we will be forced to destroy you. You are a problem for the brass. You have too much power and not enough sense to know who your betters are."

"Sir, I'm getting multiple warp threads coming in," one of the bridge officers on the *Catagain* interrupted.

"I'm seeing them too, ma'am," Mezner said. Then after a second, she added, "They're Teifen. It's the Grand Admiral's fleet."

Sara watched as fifty ships warped in, headed by Bok's battlecruiser, which was now carrying even more scars than the last time she had seen it. Several hundred more ships arrived in the following seconds. It seemed like the grand admiral had not brought his entire fleet, just a portion of it.

"The Admiral is hailing..."

That was as far as Mezner got before her jaw dropped, and she looked up at Sara.

"The *Catagain* is attacking the fleet!"

<<<<>>>>

AUTHOR'S NOTE

Dear Reader,

Thank you for reading.

Seriously. Thank you.

I know, I know… a cliffhanger. Sorry about that, but I really had no other choice. It was either a cliffhanger, or a crazy long book. I know some of you would be just fine with a crazy long book, but unfortunately my life circumstances would not allow me to continue at that time.

Some of you may have noticed that there is quite a gap between this book and Book 4; Stronghold…

Well, I had a lot going on between the two.

My wife was transferred to a new position in her company… a few thousand miles away. So, we needed to pack up the house, sell all the stuff we didn't need, travel to a city we have never been to before and buy a new house. If you have ever needed to uproot your life and move across the country, then you know what kind of havoc that introduces to your life.

And if you haven't… I don't recommend it.

Two thumbs down.

I did actually get the fourth book written during that time. But when I read it, I realized it was a big burning dumpster fire of a story, and I needed to start over.

That may have been the hardest thing I've ever done.

Finishing a book is the largest hurdle any writer needs to overcome. At least… until that author realizes that he wasted a good chunk of his life writing something he needed to throw away, and do again.

I was completely demoralized.

It took me a few weeks to finally accept that this was actually happening. I thought about just releasing it and let the bad reviews roll in… but I knew I couldn't do that to you, dear reader.

You deserve better from me.

So, I started over.

And as I continued to revise the story I became excited again. The words began to flow like they should. It became a joy to know that I could change the direction of the ship that is this series.

I hope that when you read Stronghold, you will like it as much as I do writing it.

Until then, you can check out a new series I've been working on with Justin Sloan called Supers: Rise Up.

Thanks,

Charley Case
(February 20th, 2019
Boise ID, USA)

P.S. If you could leave a review, my cats and I would be much obliged. Also if you would like, you can follow me on Facebook to see what's new.

Feel free to reach out and chat anytime.
    See you soon!

 facebook.com/CharlesRCase